DECEIT
OF THE
SOUL

SAVING THE WORLD FROM COVID-19: BEFORE THE PANDEMIC

HENRY COX

DECEIT
OF THE
SOUL

1

Huiwei could see her shadowy reflection in the full-length window as she looked out over the forested gardens next to her low-rise apartment building.

A government building – they all were in China – as was every tree and blade of grass, she mused. The steam from her tea cup slightly fogged the glass, and she sensed tremendous ambivalence knowing her assigned accommodations were extremely comfortable while so many others would never know such luxury.

Perhaps for the first time in her forty-two years, she was not in a hurry. She had a full night's sleep and enjoyed the chance to lounge in a white, fluffy cotton bath robe, letting her thick, black hair air dry for a while before she put on her uniform and headed to the Chengdu Research Center to meet with a team of biologists.

The setting seemed so peaceful. She wanted to believe that at least. But, she knew why she was there and that the People's Republic, or certain elite leaders, had already determined she had a definite expiration date. When? Not sure. Definitely sooner than later. How did she know – she shyly laughed – she helped design the protocols many years ago.

Huiwei was highly dangerous, from her feminine attributes, to her martial arts mastery, but mostly it was her intellect. She remembered the American saying from her days of post-graduate studies at Princeton, 'too smart for your own good.'

It was far too many times that she thought back to how she could have intentionally flubbed on some testing as a young girl. She was smart enough to have known. Yet, she eventually came full circle to knowing that was not possible. She had studied the algorithms over twenty-five years ago, and even programmed the variables to make the process even more impossible to beat. For her, the flubs would have stood out like a flashing red light where testing and retesting would have corrected the record.

A major in the People's Republic Air Force by the age of thirty and now a colonel, she at least was able to surreptitiously work the system to receive this assignment near Chengdu. The research facility was world renowned for its biological research in saving the Giant Panda. Without any great surprise, the real research on biogenetic modeling and sequencing had little to do with the wonderful animals she adored since she was a child. Her skills were highly valuable in Chengdu and she was able to slip in a research proposal that attained her desired location results.

Her apartment was on the outskirts of Guanghan City where she could see the Duck River winding in the distance. Through the millennia, this is where Chinese dynasties met every emerging age of technology, since before the Bronze Age; where her ancestors improved the science, methods and created superior adaptations to the admiration of the rest of the World. Even the great Chinese poets harvested many of their greatest works deep within this part of the Sichnan Province. If her days are to end, at least she could choose where.

2

Aiguo-Tao took the small, white washcloth to wipe the furious sweat from his forehead, wrapped his hand and slammed his fist into the painted cinder block wall of his small room. He could see the small traces of blood left on the paint seeping through the thin cloth. Still, his torn knuckles did not register any pain for the moment – his emotions were in override.

He heard the click of the bolt on the steel door. It wasn't a prison – but he knew he was a prisoner – on death row. "What the hell is going on!!!", he screamed, knowing no one heard him, and if they did, they wouldn't care. He still ran at the door to bang his fists in protest.

He ran the recent events over and over in his mind. He was grabbed by soldiers, at gunpoint, in the middle of the night at his Wuhan apartment. He was hooded and stuck in the back of a prisoner transport truck. If the transport had shocks, it was not obvious. The bruises on his wrists from the handcuffs chained to the bench seat were already starting to show in light shades of red and blue. He knew they would hurt even more tomorrow. But, he would not feel the pain.

Aiguo-Tao had no idea where he was after the two-hour, bumpy drive. He was dragged out of the transport, stumbling from two soldiers leading him with their hands gripping under his armpits.

When his blindfold was removed, he was standing in front of some nameless Colonel sitting at a metal table. With a sinister and calm voice, the Colonel simply said, "Major, I suggest you strongly consider how you frame your confession to your incompetence for the honor of your family and the People's Republic."

Aiguo-Tao's first thought was to exclaim '*I have no family and my only allegiance is to the Chairman and the People's Republic,*' but before he finished his first word, the butt of a rifle hit his kidney from behind. He remained silent, except for his grunt from the blow.

"Take the good Major to his room where he can contemplate his honor," was all the Colonel said.

Next, he was led down a sterile, beige hallway to an elevator, descending two floors. With the occasional, gruff shove from one of the soldiers, he was deposited in his current, sterile quarters.

3

Huiwei sat on the soft cloth of the light blue sofa and by habit, carefully poured another cup of tea. She took her laptop from the inlaid, rosewood sofa table, relaxing and curling her feet up on the sofa. She lifted the screen and typed in her three layers of security passwords to show the bright red insignia for the Ministry of State Services – Strategic Science Operations Division, along with several well-known quotes paying homage to the People's Republic and the People's Liberation Army.

As the front of her robe separated, she glanced at her lacey turquoise bra. She softly smiled, balancing her teacup and her laptop, taking a sip. She never had the pretense of being seen as a glamorous beauty. Still, she knew she could hold her own with a little primping, the right clothes and some make up – eye-catching, without standing out in a crowd. At times, her job demanded it.

Plus, maintaining her fitness and martial arts regime kept her body slender and fit, looking far younger than her age. Huiwei always enjoyed wearing her *La Perla* or *Kiki de Montparnasse* lingerie beneath her officer's uniform. It gave her balance and a silent sense of empowerment in the science and military worlds of masculine dominance, despite the hollow pronouncements of unisex equality.

She pulled up her notes on her algorithms to trace genome sequencing in generational, reproduction modeling. The file was filled with panda references but, unless the generals were planning on breeding an army of highly effective panda warriors, she understood the underlying purpose of the research.

As her thoughts wandered, she queued a highly encrypted file showing photos of her with her parents. Huiwei was only twelve years old, living in Pinghu, just north of Hong Kong, when her parents ceremoniously escorted her to the government car for her to attend a select school for high performing students.

Her parents met with a polite, well-groomed woman at their home. After the woman left, Huiwei's parents solemnly sat down with her on a woven sitting mat to explain to her that because she was blessed from birth as the bright seedling to us all, she had honored her family with such wonderful performance at school, with her mind and her agility, so that she will serve the People by attending a school for advanced learning.

Huiwei at first felt a pang of pride, then confusion, and finally shock. She asked, "What's that mean, Bàba?"

Her father did his best to hold back his emotions as he would not look straight at her to state, "It means you will honor our family by leaving home to use your talents in study at an honorable school."

Huiwei tried to keep her composure, but straight-backed, she could not hold back her tears, "Will I see you and mother?"

Her mother reached for her, but she fell into her father's lap, sobbing without being able to form any words. Her father softly stroked the back of her head, swaying with her sighs, "You will be quite busy with your studies and you might not have time for our interruption."

Huiwei's head quickly turned to the side, "That will never be true, Bàba," continuing to let her tears soak into the bottom of her father's *changsang* shirt.

When she started to relax her tears, her father picked up her small slender body and carefully carried her to her mattress on the floor of her bedroom. Her mother gently stroked her hair and offered her calming voice with words Huiwei no longer remembers.

Her energy drained from emotions, Huiwei closed her eyes and slept. It was less than an hour before she awoke. She remembered the confusion and fear she felt, laying on her mattress and hearing her mother cry in the other room and her father trying to offer her some words of comfort. In her mind, she could see her father holding her mother and rocking her gently to calm her.

The next day, Huiwei could tell that her parents had not slept, but there was no more discussion about her future. Dinner was silent, sitting in her place on the mat at the dark cherry lacquered, *ba xian zuo* table. Huiwei noticed her mother had placed more fish in her soup than normal. She looked up at her Mother. She smiled at Huiwei and nodded. No words were said.

The following morning, her mother bathed her, laid out her best outfit and she saw a travel bag packed with her clothes. The same, well-groomed woman came to the door. Her parents told the woman how honored they were for Huiwei to have the opportunity to serve the People. She knew the words were false. Yet, out of her respect for them, Huiwei felt her ability to wrap her emotions into a ball inside, bow to her parents, and follow the woman to the car.

It took Huiwei several years to track down the several photographs she had. Using her skills, she was able to take the images, rotate profiles and place her and her parents in different settings. She knew the manipulated photographs were artificial, but the emotions she felt with each one were deeply real.

She never saw her parents after that day. From time to time she would receive letters from them. The letters were short and lacked much detail. In her heart, she knew her parents had not written them. The school officials either ignored or provided curt excuses when she asked about her parents. It was quickly obvious that other students were in the same situation. Discussions were at first discouraged – eventually prohibited.

On occasion, she had overheard her parents' whispers in the night, talking of trying to escape to Hong Kong one day – never a topic to be discussed in the open. Huiwei could only hope that somehow they did.

The only positive thought she could conjure from the experience was never forgetting how she could wrap her emotions tightly inside and focus on the reality in front of her. Cold and efficient on the outside, with a small ball of warmth and love burning deep inside. It would benefit her greatly, if not save her, many times for the next three decades.

Aiguo-Tao finally fell asleep on a thin, narrow mattress on the floor. When the steel door slammed open, he could not remember where he was at first. He did not know how long he had slept, but it felt like it was only a few minutes.

He cleared his eyes and looked up to see the same nameless Colonel standing just inside the doorway with two soldiers in the hall behind him.

"Have you chosen the words for your confession Major? I trust you slept well and have a clear head now," exclaimed the Colonel.

Aiguo-Tao tried to stand up while responding, "I have no idea what confession you mean. I am an officer in the army of the People's Republic and this kidnapping is outrageous."

One of the soldiers swept around the Colonel and pushed Aiguo-Tao back down on the mattress. He knew he could disarm the soldiers in a matter of seconds – but to what end? He had no idea where he was and no plan of escape. Aiguo-Tao presumed the Colonel knew all of this as well and enjoyed his predicament.

"Your treason disavows any honor you claim, Major," said the Colonel.

As rage suddenly aroused Aiguo-Tao, he retorted, "I am a well-respected officer with many friends at the highest levels. You have made an egregious mistake Colonel!"

The Colonel smirked stating, "As of now, you have no rank Aiguo-Tao and I believe you are delusional to presume you have any *friends* who will have any interest in assisting you."

The Colonel took a deep breath and let it out slowly, "My orders are simple. Obtain your confession as soon as possible. You would be wise to consider my cooperative mood at this point as it will change dramatically the next time we meet."

"How can I confess to nothing I have done? I don't even know what you are talking about!" His words only bounced off the walls.

The soldier quickly retreated as the Colonel turned and walked out of the room. The door slammed shut again and he heard the bolt slide shut once more.

Left at the edge of the door was a clear, plastic bottle of water with the twist-off lid gone, and a dried rice cake. Poisoned or not, he crawled to the door, sitting against the wall, quickly devouring the rice cake and drinking the water.

A mixture of anger, frustration and confusion filled his mind. His thirst was greater than he ever recalled, even from his survival training exercises in the eastern Takla Makan desert. He tried to sip the water, fearing it might be a long time before he had some more. "What the hell is going on?" was the question that rapidly repeated in his mind like a bad mantra.

Aiguo-Tao was stationed in Wuhan as a chief logistics officer in coordination with the Wuhan Institute of Virology. He held the highest level of security clearance for his rank. His record was spotless, having quickly matriculated through military schools since he was fifteen.

Serving in special forces, he was decorated for his team's success in covert technical operations in Nigeria, Somalia and South Africa. He was a 'ghost' and his exploits were only known to the highest-ranking intelligence officials. Aiguo-Tao was an officer by his twenty-first birthday and he quickly advanced over the last decade, because of his acute ability to focus on the assigned objective, devoid of emotions, and execute some of the most sensitive logistics in covert operations.

His current operation was perhaps the most grandiose ever devised in military history. He played a critical role in developing the recruiting protocols, training and deployment strategy.

His devotion to the People's Republic was unquestioned where he traveled in four continents to develop contacts, conduct surveillance and understand several industries, including in Europe and the United States.

Absent an incident with an asset in Milan, his record was spotless. But she deserved the deadly loss of blood in her bathtub. When he woke up in her bed to use the bathroom, he saw her startled look when she nervously flushed the toilet and thought he didn't see his smartphone tucked into her bathrobe pocket. The *ghost* was out of Italy even before the police ruled it a suicide. He had other assets in place without her.

Despite his coldness inside, Aiguo-Tao had a type of serious affability. An attractive man's-man presence, yet non-descript in many ways. He developed assets in the best Iranian coffee shops and cafés, the most frequented trattorias in Northern Italy, the pubs and Wirtshafts throughout Europe. Perhaps his favorite ploy was the development of Chinese investment in elderly homes and care centers, especially in America, and inserting Chinese nationals educated abroad. Chinese nationals as assets were always the most reliable.

The operation took over two years of planning. Deployment was running more smoothly than could have been expected. Aiguo-Tao's future was bright and secure. He needed to be coordinating in his command center at the Wuhan Institute – "what the hell is going on?"

5

As she dressed, with each piece of her uniform, Huiwei gradually transformed into her professional persona. Looking into the mirror, she sensed her transition. She buttoned her crisp, white blouse and saw her face growing devoid of any smile. She felt her warmth winding into a small, glowing ball and stored it carefully deep inside.

She preferred to keep her silky, black hair just beyond shoulder length. It gave her more options for the different personalities and roles she had to play. Her innate advantages since she was a teenaged girl was that she could see inside the human mind as well as the intricate coding of the most complex computer. Her medical degree in psychiatry and doctorates in computer engineering were a logical mix to her. At times, she wasn't sure there was much of a difference – understanding the coding was all that mattered.

By the time she was fifteen, she was already a black belt in more than one martial art with an acute talent for knowing, and finding, pressure points. This led to her becoming an exceptional, self-taught acupuncturist, and herbal healer, initially to heal her own battle wounds.

The human neural systems were simply pathways for electrical currents to execute the intended program, much the same as the integrated circuit programs she designed thousands of times – it was just knowing the coding.

Some nights, she would dream of representing the People's Republic on its judo or karate Olympic team. By seventeen she realized such a dream was fantasy, because her highly tuned muscle memory reflexes included too many moves and strikes that would disqualify her.

These combinations of talents spared her from being part of the untold stories of sexual assault encountered by many of her female colleagues raised through the select educational programs, from gymnastics to military training.

Only once did she recall letting her persona down. At twenty-five and relatively new to field operations with the Ministry of State Services, she was attending a foreign embassy gala, involving a contrived date with an MSS official. Afterwards, he mistakenly believed that her eye-catching, and somewhat exposing gown, was meant for him and not the covert operation. Upon retrieving the data from the remote cloning device she had programmed and deployed, she had a sense of youthful pride along with a need to release the anxiety built up with the highly dangerous exploit.

Vulnerability? Wrong signals or not, he tried to push her down on the couch. Thirty minutes later, he woke up, pant-less, on the hotel bed, minus one testicle and an expertly sutured scrotum without a drop of blood to be found. Out of his own pride or embarrassment, the incident never reached any official report – she already knew that outcome. With whatever rumor mills exist in human nature, she never encountered a similar event.

Checking her tightly bunned hair, and pulling on her uniform jacket, she thought about Aiguo-Tao. A major in the People's Liberation Army. A highly decorated special forces combat leader. Least known, unless you can obtain access to highly classified documents, he was one of the most successful ghost operators in the MSS. When she reviewed his classified background history, she did not look any further for a target.

Zhu Aiguo-Tao, born and raised in Fuzhou, less than 170 kilometers from Northern Taiwan, across the East China Sea. His parents, part of an underground, Christian church. The church leader had been *outed* and taken into custody.

Out of fear, his parents were part of a small group who arranged transport to Taiwan. They anxiously awaited their fifteen-year-old son, delaying their departure. Aiguo-Tao finally appeared just before sunrise – with a group of PLA soldiers. The group and the boat pilot were taken into custody. While tied up, they were beaten by the soldiers. Standing next to Aiguo-Tao's parents, the commanding officer openly thanked Aiguo-Tao for his patriotism by turning in the "treasonous scum."

As Huiwei read the coldly worded account, she pictured his parents bruised and bleeding, with their hands tied behind their backs, pleading with their young son on how and why he would do this. She saw the tears in the mother's eyes, the questioning disappointment on her face and the shamed face of the father not willing to raise his eyes now swollen shut.

Reading on, the officer decided to fulfill Aiguo-Tao's true sense of honor to the People. He handed young, Aiguo-Tao his pistol and ordered him to shoot his parents in the back of the head. He shot his Mother first, then cursed his Father before pressing the barrel to the back of his head and pulling the trigger.

The officer ran the report of the events up the ranks. Aiguo-Tao was tested, performing reasonably well, and entered a prestigious military school to complete his education.

Huiwei stared at the mirror, blind to her own reflection, as she remembered reading the report and how that ball of human emotion burst through her, recalling her own parents and how much they wanted to keep her from leaving, helpless, left to their own tears and remorse after her car drove away. She cried, hard. Something she could only vaguely and remotely remember happening to her as a thirteen-year old girl . . . maybe fourteen . . . doesn't matter, she doesn't weep – certainly not for things she cannot control.

She finished buttoning her jacket, straightened the ribbons of military decorations, finally seeing her own reflection in the mirror, "How does it feel to be the *treasonous sc*um Aiguo-Tao?"

6

Aiguo-Tao sat on the thin mattress, crossed his legs, ate the two, new rice cakes and drank half the bottle of water left for him. Then, he closed his eyes and focused on slowing his heart rate.

Waterboarding, isolation heat chambers, sleep deprivation with the loud, most obnoxious music ever created – East European techno-rock. He had been through all of the testing, beating the parameters, even to the point where his vital signs were past any healthy limits for most.

He never liked torture techniques or even interrogation. He didn't need them. In his mind, either the person turned into a reliable asset or he walked away. If the target figured out too much or was allied elsewhere, a bullet or a quick death resolved matters. Aiguo-Tao understood the need for coerced interrogation, but it was a prolonged process more frequently resulting in misleading information or admissions to anything to avoid any more anguish or pain. Sorting out the credibility was guesswork. It was not results-oriented for an operational goal.

Still, he knew the protocol. When the small, intense strobe lights started pulsing from their stations embedded in the corners of the room, ten feet up, he also felt the hair on his arms slightly rise and fall – high frequency sonar that most humans would never detect without knowing the inaudible reactions. The effects were often quick. Panic, an adrenalin boost in a fraction of a second, that would never plateau until the person passed out from shock. Even unconscious, the victim's physiology remained bombarded by the pulsing light putting the nervous system in a state of frenzy, like being caught standing in the middle of a busy freeway not knowing which way to turn or move.

The sonic waves continued to blast the brain with the confusion, sometimes resulting in cranial aneurysms, severe headaches, nausea and vomiting, or at least a scrambling of the neuropathways. He had personally coached assets in Cuba and South Africa to set up these systems to attack foreign embassy residences. Interrogation was not the goal then, nor was the more distant proximity as intense. Even then, he witnessed the debilitating effects.

Avoid the panic, control every system from respiration to blood flow, even digestion. His biggest enemy was his own skin, the largest organ in his body, unable to cloak itself from these invaders.

Calmly repeating one last time, "What the hell is going on," Aiguo-Tao's mind drifted and drifted, traveling to the fine razor edge of cognitively staying awake, yet relying on his subconscious to consume him.

Only sixteen, barely a year into the military-prep academy, he failed.

At least ten feet, maybe twelve, up the fifteen-foot climbing wall, covered with barbed wire, embedded glass chards and an assortment of other hazards, he remained focused and calm.

He could hear his classmates cheering him on – *"Jiayou, jiayou, jiayou."* *"He's going to make it!"* The taste of iron crept into his mouth from cuts on his face. He saw the blood dripping from the many cuts on his forearms and hands, and felt the moisture seeping into his field pants which were surely shredded by now. The 'wall of a thousand cuts' was a literal, not a figurative name for the training exercise.

"Xiajiang!"- drop. That's all he had to say, and the trainer on top of the wall would toss the rope down to let him finish the climb, or with less honor, repel down. The hand-holds were intentionally scarce and narrow, requiring a defiance of gravity with the tips of his fingers and the edges of his boots.

He knew he had made it further up the wall than most of his classmates would ever accomplish. Most would likely fall to the pit cushion below, not even being able to hold-on for the rope - but that wasn't the point.

The pangs of sharp pain from his fingertips to his legs were maddening. Aiguo-Tao could sense the panic gripping him, feeling the muscles in his neck strain to balance and keep his body tight to the wall to suffer another cut. The edge of his left boot barely slipped, only for an instant, but he felt the sharp object stab into his muscular stomach. He knew it broke through the skin like a short-bladed knife. Suddenly, he felt the pain he had been ignoring and the surge of panic waft through his body like a cold chill.

"Xiajiang!" shouted Aiguo-Tao. Humiliation consumed him as he grabbed the rope and climbed to the top. His classmates still cheered him and the trainer gave him a rare pat on the back to signal he had done well. He respectfully nodded, while he silently yelled at himself, *"Never again!"*

Before he left the infirmary that night, covered with taped gauze bandages and various stitches to close his wounds, Aiguo-Tao stealthily slipped a candle he spotted on the reception desk into his pocket, along with a packet of matches.

That weekend, during his free time, he began his self-training to never let pain or panic interfere with his objective again. In an isolated area near the training grounds, he sat crossing his legs. He lit the candle and closed his eyes as he lowered his hand to the flame. He worked to gain control of his senses, to let the pain soak into his mind and dissipate and to feel how close and long he could keep his palm above the flame without serious burns.

In the gymnasium, he would repeatedly push the body-bag as hard as he could, letting the return swing hit him in the face, the groin, his ribs or any place vulnerable to pain. He would even launch his body into the safety padding on the walls or do Plyo push-ups letting his body smash to the ground.

When an instructor saw him engaged in his lunatic behavior, he started to rush to intervene, but the trainer grabbed the instructor's arm, "Leave him be! Let his mind learn to be blind of the pain."

By the time Aiguo-Tao was recruited into special forces, he was already catching scorpions to let them sting him, and visiting the local apothecary to obtain herbal poisons and tame his system, consulting with healers about the limits of non-lethal doses. The sweats, stomach cramps and vomiting grew absent over time. He was not a masochist of any sort, he deplored pain. Aiguo-Tao's body was simply, perpetually healed from pain.

While the strobes flashed for hours on end, Aiguo-Tao remained captive to the vivid visions of his past and his journey from the human realm of panic.

He did not notice the strobes turned off, the sound of the door bolt or the footsteps of the guards, until one slapped him across the face. Purely by blind reflex, before his eyes opened, he grabbed the guard's wrist, bending it to force his submission and kneel to the ground as Aiguo-Tao grabbed the barrel of the semi-automatic rifle and had the strap wrapped around the guard's neck, with the muzzle pointed at the second guard.

Blinking his eyes open, Aiguo-Tao removed his finger from the trigger and forcefully pushed the guard away with the guard landing on his hip and frantically trying to regain control of his rifle. Scrambling to stand up, the Corporal fixed the aim of his weapon on Aiguo-Tao.

The Master Sergeant shouted, "méiyǒu, tingzhi, tingzhi," *no, halt*, pressing his hand down on the barrel of the Corporal's rifle.

Aiguo-Tao remained sitting with his legs crossed as if nothing had happened. "Please, do not do that again."

"Colonel Zhào wishes to speak to you. Please come with us Major," said the Master Sergeant.

The Corporal tersely retorted, "He has no rank. Now get up before I shoot you."

The Master Sergeant glanced at his companion, "Corporal, you should know you are still alive. Please come with us Major. There will be no shooting today."

Aiguo-Tao, nodded to the Master Sergeant and stood, extending his fisted hands, "At least the Colonel now has a name," he said.

The Master Sergeant acknowledged the gesture, "I don't think restraints are needed. Perhaps they would not make a difference if they were. This way Major. Colonel Zhào is waiting."

7

Huiwei's room was on the third floor – the top floor. She entered the elevator and pushed the button for the lobby. The lift suddenly slowed, stopped, and the door opened to the second floor.

She saw a balding man, probably sixty or sixty-two, and in need of some routine exercise. Tailored suit, polished black shoes and a gold, Rolex watch – respectable. He was fumbling with his two bags and a computer satchel, to close his door. He raised his hand toward Huiwei, signaling to hold the elevator. She pushed the button to hold the door open, hoping an alert signal would not sound. He scurried into the elevator still trying to coordinate his luggage.

"Thank you, Miss. This has been a very rushed morning."

His jowls slightly flapped as he shook his head, taking out a handkerchief to wipe the sweat on his forehead.

Huiwei politely nodded, seeing the satchel slipping down. She kneeled to grab the shoulder strap to hand him. She momentarily paused when she spied a room key on the floor, peeking out from under one of the bags. Blocking his view with her back, she pinched the corner of the card pulling it free. She started to hand it to him, but changed course with a single motion, slipping the card into her jacket pocket as she stood and handed him the strap.

"Thank you, again, young lady."

Staring straight ahead at the door, Huiwei softly said, "Colonel."

"Oh, yes. I'm so sorry Colonel. I know better. Thank you . . . Colonel," he said.

"You're welcome. I hope your day will improve," said Huiwei.

"It will. Last minute call and all. I need to catch the train and I hope my taxi is waiting. I won't be back to my flat for several days now. I have to get home, and no time to first get to my office in Chengdu. Perhaps I will be able to buy you a cup of tea when I return on Monday. Your kindness reminds me of my daughter. At least before she was married."

Huiwei understood the compliment along with his sense of humor offering a blunt jab at his son in law. He probably keeps her away from her family as much as possible. Isolation from those who would build her self-esteem. A control-freak. Her father seems very worthy of his daughter.

The door to the lobby opened. Grabbing his bags in a more orderly fashion this time, he said, "I certain hope your day begins better than mine, Colonel."

"It already has, thanks to you." Huiwei logged a mental note of his room number, 201, "And, thank you for making me smile."

The man rushed off seeing his taxi waiting outside.

Before she took a step out, Huiwei heard the desk attendant spout, "Good morning Colonel Lí. A late start for you today. Shall I call for a car?"

Huiwei was weighing whether she was more concerned that the desk attendant knew that 9:00 a.m. was a late start for her, or the mere fact that she had never met this person before and he recognized her on sight. He also failed to assist the guest with his bags to the taxi, or to even open the door for him. She could process this later. She needed to get to her office and have on site access to the mainframe.

"No thank you . . ." she hesitated, intentionally, as if not finishing her response.

"Wang lei, Colonel Lí," she instinctively knew he would fill the gap with his name. Wang lei? she thought, a rather common name and unlikely his real name by the way he said it. Maybe in his late twenties . . . perhaps an Airman, or Second Lieutenant, wearing an off -the-rack, black suit.

Now, only a few feet away, she fixed her eyes straight at him. With a friendly voice she said, "Well, Wang lei, since this is a civilian residence, you may call me Huiwei. Wang lei, is that your given name?"

Avoiding her eyes, he said, "Uh . . . yes, most certainly."

Quickly gazing up once more, to gather his thoughts, he lowered his eyes and continued, "If you don't mind Colonel Lí, my instructions are to refer to the residents on a formal basis."

Now, finally looking at her, "And I do not want to lose my job, if you are so kind."

Definitely military. At least he was honest about not wanting to lose his job.

"I believe I'll take a taxi to the train station and into Tianfu Square. A car will not be necessary, Wang lei." She tried not to smile using the name, but she also knew that the game was changing faster than she had hoped.

"Colonel Lí, that won't be necessary and a car would be much quicker to the Research Center. It's at least seven kilometers from the Square," he said.

Now, she tried to calculate whether she was more concerned with the obvious surveillance, or his absolute ineptness in so openly revealing that he was given a profile on her to memorize. If he is training as a junior agent in the MSS, she hoped he would be weeded out sooner than later. He, or someone, will not survive his next birthday.

"This morning, I prefer the uninterrupted ride of the bullet train. It's calming, and only a quick subway ride to the Center." Huiwei already knew what was coming as she strolled to the door, but she wanted to play out the scene to uncover more variables from Wang lei – it was more like he was dropping *slices* of bread as opposed to crumbs.

As she began pulling the chrome handle on the large glass door, Wang lei scurried to stand between her and the opening door.

"Given my desire to do my best, I have already summoned a car for you Colonel. I hope you understand," he said.

"Yes, I understand . . . fully." She withdrew her hand from the door handle, turning back toward the fashionable lobby.

Huiwei walked across the parquet, walnut floor, and stepped to the plush white rug bearing the symbol of an orange, jumping koi fish, beneath the large, glass tea table. She sat politely on one of the white cushioned sofas, lowering her black leather satchel to the cushion next to her.

"Your courtesy is appreciated Wang lei. Do tell me what happened to the regular attendant, Zang Do. I do hope his mother is doing better since she's so far away," she asked.

He looked down, as she sensed he was processing the information in DSL for a 5G network.

"Perhaps he was too lazy as I understood that I would need to call him in advance to bring a car around," she said.

"It is my understanding that there was a family illness, his mother as you mentioned. He was requested to return home, out of town, to assist. I believe it may be for some time." Wang lei finally said.

Of course, Huiwei conjured up the name, Zang Do. The morning attendant was a polite young woman, named Chén. She is taking night classes at the university, living with her father and younger brother. Her mother had passed away several years ago.

On several mornings, Huiwei had enjoyed helping Chén with statistics calculations from her textbook, while Huiwei waited for a taxi. She hoped Chén was okay and whomever *they* were had placed her safely in another job.

Wang lei must have an uncle with some political pull and a mother who is a nagging sister to be able to get him into any type of surveillance position. It was most certainly not on any sort of merit. He will likely figure out his glaring mistake, later – there is no Zang Do or bedridden mother. It will not make it to any report, unless he is so ignorant or wanting to be assigned to a civilian manufacturing barracks, working fourteen hours a day making microchips or the latest basketball shoes. His festering confusion, knowing he is in over his head, without a place to turn, will make him a potential cornucopia of information for her.

Out of the corner of her eye, she saw one of the security cameras in the lobby. One camera in her hallway, one in the elevator, two in the lobby and at least two more out front. Most surely the stairwell is covered as well. She will need to take a better security inventory later on – she knew she already should have. Her room? Another reason to get to the engineering lab at the center so she can reprogram an electronic scanner.

Taking away her flexibility to use a taxi at will, or the train, definitely changes the variables. With the thought, Huiwei plaintively pressed her extended forefinger to her mouth.

"Wang lei?"

"Yes, Colonel Lí," he said, as if Huiwei was his enlistment Sergeant screaming, *attention* in his face. Huiwei seriously hoped he never played poker, unless his uncle was also willing to cover his gambling debts.

She casually spoke to him now, "Given my long hours, I greatly appreciate the attention to security here. I presume there is a bank of monitors in a security room and I was wondering whether you had access to it should I have any incident of concern."

His eyes perked up, "Security access . . . yes, Colonel Lí, I . . .," and then his speaking trailed off, looking down at the floor now to reassess his response.

"I am simply the desk attendant, Colonel. I don't know what security features the building has, except the keypad when the front door is locked. Sorry, I can't help you with your inquiry," he said.

She also knew they had access to any room with a master, electronic keycard, if a resident was not inside with the security door jamb in place.

The variables were mounting and the odds of escaping her fate were rapidly changing. Unfortunately, if nothing else, the reality was that Huiwei was good with numbers and odds.

Okay, he has access and at least some password security level. Huiwei walked toward the door as she saw the black, Hongqi H7 waiting in front. Wang lei opened the door for her as she walked past. She could see the sweat lingering on his forehead and imagined he felt like he needed to change a perspiration-soaked shirt by now.

She nodded to the driver as she opened the door for Huiwei. She could immediately tell that the driver had far more discipline than Wang lei, and certainly more experience. It would be a silent drive to the Center.

8

"Please sit major," said Colonel Zhào, gesturing to the metal chair with his hand, palm up.

Aiguo-Tao silently complied and nodded to the Master Sergeant who asked for his hands to clasp the handcuffs. The handcuffs were attached to a chain running through a thick metal ring welded to the metal table – clearly bolted to the floor.

"I trust you understand my need for some precaution since you are now on ground level and I would prefer to avoid further demonstrations of your skills," said Zhào.

"Rumors travel quickly in this facility," responded Aiguo-Tao.

Zhào slightly raised one eyebrow, saying, "And, the speed of light is even faster through our camera monitors." Zhào paused, amused by his own sense of humor. "Your file, at least the parts that are not blacked-out, obviously do not give you justice for your skills."

Zhào sat down in the metal chair across the table from Aiguo-Tao.

"Should you escape, I'm not sure where you would go without meeting a bullet in short order, despite the bodies you might leave in your wake, perhaps my own." Zhào said, detecting no reaction.

"Ah . . . and due to my own bias for self-preservation, you may presume that our acquaintance will end before you are able to devise any plan in hopes of success." Zhào thought he detected a slight, momentary grin.

Aiguo-Tao remained silent, sitting erect, while calmly looking directly at Zhào. Before he sat down, his mental reflexes had already logged the details.

The sterile, dead-end hallway back to the elevators, 30 meters, another hallway, maybe 10 meters, suspended ceiling tiles, two offices on the left side, windows? maybe, an exit door at the end, locked with an electronic keypad, bulletproof glass, armed personnel on the other side – one visible, distance to exterior exit - unknown. The room, beige concrete walls, no drywall, no windows, one steel door, solid ceiling, no panels, metal grates bolted to the ventilation duct and across the bright, recessed LED tube lights in the ceiling, gray painted concrete floor, one metal table, two metal chairs.

The Master Sergeant had exited the room, locking the door from the outside – armed, in the hallway. Before Aiguo-Tao had entered the room, he saw a young, second lieutenant at the exit door – five-digit key code, first three, "1" "5" "0," the lieutenant moved and blocked any further view. The Corporal, absent, hopefully getting an ear-full from that second lieutenant, sowing his wild oats of new authority, with the incompetence of the younger man.

Aiguo-Tao tried not to look away. Something was missing from his mental catalog. He momentarily flicked his eyes, up to the left, then the right and resumed his calm focus on Zhào.

"Yes, major, I can see you surmise correctly. There are no cameras, recording, electronic devices, or weapons in this room. Thanks to a Mr. Faraday, such devices would not work anyway," said Zhào.

Zhào was perhaps in his mid-fifties, with some graying hair. He was still somewhat fit, with broad shoulders and muscular hands, but his days of routine physical training were obviously behind him. Aiguo-Tao noticed the stretched and deformed skin that ran down the right side of Zhào's neck disappearing beyond his shirt collar. Serious burns and skin grafting – most likely an interesting story to be told. He did not wear any ribbons or patches of decoration or identity, only the three, stitched, silver leaves of his rank on each epaulet of his light-blue, People's Liberation Air Force shirt.

It always left a bad taste in Aiguo-Tao's mouth when he thought about how China had somehow mimicked the United States military in its insignias and uniforms. At least a full-colonel had three clusters instead of an American eagle. He presumed his rank would soon show the three, gold clusters in the PLA. *What the hell is going on?* he thought once more.

Zhào sat back and folded his hands on his stomach, "I respect your preference for silence Major, however, at some point, quite soon, our conversation will be much more unilateral from you rather than me."

He paused, repositioning his stare at Aiguo-Tao, "The tone of that conversation, remains to be seen, but is mostly in your control. You owe me no favors. After all, we've only recently become such good *friends*. Nonetheless, your cooperation will be greatly appreciated. Let's discuss your confession Major."

"That is where you evidently have the upper-hand Colonel, or more likely a serious misunderstanding of any facts." Aiguo-Tao adjusted his posture, leaning forward with his forearms pressing against the edge of the table.

"Please, look at me. Stare straight into my eyes. I have no idea what you are talking about Colonel Zhào," said Aiguo-Tao, emphatically, yet with calm.

Zhào obliged him, realizing that when facts in an interrogation become clouded by inconsistencies and credibility, a mother's simple tool was most effective, 'look me in the eyes and tell me.' Aiguo-Tao obviously understood this axiom as well.

"Colonel, I will be candid with you," began Aiguo-Tao.

"Please do Major. That is all I ask," responded Zhào.

"You have walked through your several paths of interrogation with me. A surprised and forceful incarceration to instill fear. Isolation and deprivation, even followed by photosensitive disorientation and hypersonic bombardment. I presume you already realize that my tolerance for physical pain would render archaic torture worthless, more likely resulting in my death as opposed to information," he said, and paused.

Aiguo-Tao continued, "My guess is that you are, yourself, no stranger to pain and you would not be here if you had not survived with honor. Your sense of empathetic coercion is tactful, but ultimately ineffective. I think it is important that we start on the same page here, and most importantly, that you understand I have no idea what you are talking about. My only question is, what the hell is going on Colonel?"

Aiguo-Tao took a slow, deep breath continuing to look directly at Zhào. He saw the red capillaries in Zhào's watering eyes, and watched him cough into his white handkerchief and slip it back into his hip pocket.

Zhào contemplated Aiguo-Tao's words, perching his thumbs together and bringing them to his chin before he leaned toward the table, "First, you should understand that I am likely as good at my job as you are at yours – or believe you are. Second, I appreciate your attempted lecture on interrogation methods, novice as it might be, and even somehow detecting sonic disorientation. Third, I admittedly am at an abnormal disadvantage, since the details in your record, apparently, are largely blacked-out if not erased completely."

Aiguo-Tao interrupted, "Colonel Zhào, then hopefully you understand the impossible dilemma you propose. There is nothing to confess. I have no idea of why I am here. And, to even attempt to discuss my activities, a *confession* as you erroneously propose, would appropriately be a death sentence for me in breaching my security protocols."

Zhào hesitated, pulled his handkerchief out to cough once more and continued, "I understand that the nature of your work is highly classified, which is why there is no recording of surveillance of our discussion. In fact, given the parameters I have, I believe it would be in my own best interests to know as little about your operational activities as possible. Nonetheless, fourth, my directives are to obtain your confession and, again, I am very good at my job. Time is running out Major."

"You have no idea Colonel. As good as you may be at your job, I highly presume it does not include prophecy. Time *has* run out," retorted Aiguo-Tao.

Zhào stood, walked to the door and knocked. The Master Sergeant opened the door, flanked by an Air Force Sergeant. "For now, the Major may return to his quarters," pronounced Zhào. The Master Sergeant moved toward Aiguo-Tao to remove his handcuffs.

In less than a span of three seconds, the Air Force Sergeant moved to grab Aiguo-Tao's left hand, to firmly hold it on the table, while transferring a serrated, stainless steel blade to Zhào. In one, orchestrated motion, as soon as his hand was slapped on the table, Zhào sliced through Aiguo-Tao's little finger, leaving it dismembered, with a slight wiggling, on the table, and slammed a cauterizing device on the wound to immediately stop any blood flow. Aiguo-Tao smelled the distinct odor of burning flesh – his.

Aiguo-Tao stared at the small pool of blood realizing he had been caught off guard.

His mental file card rapidly flashed in his head - his wrists remained in the handcuffs, both Sergeants pressing down on his shoulders, a surgical knife, two Norinco CQ rifles, two QSZ-92 9mm handguns, K-bar knife Master's right boot, open hall, two targets past door, maybe three, only three code numbers.

He would replay the events later, on his own time, to learn from his mistake. Aiguo-Tao felt no pain, yet his anger flooded his senses.

"You have no idea what you are doing and the harm you have truly already caused," he intensely proclaimed. 'Now focus, focus', he repeated to himself.

Zhào left the room, walking to the exit door to leave. He turned toward his *project* while opening the door, and spoke loudly enough to carry the hallway, "Major, *archaic* as you might classify it, please remember, I am good at my job."

Aiguo-Tao squinted his eyes with an eerie glare at Zhào. He turned his head away straining not to smile and running it through his head, "*6 - #, the Chairman's birthday, 1-5-0-6-#, 15 June.*"

The Master Sergeant quickly placed a second pair of handcuffs on Aiguo-Tao before releasing him from the ones bound to the table. The Air Force Sergeant slammed a hood over his head, tightly cinching it around his neck. The guards raised him from his chair an escorted him to the door.

Aiguo-Tao tensely and silently walked to the elevator with his escorts guiding him to his cell. He could feel the barrel of the pistol pressed into his neck while the Master Sergeant asked for his cooperation to remove the handcuffs and hood.

His burst of fury had subsided almost as quickly as it set in. Emotions over focus would not serve him any purpose. Disarming and killing the guards would not advance an operational goal, at this time.

9

The car pulled into the lower level, restricted parking enclosure and up to the curb in front of the security entrance. Huiwei was already stepping out of the back seat before the driver could reach her car door. The driver remained silent and stern holding the backdoor open and ready to close it behind Huiwei.

Huiwei stepped onto the walk area saying, "Thank you for the ride . . . sorry I don't know your rank."

"No rank Colonel Lí. I'm just a driver."

Addressing the driver again, Huiwei added, "Please do give my best to your husband and children."

With a surprised look, the driver responded, "Sorry Colonel . . . I do not have a husband or children."

Turning toward the glass doors to the building, Huiwei gave a slight smirk, "I know. And, don't be sorry, I know they wouldn't be."

The driver's face showed a confused look, slightly shook her head and walked back to the driver's seat to set out for her next route.

Huiwei walked on, to the security doors, carrying her satchel over her right shoulder and stretching her security identification card from the retractable clip on her jacket lapel.

She scanned the card, heard the door click, and approached the team of security guards to go through the metal detector, then scanned by a wand, and to have her satchel scanned and searched. There was a freestanding cubical, with a gray, plastic curtain, should more invasive searches be determined.

Her lucky day. The security guard, Huan, recognized her.

"Please, come on through Colonel Lí," as Huan waived off the guard with the wand and another on the baggage belt. She always appreciated his small gestures of kindness and thought her father would be much like he was.

"Thank you Huan. I am running late. Please, give my best to your wife and grandson," she said, smiling.

Huan smiled, "I will Colonel. He's almost six now and I think he's coming to see the Giant Pandas next week. I can give him private access without the line. A small perk of the job." He greatly appreciated the fact that Colonel Lí always remembered his name and asked about his grandson.

She smiled back, "That's wonderful. He will be proud of his grandfather."

Huiwei heard the squeak of her rubber soles on the polished, granite tiles. She walked past the corridor leading to the information center where more security existed to gain access to the mainframe and data server rooms. She pranced up the open stairs constructed in granite, chrome and glass.

Her office was on the first floor so she had ready access to the information center. She reached the glass door claiming, "MSS

Strategic Genome Research" with an etched drawing of a Panda. Huiwei scanned her I.D., logged her thumbprint on the scanner and pulled the door open. No one even seemed to look up as she passed the open workspace with about twelve, mostly non-military people, fixated on their computer screens.

She reached her office and dropped her satchel behind her desk as she sat down. The three-by-four-meter office was small, but she had enough clout to earn a window, and a view of the gardens, as opposed to the crowded streets.

She pulled a private, encrypted, iPad out of her desk and pulled up the streaming of the State news channel out of Beijing.

Then she turned on her desk computer and entered a series of passwords and prompts. One hundred-three stokes later, the secure screen for the Wuhan Institute of Virology popped up. She knew the backdoors, she created them.

She opened the communications database with the firewalls tumbled down from her access coding. Technically, she could access the site from her laptop, but the cyber footprint would be far too easy to track. At the Center, she could route her access through the mainframe, and innocuous IP and URL sources.

The State news commentators seemed to be focused on the usual stories protesting the U.S. trade policies, the superior economics of China and the importance of citizens to adhere to designated protocols to maintain their social scores. An interview of a female occupant in one of the Uyghur encampments, in Xinjiang, extolling the wonderful accommodations, work opportunity and benevolence of the Chairman. Nothing yet.

In the Institute's communications database, Huiwei typed in keyword searches. Her point of curiosity should not require her to program a special search protocol, or risk some caffeine riddled programmer from noticing an errant program they can't access.

There it was. The early signs. Security protocols were obviously activated. They typically called for one-line, or somewhat cryptic, brief statements:

Containment protocol reviewed - request direction

Executive security conference, mandatory 1 p.m.

SCIO SARS protocol review – conference Ministry of Transportation (secure)

In the past, China's response to crisis management was relatively simple. Contain the communications, remain silent, eliminate any hostile sources, deny, and publish the re-determined narrative – gag and redirect.

Since the SARS outbreak in 2003, the Central Committee and the CCP quickly learned that the scope of Internet communications and the increasing intertwining of global commerce not only was a boom for China's economy, but a bust for the Ministry of Communications, now dispersed and folded into other ministries for crisis communications control. The State Council Information Office, SCIO, was at the top of the food chain.

Since graduate school, at the Tsinghua National Laboratory for Information Science and Technology, Princeton, and a semester at MIT, Huiwei had long studied the human dynamic statistical modeling for many events in history, including the impact of communications. The propaganda machine of the *Commission for Public Information* in the United States during World War I, the Soviet *Ministry of Information* with its disinformation and foreign insertion strategies, even prompting, if not creating, the U.S. anti-war movement during the Viet Nam War and the election of President Johnson.

Anymore, Communications strategies were as much about controlling the communications in the homeland as it is to impact the communications in foreign countries.

Her predictive models were premised on proven basics. People are malleable in determining truth. At the individual level, it's almost child's-play. At the group dynamic level, it was only a matter of inserting credible variables. At a national level, it was more about identifying the existing variables, pinpointing the right group, the weak links in the chain, then inserting designed variables from different directions, sometimes intentionally contrary to the other, and watch the wildfire consume the forest.

Determining the variables and accurately knowing the predicted outcome was what made Huiwei so dangerous, or beneficial, depending on where a person sat at the table.

Her career gained credibility with her accurate modeling of human, political and economic impacts beginning with the SARS outbreak, continuing with the Beijing Olympics, earthquakes and other crisis situations. Young and female, in 2003, her research and recommendations on SARS was often ignored, or superiors took full credit for those elements successfully implemented. It took a few more years before her predictive modeling algorithms were rediscovered – with a newly found appetite for her genius.

An ambitious Major General attempted to implement one of Huiwei's protocols, as his own concept, without fully understanding the coding design. His attempt to gain great favor with the SCIO ended disastrously and with his unceremonious cremation. In the aftermath, technology engineers unraveled the programming, discovering Huiwei's original footprint and design. The brilliance of her predictive modeling, in capable hands, stood out like a single, white water-lily in the middle of a garden pond.

Once more, she found a certain amount of trepidation with a spotlight on her intellect. The rapid promotions should be appreciated, yet any anonymity to her life would seep slowly, then vanish. She had been down this road before.

Changing her search words, and playing off of the tidbits she found, Huiwei dug deeper:

SCIO directive to Ministry of health, wet markets Wuhan Univ. Wuhan – Zhongnan Hosp. – containment directive MSS – Zhongnan med. Personnel ID – interrog.

Huiwei felt a chill run through her spine. The crown was out of the castle. A newly, hybridized corona virus that was only known to a small group of virologists at the Wuhan Institute. This was once true for SARS and MERS as well.

She now used a hacking code to access the SCIO – the masterminds of China's communications control. Knowing the embedded protocols in the government systems, once her program entered into the SCIO system, it would simply blend into the background as a legitimate MSS file. It was, perhaps, the most protected computer system next to the MSS. There would be nothing unusual about her footprint in the MSS programs, since she developed, wrote, or reconfigured the coding for many of the programs.

Dx fault – config med rec Zhongnan Hosp.
Rhino soup, pango + test insert
MSS maj. Ag-l s/d recon. Ear. Rpt. → Col. Zhào

There it was. There were more, but that was enough to confirm.

The SCIO, and in turn, the Central Committee, were entering panic mode. Merit was not always a virtue in climbing the political ranks. Political dogma and networking often won out. Members of the Central Committee often had one- foot-in and one-foot -out when dealing with traditional doctrines and strategies of the China Communist Party, CCP, and the realities of Global interactions – wealth opportunity was also not a missed factor.

Huiwei mentally recalled her background research. There are four, common, corona viruses around the World, 229E(alpha), NL63(alpha), OC43(beta) and HKU1(beta). The first one was identified in the 1960s. The initial belief, or excuse, was that these viruses infect humans through small, wild animal sources, such as feces.

Animals are always an easy target in public relations. It is not the type of virus that is easily transmitted from an animal to a person. Still some debate if it is possible in the wild. Most would not know they have it, although some serious reactions have been suspected. Coronas, and similar viruses found in animals, like protein-folding prions, involved with mad cow disease, simply are not highly transmittable to humans, and certainly not a pandemic concern.

When Huiwei worked on the SARS modeling, her intellect drove her to find as much background data as she could, the potential variables. In that process, she was uniquely perplexed. First, it appeared to her that China, through the Wuhan Institute, literally *owned* the corona virus, in all its forms. There had been an entire series of research teams over the years in a sizable facility for this seemingly innocuous viron. Second, virtually all electronic records before 2000 had been destroyed or never entered into a database at all. In a sense, the research teams never existed, not even the ones she had met.

Tracking down the few retired workers she could, off-the-record, Huiwei began to fit the pieces of the puzzle together. It appeared to her that in the early 1990s two young researchers were interested in corona viruses, because they had unusually long RNA, genome strands, often over 30 kilobases. While DNA sequencing was becoming the Midas-touch for research with the progression of supercomputer applications, RNA was at best the bastard child of research. After all, who wanted a dancing virus when you could clone a sheep or make warrior pandas.

There was some unrecorded or destroyed breakthrough. The young researchers found a method to manipulate and re-sequence the RNA genome. The virus had an affinity to attack the respiratory system and anchor itself to the tissues, including the lungs. The names of these researchers completely disappeared from any government records. Likely, the reward was their permanent disappearance.

Huiwei surmised that someone up the chain of command stumbled across these early results and recognized the potential applications. She knew that MERS and SARS were far different than the original four viruses rather benignly floating in and out of human contact, and the effects were certainly more devastating.

Huiwei had a talent for seeing seemingly unconnected variables and finding the connection – that was her calling card. She did not believe in coincidence. Wuhan Institute had these viruses that by all accounts did not exist in the World outside the laboratory.

"Bat-soup," she shook her head – 'Rhino.' She knew that with SARS, the SCIO went on a campaign to manufacture test results showing that it originated with *Rhinolophis sinicus*, a common bat, that somehow infected wild, civet cats with exposure to humans. These creatures sometimes reached the 'wet markets' of China where wild animals were sold for food. On the heels of the H5N1, Avian flu virus, in Hong Kong, blaming wilds birds for infecting poultry, it was not a public-relations stretch to defame the bat population.

More importantly, perhaps, she knew that most people do not have warm, fuzzy feelings for bats – thus, a perfect social, target variable to predict human behavior patterns. "Pangos?" Another easy target. The rather innocent, insect eating pangolins. A rather ugly little creature to most, with a scaly hide, much like the armadillo in the United States.

The other cryptic lines were easier for her to discern. The SCIO was ordering medical records at the hospital to show diagnostics errors by the medical staff. Most likely those health professionals will have a shorter lifespan than they presumed, or are providing medical services in a re-education camp, just by being in the wrong place at the wrong time – they knew too much already, and didn't even know it. Laboratory tests will be manufactured to document the significant infestation of the virus in bats and pangolins, allegedly sold in the Wuhan, wet-markets.

The critical communications of interest to Huiwei was that her chain of evidence for security access will lead straight to an MSS major name Aiguo-Tao. "s/d," *search and destroy*, seemed a bit dramatic, yet perhaps accurate.

She felt the perspiration growing in her armpits and her neck, damping her shirt collar. She was fully aware she had orchestrated the contamination of the newly mutated virus in Wuhan. She could only pray to gods unknown to her that the protocols she left embedded in the research information were quickly reviewed and followed to control the spread. People would die. Her hope - it would be minimalized.

There were many variables she would have wanted first. However, based on the MSS documents she tripped over in the database, time had run out. Verification was impossible without being exposed. She presumed the mentioned vaccine worked, but there was no time to research its development records or testing on animals . . . hopefully humans as well.

A staff assistant knocked on her door and entered the office, "Colonel Lí, I believe the panda genome team is waiting for you to join them in the main conference room on the third-floor."

Startled, like waking from a dream, Huiwei responded, "Thank you. I'll be right there." She began to carefully enter her code protocols to close out the files and erase her cyber footprint.

Now, her hope rested in whether she had created a serious enough disruption to interfere with Aiguo-Tao's assets. There was a pandemic to stop.

10

Aiguo-Tao rested after his self-determined exercise regime of push-ups, sit-ups and aerobics using the limited space to attempt various Parkour movements. His frustration was the limits of the small room to build up enough speed and momentum to run at least a half-circle on the walls, before flipping to the ground.

He took a few sips from a new bottle of water, holding his left hand out, and staring at his three fingers and thumb.

The cauterized knuckle had a twinge of discomfort, but any pain was non-existent. He had vaguely heard of *phantom limb sensation*. Now, he was mesmerized with staring at his hand and actually feeling the little finger that was no longer there.

Sitting on his mattress, Aiguo-Tao stared into thin air trying to gain some estimation for what day and time it was. *"How much time has passed?"* he whispered. He had slept, how long he did not know, not long. He had completed his exercise regime twice. While sparse, the guards had opened his door to provide water and rice cakes two more times. He had anticipated encountering Zhào by now.

He mentally outlined the logistics of his orchestrated operation. So many pieces in locations far apart. His planning was flawless – he knew that. The inevitable problem was always the human-element of execution.

It was almost eighteen months ago. He was called into the strategic planning room in the underground, concrete bunker near Beijing, and was directed to the end of the large conference table nearest the door. The table was sparsely occupied by seven other individuals displaying uniforms from the various branches of service, and civilians – some scientists among them.

The room seemed dimly lit with the dark grey walls absorbing most of the indirect lighting. In front of him was an open laptop that displayed the graphics and information shown on the three large flat screens, suspended from walls at the opposite end of the room. The laptop and screens were a shimmering white, blank, except for a file prompt, "*Password required.*"

At the other end of the table, silhouetted by the ambient light of the screens, sat a slightly portly woman wearing a dark suitcoat adorned with several medals pinned to her breast pocket. He felt confident she was a high-level official from one of the ministries or perhaps even a member of the Central Committee. Wearing such decorations by a civilian was considered an affront to any member of the military – except for the narcissistic tendencies of powerful officials.

The woman wore reading glasses attached to a gold chain around her neck. She looked up from a file folder in front of her, directing her focus on him, "Major Zhu Aiguo-Tao." He bowed his head, standing at attention. "Please sit."

She nodded to the side, and a young female PLA officer seemed to appear out of the shadows and placed a tea cup and saucer in front of him, then poured the tea from a blood-red, ceramic teapot. He could see the steam rise from the cup and noticed the insignia of the CCP on the matching red cup. He gave a slight bow to the young officer and respectfully took a sip of tea.

The woman continued, "Major, I am Sun Jun-Lai." Aiguo-Tau recognized the name – he was impressed.

"As you likely know, I am the Assistant Secretary of the SCIO and sit on the Central Committee. Your security clearance level has been elevated so that you can see the information I am about to show you. Based upon your record, I do not question your loyalty or sense of discretion. However, you need to understand there are fewer than a handful of others outside this room that know what we are about to discuss and the utmost confidentiality must be absolute." Aiguo-Tao gave a slight bow of his head.

"Doctor Qiao, please proceed," she said.

A rather older, thin, bald man tapped on his laptop, filling in the file prompt, revealing only asterisks on the screen. The screens and laptops showed a graphic of two twisting strands, labeled, "RNA."

Dr. Qiao spoke, "What you see are two different strands of viral RNA. The shorter one from rhinovirus, the common cold, and the longer one from a common corona virus found in various small forest animals around the World. RNA, as opposed to double helix DNA, mutates quite easily on its own; however, artificially modifying the RNA sequencing in a laboratory, with any predictability or long-term control is extremely challenging. Without delving into the potentially boring microbiological, recombination polycistronic details, given the extended sequencing of the corona virus'

RNA, we have had remarkable success in controlling certain artificial mutations."

Dr. Qiao continued to advance several slides showing microscopic images of the various corona viruses. They were colorful spheres with unusual hairy spikes poking up with little caps, like crowns, on the ends.

"The coronas in the wild are relatively harmless. In the bigger scheme of things, statistically speaking, they seldom reach human hosts with any concerns. It favors the respiratory system and does not have the same expansive desires as with its deadly cousin Ebola. Without belaboring historical events, SARS is a corona virus and developed in our research laboratories. Mostly, becoming an unintended control test, by human error. However, Hong Kong was an excellent petri-dish," Dr. Qiao said.

The shuffling of the individuals in their chairs was almost simultaneous and audible.

A PLA general interrupted, "What would prohibit it from mutating into a more serious situation, doctor?"

Dr. Qiao's eyes seemed to light up, "Ah, general, an excellent question and critical point. Viruses as you obviously know, from your question, love to mutate, mostly because of some environmental pressure, a type of epigenetics. A mutant, however, only survives to reproduce, replicate, if it advances a usable purpose, it replicates. Mutations are a bit trial-and-error and most do not survive. We have been able to sequence the corona so it basically has nowhere to go. It will mutate, but the mutant viruses will not likely replicate with a functional change. Maybe some resistive forms, but not a different variant, functionally. SARS improved our understanding of this process. It survived and replicated for a while, but without finding a purpose to change, it fundamentally disappeared. Basically, within a year, you could only find SARS in preserved, laboratory samples."

The general grumbled again, "But if other countries have samples to study won't they find these attributes?"

"Again, general, an excellent point. Politics often control scientific research. Again, as you know general, once the SARS effectively died out, there was no political motivation to look further. The panic was over and so was much of the research funding. More interestingly, we believe our newer corona has a potential 'rebound' capacity. It will lie dormant, even within a cured host, and possibly return. Only an observation for the moment as we pursue testing." Dr. Qiao paused.

Dr. Qiao, then looked at Aiguo-Tao, "Major Zhu, more detailed scientific briefing will be provided for you in preparing your operation. For now, the central point is that our corona virus is quite unique from other viruses contracted by humans and has an extremely high contagion-level – it's easy to pass along. It is not the common cold, nor are there preventative vaccines or natural immunities in the human population, often referred to as 'herd immunity,' as there are with various influenza virus strains. It will, however, bring things to an economic standstill."

"Thank you Dr. Quio," interrupted Secretary Sun. "The World has changed. The People's Republic, nor any other major power, can predictably engage in major warfare and sustain a known, favorable outcome, especially in economic or political terms. Our destined dominance, however, can be predictably controlled by a strategic viral outbreak in the most economically developed countries where our belt-and-road strategies are more limited, until our 5G networks are adopted in the West. While certain portions of an affected population will succumb to predictable mortality rates, likely respiratory failure, most will not. It is not a tool of extinction, but rather one of economic disruption. Isolating the impact on the population of the People's Republic, or other geographic areas, is achievable within acceptable parameters. General He'?"

A confident, bass voice spoke up, "Thank you Secretary Sun. As you can see in the charts on your screens . . . our strategic planning for over two decades has progressed to the point of maneuvering capitalistic greed to where the People's Republic effectively controls the production of pharmaceuticals, or pharmaceutical components, for most of the common medicines in the World. This includes antibiotics and vaccine production. The last aspirin was made in the United States in 2002. In other words, we control the spigot to the health of any population around the globe."

Aiguo-Tao recalled his prolonged introduction to the operation that would consume him for the next eighteen months. Charts and maps were displayed showing the impacts, deaths, political and economic changes resulting from epidemics over history. From theories on the viral extinction of the dinosaurs, to the several major plagues, smallpox, the Spanish flu and into more modern health events such as polio, to HIV-AIDS, Ebola, and more recent influenza viruses.

Lú Ho-sun, a somewhat youthful and fit PLA officer, for a Major General, introduced himself and his role in supervising scientific research for the MSS. He showed the geographic mapping of highly detailed models specific to the newly developed virus. The modeling was based on a variety of unique factors and variables, such as asymptomatic contraction, vulnerability factors, latent and rebound infection properties, and timetable rates of infection in relation to population density, then overlapped by economic, political and media influences. Of key interest to Aiguo-Tao was the ability to leave the infection sourcing with a relatively untraceable footprint to 'patient zero' as the virus fades out of the population while governments scramble for a cure.

Aiguo-Tao was not a scientist. What impressed him was the strategic, operational relevance to the modeling data. He may not understand the science, but he clearly understood the operational deployment and outcome aspects. He recalled the admonition of a shooting instructor, *"You don't keep your trigger-finger on auto-fire once the objective has been neutralized."* The wheels in his head immediately started spinning to go through the maze of options to find a path for operational success.

Sitting as a prisoner, he knew the operation was in motion. It heavily relied on human assets, compartmentalized in several parts of the World. Human factors always create unpredictable challenges. Decisions and directives need to be made without hesitation with real-time information. The operation depended on it – it depended on him.

He folded his lower lip over his teeth as he contemplated potential pitfalls, finally tasting the blood from unconsciously biting down. Shaking his head, he said, "What the hell is going on, why am I here?"

11

Huiwei was certainly distracted by her own thoughts during the meeting with the genetic micro-biologists. Overall, pure scientists tended to cast a partially deaf ear to the military, especially when in uniform. Despite any educational qualifications, they were the "real" scientists and military officers were soldiers first.

To a limited extent, she recognized the truism to their stereotypic perception. Officers frequently had multiple objectives, were controlled by political realities, and had a different chain of command. The scientists honored the CCP's need to politically control information and facts, but they still primarily relied upon scientific fact to accomplish their goals.

Fortunately, Huiwei's reputation in computer modeling, along with her actual research results, preceded her at the Institute, especially with Dr. Ching, the genome team leader. Her father had been a respected PLA Colonel and she was familiar with Huiwei's medical background and acute grasp of biological impact modeling going back to the SARS outbreak.

Huiwei struggled with anxiousness to get through her presentation. Mostly, it was her unique methods in predictive variables to provide more specific guidance on the sequencing to factors they already knew. In a nutshell, Huiwei could be categorized as an 'evolution denier', at least when it came to higher life forms and Darwinism.

With improved modeling from super computers, her results showed that there simply was not enough time, even over the 65 million years since the end of the Cretaceous period, to go from a limited number of surviving rodent and bird species, to early simians, genetically evolving to early hominid apes, advancing to ancient homo genus species, and eventually modern homo sapiens. Mathematically and statistically, she could show truer realities arising from untapped polygenetic modeling and even some epigenetic concepts, yet evolution theory had become a religion for most scientists, and they could only interpret data with adaptive or selective evolution at the center of their universe. *"It's called a 'theory' for a reason,"* she would scream in her head.

Intentionally avoiding the e-word, and the inevitable debate, Huiwei explained, "At the end of the day, we are fundamentally looking at predicted sequencing that leap-frog's the problems with random DNA mutation. In nature, perhaps 99.9% of mutations in any complex lifeform fail – pandas nor humans are RNA controlled viruses. The majority of genetic mutations are, in fact, harmful to the species. The mutant often dies an early death and certainly never matures to a reproductive capacity. We know we can easily create DNA mutations with such technology as radiation, yet radioactive mutations more likely lead to death not improvement of the species – except for Godzilla perhaps."

She received the anticipated, but reserved laugh from the scientific group. "Still, even with a perceived survival improvement in the species, our friend Godzilla will almost always be reproductively sterile and the improvement dies with the mutant. Cross-breeding creates the same adaptive problem as seen with our farm friend the mule. A superior work animal, yet unable to reproduce. Thus, we have the dilemma of not only identifying useful genome changes, but also ones that will lead to adaptive reproduction and not lost in the scramble of recessive genomes, that may or may not die off in the gene pool, waiting for genetic chance to reappear. RNA virus implants, for example can have a multi-generational impact on allele piggy-backing, thus focusing on recombination as opposed the traditional mutation concepts."

Several in the group nodded their heads in agreement. "This predictive modeling becomes more difficult with each higher level of species, presuming humans are at the top – a presumption that our whale friends might like to challenge."

Another slight laugh from the group. "My research will hopefully accelerate the identification of adaptive genome remodeling, recombination, and artificial sequencing in multi-generational reproduction." She wanted to add, "For our super panda warriors," but she was able to restrain the temptation.

Dr. Ching smiled, expressed her appreciation for the presentation, and asked for any questions. Fortunately, the group was not in an overly inquisitive mood and Huiwei was headed back to her office.

She had a lingering question stuck in the back of her mind from the cryptic email on detaining Aiguo-Tao. "à Col. Zhào," Why, "go to Colonel Zhào", and who was she . . . or he?

With a sense of hurried curiosity, Huiwei logged in her codes to enter the encrypted MSS files. She quickly found the name, "Colonel Zhào Gan-Lí." The file was not difficult to find, but the amount of unredacted information after about 2001, was brief. In 1980, he graduated from the PLA Air Force Flight College, in Changchun. He advanced normally in rank, but his aviation skills were where he stood out – combat fighter pilot, combat pilot trainer, advanced aerial surveillance pilot, putting him in the MSS ranks. No known spouse or family was noted.

While Huiwei needed to peruse a number of redacted documents, she assembled a reasonable picture from the jig-sawed pieces of data. In the late 1990's, Russia remained stumbling after the fall of the Soviet Iron Curtain and new leadership rose and fell within the once powerful military. Every country felt a need to know as much as possible about the rebuilding of the Russian military, with particular interest in locating the remnants of its nuclear assets.

On October 12, 1998, Zhào was flying a high speed, low surveillance aircraft. He was intercepted by two Soviet MiG 29's. Although his aircraft was not a fighter, it was combat equipped. Zhào was able to seriously damage one MiG and the other retreated, but in the process, Zhào's aircraft was hit. The remarkable factor was that as Zhào ejected from his cockpit, he deployed a specialized TBX, thermobaric, charge that would effectively incinerate the black box and surveillance data collector, along with a good portion of the aircraft. Any usable data was destroyed, but he was left with life-threatening, high-heat burns. Upon capture, near Krasnoyarak, the Russian GRU attempted to interrogate him, apparently without much success. To avoid having Zhào die in their custody, he was part of a prisoner exchange with the People's Republic in 1999.

As best has she could piece together, especially with her medical knowledge, Zhào received multiple surgeries which she knew were extremely painful and in 2015 he underwent chemo-therapy and radiation treatments for thyroid cancer. Absent a compromised immune system, it appeared he was healthy enough to return to active duty.

Grounded, Zhào was trained as an MSS interrogator. His operations record was largely blank after 2002.

Huiwei knew her office had been searched, probably on a regular basis. She opened a desk drawer, rummaged under an assortment of pens and highlighters, finding a pink, plastic case to carry tampons. Unnoticed to most, the innocuous case required her fingerprint to open it. Her presumption, when she designed it, was that even if it was a curious junior agent, the person would look and feel foolish fumbling with a pink tampon case during a search. Huiwei knew predictable human behavior.

Opening the pink case, she checked to see if the high efficiency, lithium-ion battery for the electronic scanner remained operational – it was. She periodically scanned her office to know where, not if, the micro listening or video devices were located. Using a small cable, she plugged the scanner into a USB port on her computer, accessing an updated, electronic security program she wrote.

The download complete, Huiwei called the security station requesting they call for a taxi. As she finished packing her satchel and began to head for the door, her phone rang. The identification screen on the office phone, scrolled, *"SECURITY."* *"Took them long enough,"* she whimsically said.

Picking up the receiver, she politely said, "Ni hao," *hello.*

In response she heard a young female voice, "Is this Colonel Lí? This is the security office."

"Yes, this is Colonel Lí. Has my taxi arrived?" she remained standing, turning toward the window. She could hear the low rumble of a muffled male voice in the background on the other end of the line.

"Colonel Lí . . . we have taken the liberty of arranging a private car for you . . . from the Institute . . . as one has become available. We trust that would be preferred," said the person on the other end. So, who is *"we"*, she thought.

Huiwei responded, "That will not be necessary. A taxi will be fine. I need to run a quick errand and then I can take the train."

The woman's voice was now obviously stressed, "That will not be a problem . . . the driver will be able to take you where you wish . . . and drive you to your apartment . . . it will be no trouble."

Huiwei thought about just curtly hanging up, but politely said, "Thank you. I'm leaving my office now," then replaced the receiver to the phone base on her desk.

Turning back to look out over the garden, Huiwei contemplated her next move. Evidently, *"we"* and *"they,"* are not wanting her exit from the Province to be unnoticed, she mused.

During her brief time in Chengdu, she had developed a limited acquaintance with Jun-Ling, the owner and healer at an apothecary shop not far from the train station in Tianfu Square.

Jun-Ling was a soft-spoken, studious looking man, perhaps in his mid-fifties, or sixties, it was difficult to tell. He wore round, thin framed glasses and a drab-grey jacket over his shirt, much like a short lab coat.

Huiwei shared with Jun-Ling that her father had run a pharmacy and apothecary shop. She shared some of her memories of being honored to go to work with him as a girl.

She also discussed her own knowledge of acupuncture and herbal therapies, attributing it to her father and not medical school, or trial and error. He was obviously very reserved in attempting a casual discussion with a uniformed, PLA Air Force Colonel.

He did appreciate her knowledge and was becoming more affable, with each visit, as he vetted her with subtle technical and practical questions. Huiwei enjoyed his wisdom-interrogation technique. She intentionally omitted, even lying, about significant details regarding her background, where she grew up, her family, education, and military experience. She was sincere about going with her father to the pharmacy and apothecary shop he managed.

Earlier, anticipating her lack of transportation preference, Huiwei had called Jun-Ling with a list of supplies and herbal concoctions. She knew that some of her requests might be met with a raised eyebrow for the average consumer, but, evidently, she had passed his inquisition process. He promised her order would be assembled and waiting for her at the end of the day.

Huiwei walked out of the lower-level door. She saw a young man, in his white shirt, thin black tie and black suit, standing at attention next to the open backdoor to the car. When she approached, he gave a slight bow of his head simply stating, "Colonel Lí."

Huiwei got in the car, the door closed and the young man moved to the driver's seat. "My understanding is that you need to stop before we drive to your apartment in Guanghan."

"What a mind-reader you are," thought Huiwei.

While expressionless, he seemed like a close friend compared to the driver in the morning. She thought about how popular her file photo and certain personal information was becoming with others.

"I need to go to this apothecary shop near the Square. My apartment is quite nice, yet lacks a relaxing aroma. Then, I need to find some things at the food stalls across the street, if your time allows, of course," she said.

He nodded his head looking into the rearview mirror and she handed him her iPhone showing the location on the GPS map.

Stating an address number in Changdu can be more complicated than simply showing the visual location. In giving drivers locations, she thought about the ease of it in the United States, where the streets north and south simply ascended or descended in numerical and the east to west streets had known names – Boston being an exception, of course.

The driver looked at the map, "Yes, I know exactly where that is, and perhaps a shorter route than other drivers." He handed back the iPhone. Huiwei slightly smiled, saying to herself, "*Oh my, a real human being on my tail. A mother who taught her son manners, and extra points for at least some intelligence.*"

Huiwei first went to the food stalls on the open sidewalk, entering a couple of the adjoined business, then walked across the street to the apothecary shop.

Jun-Ling was not there. Huiwei identified herself and the clerk, an older woman with frizzy hair and the same drab-grey lab coat, acknowledged her. She found the wrapped package, showed Huiwei the hand-written ticket and Huiwei paid the price stated on the receipt, leaving a ten Yuan note for the clerk. The sullen face of the clerk brightened with her best effort for a smile.

She nodded, and Huiwei left to go find her driver. Not a difficult task since he was standing next to the shop's door and peering in. As nice as he seemed, he had not advanced past covert surveillance for eight-year-olds, trying to find out what mother is buying for a birthday gift.

They walked to the car, he asked for her bags and reached across the backseat to set them down. Then, she got in the backseat. Once the sequence of polite chauffer theatrics ended, the car took off and headed to Huiwei's apartment.

12

Aiguo-Tao heard the door-bolt releasing. He saw the barrel of a rifle poke through as the door slowly opened, then the face of a young soldier who held another water bottle and rice cake. The sheepish look on his face told Aiguo-Tao that his reputation, now, preceded him.

Sitting on his mattress, Aiguo-Tao barked, "Tongzhi . . . *comrade.*" The young man reflexively dropped the water and cake, trying to awkwardly raise his rifle. Calmly, Aiguo-Tao said, "Thank you, tongzhi. I was expecting Colonel Zhào by now."

The soldier held tight to his rifle, now pointing it toward the floor, as he saw the prisoner sit with crossed legs and almost motionless.

With a nervous voice, trying desperately *not* to sound nervous, he responded, "Colonel Zhào was not feeling well . . . perhaps bad fish." He, then looked wide-eyed, almost angry, "I will not talk to you. You may eat your cake now."

In the shadows of the hallway, Aiguo-Tao saw two figures appear. The young soldier hurried away and the Air Force Sergeant stepped inside with the PLA Master Sergeant behind him.

"The Colonel is ready to speak with you again," as the Sergeant motioned with his hand for Aiguo-Tao to stand, stepping aside so he could walk out the door in front of his guards.

In the interrogation room, the Air Force Sergeant attached the tethered handcuffs while the Master Sergeant stood near. Aiguo-Tao slid the one-meter chain a few inches each way through the metal loop welded to the table and watched as Zhào used his handkerchief to dab away the sweat on his forehead, before using it to cover several boisterous coughs.

Zhào gathered his composure, then spoke, "Major, I hope that my generosity in providing a day's rest is not misinterpreted and has given you time to reassess your cooperation. As noted, whether removing each finger would accomplish my goal, it would be a some-what prolonged . . . and painful process."

The Air Force Sergeant, then carefully placed the scalpel with the long, serrated blade in front of Zhào for some sort of dramatic effect – that was lost on Aiguo-Tao.

"Major, I am running out of time and patience, mostly time. Your statement, confession if you will, is needed, and I will get it," said Zhào.

Interrupting, Aiguo-Tao calmly stated, "And, once again Colonel, it remains impossible for me to give a confession to matters I do not know."

Zhào quickly pulled up his white cloth and coughed several times once more. Aiguo-Tao saw the small spots of blood on the cloth in different hues of red to brown. *"Dried blood? Zhào has been coughing for some time,"* he presumed.

Zhào dabbed his forehead and began speaking again, "Perhaps we can get to the matter, as well as focus your memory to what you say you do not know. When I was called to investigate you several days ago, I went to your laboratory facility in Wuhan. I personally inspected the security records with highly trusted computer security officers from the MSS."

Aiguo-Tao concentrated on maintaining an expressionless face. He was in charge of all security in the laboratory building at the Wuhan Institute. What was he talking about?

"I do not know, nor do I want to know about the project you were assigned to. The obvious facts are that you were in charge of the security for the project, whether it is some clever explosive, deadly gas or miscreant toxin . . . containment was compromised."

Aiguo-Tao sensed that his poker-face waivered.

"See . . . Major! From your expression, I believe your memory is bouncing back. Now, of course, despite your attempts to cover up your access coding – very good, I might add . . . it took a while to trace things; nonetheless, the containment breach, as you know, was your own."

If his face showed any expression, it was confusion, now. *"This is impossible,"* he thought. The operational batches could only be handled by himself or the two technicians he selected, using an environmental chamber, glove box. A computer program generated randomized security codes paired with their biometric print. Even *he* did not know their codes or when they changed.

Cheap, 4mb flash drives were swabbed with the virus, along with several pieces of local currency for the target country, then put in a vacuum-sealed plastic casing, and placed in small, hard plastic delivery containers. It would take several blows from a 4kg sledge-hammer to break open the container.

Three to five flash drives, with some currency, were delivered to each asset. The containers were decontaminated, electronically labeled, and then programmed outside the chamber with the individualized biometric code for the asset. Only the asset could open their own container once it left the laboratory.

Assets were instructed to insert the flash drive in various, computer devices that were commonly shared, such as the point of sale, *POS*, devices to charge credit cards at a bar, or at a reception desk. Then, they were instructed to leave the device on a table or in another public area to let some unsuspecting stranger dispose of it anonymously. The flash drives contained one or two downloaded apps for smartphone kids' games. Then, leave the currency for tips, or just in places where a person would pick it up and take it.

The assets believed they were downloading some virus. They were – just not inside the computer. In a humorless mind, Aiguo-Tao enjoyed the double-entendre he created.

"As you see Major, I am not seeking your confession on what you did or how you did it. We have the records. What the Ministry demands is your confession and identification of your benefactor."

"Benefactor?" Aiguo-Tao whispered, still confused.

"Yes, Major, whether it was a government or an intermediary dealer, we need to know who bribed you. You'll never see the money of course, but the Ministry gives you credit for the difficult transaction trail. Personally, I would like you to explain *why* as well; however, that is not critical. I've been doing this for some time, and you certainly do not fit the profile of a traitor, especially one of this magnitude," Zhào said.

He could no longer remain silent with a cloud of thoughts spinning in his head, "Colonel Zhào, I do not know what information you have, but I assure you I am not a traitor!"

Despite the swirling confusion, Aiguo-Tao fought to regain his focus. Above all, he knew there was nothing, but a false confession he could provide, and, regardless, his death was shortly imminent.

"As you may realize, evidently your little escapade resulted in some of your former colleagues to seek medical care. Whatever this thing was, you knew it was harmful, yet you contaminated the cafeteria in the main building and local businesses. I can only presume this was a nervous accident on your part, thinking you would get away with it. We presume whatever else you escaped with is long gone to your source, but we are working on that."

Zhào began another coughing fit, struggling to find his handkerchief in his hip pocket. The Master Sergeant pulled out his own handkerchief and reached across the table to hand it to Zhào.

Aiguo-Tao saw the Master Sergeant's pant leg rise while stretching out and spied the sheath of the K-bar, combat knife strapped to his ankle. He pulled the chain through the metal loop extending as much slack as he could, forcefully grabbed the Master Sergeant's calf, pulling the knife free and sending his target in a hard tumble.

As the Master Sergeant tried to reach into thin air to regain his balance, he knocked the other Sergeant into the prisoner. Aiguo-Tao, focused to bring his choreography into slow motion, to create one continuous movement, plunging the combat knife into the Air Force Sergeant's back, above his belt, into the tenth-thoracic vertebra, twisting to sever the spinal-cord, releasing, and stabbing the razor-sharp blade into his kidney with another twist. Leaving the blade embedded, the sergeant screamed, falling away as Aiguo-Tao grabbed his QSZ-92, 9 mm pistol, pressing the muzzle to the joint of his left handcuff, firing, as the metal bracelet blasted apart.

Pulling the chain through the loop with his cuffed, right hand, Aiguo-Tao reached across the table, grabbing the scalpel in front of the Colonel, as Zhào, continued to cough and was attempting to push himself back away from the table. Too late. The adrenaline-fed frenzy of the slash severed his carotid artery and trachea as Zhào reached for his throat, falling with a crash out of his chair, and his coughing ceased.

Aiguo-Tao was in conscious, auto-pilot mode, flying on adrenaline and muscle-memory from his thousands of hours of training. Zhào's spurting blood barely touched Aiguo-Tao as he had already flung himself on the Master Sergeant. He was trying to stand-up, and Aiguo-Tao wrapped the handcuff chain around his neck bringing him back down to the floor on top of Aiguo-Tao.

He felt the Master Sergeant's body go limp, but he knew he had not yet caused that reaction. "Peng you, peng you," *friend*, he cried with a gurgled voice.

Agiou-Tao cautiously held his grip on the chain and his leg hold, "And, how would you be my friend Master Sergeant?"

Searching for parsed words through the chain, he said, "Wife . . . nurse . . . staff . . . killed . . . save her . . . and son."

Removing the Master Sergeant's pistol, Aiguo-Tao remained confident in his control, sitting up the Master Sergeant, leaving the chain securely around his neck.

Huan-Jun nervously explained that he has a ten-year-old son and his wife is a nurse working in Wuhan. He has made several trips to pick-up prisoners in Wuhan, even doctors and local officials. Huan-Jun presumed their fates were not good.

His wife says there is something very strange going on. People are getting sick, medical staff are being interrogated and sometimes not coming to work the next day, or the next day. He does not mean to dishonor his uniform, but he needs to get his wife and son out of the Province, even if he needs to return to his post.

Huan-Jun indicated that he is not interested in whether it is Colonel Zhào or Aiguo-Tao who is lying, but he believes Aiguo-Tao, and knows he is his only hope to help him get to his family.

Aiguo-Tao knew that only two or three days ago he had an operation that was running smoothly. He still did not know how much time had passed, he did not know where he was, and he did not know what resources he had available. He also did not like leaving things to chance.

Mentally running through his options and situation like a high-speed app for covert special forces, and having observed Huan-Jun, he decided he needed to take a chance. A person with their own objective for a similar goal was an ally and not an unpredictable hostage. They both needed to escape. Quickly.

Aiguo-Tao ejected the chambered bullet in Huan-Jun's handgun and removed the magazine, putting it in his own pocket. He had Huan-Jun give him the sheath for the combat knife attaching it to his leg, removing and wiping off the knife to slide back in the sheath. He also tucked the loaded pistol from the Air Force Sergeant in the back of his pants with his shirt hanging over it. His belt had long been removed and he hoped the gun would stay in place.

He saw the powder burn on his wrist, along with his cauterized knuckle. Any pain remained a shadow in the back of his mind as he loosely fastened a zip-tie restrainer around his wrists, in front of him.

The semi-automatic rifle was a coin-toss in his head. Aiguo-Tao finally reasoned that remaining within arms-length of Huan-Jun, he could disarm him, if needed, before he could do any harm. The rifle would be a significant asset depending on the situations they might encounter. They closed and locked the door to the interrogation room and left.

As Huan-Jun ceremoniously marched his faux-prisoner in front of him to the exit door, he stopped to push in the keycode.

"One-five-zero-six-pound," said Aiguo-Tao.

"Seriously?" Huan-Jun replied, as he shook his head in some disbelief while opening the door.

There was one guard in the hallway, sitting in a chair. He quickly stood up at attention as they walked by. Huan-Jun nodded, not to release his hand from the prisoner. The exit door to the outside was only a few meters down another corridor, as they both looked out the door's window into the graveled area.

"No one would question me using one of the prisoner transport trucks. I could likely get a four-wheel, personnel transport, but it would require checking it out with a clerk, paperwork, and possibly a phone call for approval," said Huan-Jun.

"What's the smallest vehicle without questions," asked Aiguo-Tao.

Huan-Jun nodded with his eyes at a drab-green utility van with a PLA insignia on the side, "It's a low-security prisoner transport. Sometimes, we use it to pick up supplies. One problem . . ."

"What?" said Aiguo-Tao.

"You are a prisoner. If someone was looking, I need to load you through the backdoor. There are benches on each side, but a heavy metal grate between you and the driver – me. You would be a captive in the back with locked doors," said Huan-Jun.

In reply, Aiguo-Tao slightly smiled at him, "Could a prisoner shoot the driver through the grate?"

"Shi," Huan-Jun replied with an ungrateful tone.

"Then, I am not captive Master Sergeant. Let's go," said Aiguo-Tao.

13

Huiwei arrived back at her apartment. All she could think about was that there were too many unknown variables. She liked predictability. With adequate information, she could determine varying paths to alternate certainties. She realized, however, there was no certainty in her immediate future. She let out a sigh.

She had pulled her pink tampon case out of her satchel and scanned the apartment. Surveillance devices were getting smaller and more difficult to detect, even with a scanner. One under the table top next to the front door, and one on the lamp next to her work desk. None outside on the small balcony.

She was slightly miffed they did not think it important to place one on the headboard of her bed. *"So that's what you think . . . I can still kick your ass in or out of bed,"* she said in her best library-voice, only pretending that she hoped someone might hear her. She surmised that every apartment in this building had similar devices planted, to activate when desired. She was confident that hers were active. At least she knew the devices were there, and *where* they were.

Huiwei knew the protocols. In an event, like the one she created, there would be identification of those who had operational knowledge. The names, personnel history, social ranking scores, scope of operational knowledge, with crisis-risk rankings, and other variables would be fed into a series of algorithms.

An artificial intelligence methodology would spit-out the identifications along with recommended action. The A.I. was good, very good, she helped design it.

While her personal touches in the code might divert attention from her for a while, eventually the MSS and SCIO officers would see her name recommended for enhanced surveillance.

Even without her surreptitious intervention, she would have been caught in the net on down the line for risk assessment. As the crisis expanded, surveillance would be factored with risk assessment for the person. A flag for a higher risk would lead to interception, then containment – a prisoner, presumed guilty. The next flag - interrogation. If fortunate, re-education, more likely, a cremation table at the appropriate time. Even the highest-level officers and officials could not escape the program – they all had profiles swimming in the database. Of course, she effectively leap-frogged the process for Aiguo-Tao. Hard evidence of treason, did not require an algorithm.

She was not exactly sure where the program had placed her at this point, but she knew time was running out. It had been all too easy, to her, to develop a program that even she could not beat at chess – and that was twenty years ago – her programming skills had improved since then.

By the time she learned about the corona project and the level of her involvement, time had run out – it was already in active operational mode. She had very little time to act and even less time to plan an escape. It had been over three weeks from when she processed her request to work on a project at the Chengdu Research Center.

Huiwei neatly hung up her uniform, slipped on a pair of hiking shorts and partially buttoned up an old field training shirt with the shirttail hanging down. Walking barefoot into the kitchen, she looked more like she was going camping with a group of college kids as opposed to preparing dinner.

She unpacked her shopping bags on the kitchen counter, separating her apothecary chattel from the items for dinner – although both would eventually share the stove.

She cleaned, chopped and diced away, opening her laptop on the counter and clicking through various journalist blog sites.

Wuhan - Medical staff at a local hospital were observed in what appeared to be protective gear while receiving patients, including one person in a bio-hazard suit. One family member stated that her husband had become ill with a high fever and could not breathe. Others reported similar symptoms for their family members . . .

Hubei Province – Wuhan – Local health officials were seen ordering merchants at a local food market to close up their booths, putting cages of live animals in trucks and driving away. A statement from the city office said some vendors at the market in question sold wild animals believed to be passing fleas to live domestic animals for sale, such as ducks, chickens or even dogs. For the time being, live animal sales are being suspended pending further inspection and testing of animals . . .

With the tight control of information to the public, Huiwei often relied on journalist's blogs. They often times used false names to avoid arrest. On the Internet, they could receive crypto-currency payments from news sources outside of China. She knew her social score could be impacted by pulling up these sites, but she also knew how to route her URL around the customary sniffer programs for social media scoring.

She added more fresh spices and cut vegetables, smelling the aroma of her sizzling meat dish. Besides being hungry, she also knew she would need greater focus with some of the herbs she planned to prepare later.

Wuhan – City Hospital – Given the reports of medical staff using bio-hazard equipment to handle patients, this reporter was able to talk to several staff members who would only talk off the record. One physician commented, "We are not sure what we are dealing with at this time." An emergency room nurse said there are many patients arriving very sick, with high fevers and showing the same symptoms, even though they live in different parts of the city. Based on observations, one thing seems certain . . ."

Huiwei blinked her eyes at the laptop in surprise and clicked at the mouse pad. She was reading the story as it was being posted in real-time. The journalist never finished the sentence, suddenly a quick flash, and the screen was blank.

She stared at the blank screen and a chill hit her spine, then she quickly logged out. She knew that her digital handprint was already set in the wet concrete on the digital path, but she hoped the scanning program could not find her initials scrawled next to her handprint. *"This is not good,"* she whispered. Her appetite subsided.

Huiwei turned off the stovetop burner and moved the pan. She went to her closet, grabbing a plastic, traveling shoe baggie, taking out her running shoes, ignoring the mildewed smell, and slipping her hand inside a hidden sleeve.

Removing the cell phone, she turned it on to make sure the battery was still charged. She sat on the floor of her small balcony with her back against the wall and her knees pulled up toward her face. She had two calls to make. One local, and one to Hong Kong, hoping he was there. Huiwei held her breathe, *"please don't go to voicemail."*

14

Aiguo-Tao shouted over the road noise of the uninsulated utility van, "I told you to stop. Pull over, now!"

The van slowed and came to a stop, with a slight lurch. "Security cameras on the road. I needed to get past their line of sight," Huan-Jun somewhat tersely replied, remembering that his prisoner also had a pistol, probably already pointed at his head.

"Okay. Understood," said Aiguo-Tao.

His trust in Huan-Jun would never be absolute, and it remained a moving scale. He also knew that his captor's familiarity with the facility, even their location, was his best chance at a rapid escape.

"Where are we Master Sergeant?" he asked.

"About 160 kilometers southeast of Wuhan near the Jiangxi Province border. Not far from the PLA base outside of Jiuiang. I need to get to Wuhan. To my wife and son," replied Huan-Jun.

Aiguo-Tao had already determined that his best exit was the Southern shores. He had assets in Taiwan and Hong Kong, depending on where his undetermined transportation plans took him.

Huan-Jun found the key to the lock on the metal grate and watched as

Aiguo-Tao climbed into the front passenger seat. Resting the pistol on his lap, he looked at Huan-Jun.

"Then, we may have a problem as we are going in quite opposite directions. The need for my haste, as you understand, is considerable. I do not believe it is in my best interests to allow you to part my company so soon, especially as my absence will not go unnoticed for long," he said.

"I know you have spared my life, even if to your own benefit, and you owe me nothing. If I do not get to my family, I fear their fate may be worse than my death," said Huan-Jan.

Aiguo-Tau thought for a moment. He saw his plan forming in his head, but many pieces had not yet connected.

"For now, you may drive north. However, I need to find new clothes before we travel far," Aiguo-Tao directed.

"Thank you Major. There is a store not far. I know the owner from picking up some personal orders for the staff. I believe he may be able to help," said Huan-Jun, as he felt some of the nervous tension releasing.

Aiguo-Tao knew he was operating on a very short timeline. He either needed to find an extremely remote rural site, with computer access, or get to the Southern coast. He decided, south, was his better option, but air travel was the only avenue to quickly cover the distance. The commercial airport outside of Wuhan created more options than he might find in the small PLA base at Jinjiang.

15

Huiwei tried to remain calm and chose her words carefully when Jerome Xi answered the phone. It is always possible that either end of their conversation, ends up getting flagged by artificial intelligence in a national security, super-computer.

"Jerome, I know it's been a long time, but this is Huiwei . . . Lí Huiwei, in . . ." she was saying, getting cut-off.

"Huiwei! Of course! Let me see...um...aren't you the beautiful woman who can kick my butt on the training mat and in . . . well . . . interesting you would call as I was just thinking about you," he said.

"You always were such a romantic. Not enough Chinese blood in you, but thank you for thinking of me," she responded.

"Don't hit me when you see me next . . . it hurts when you hit . . . I promise to think about us showering together tonight if that helps . . . but it had to do with some entertaining stuff coming across the wire . . . or I guess, the unsanctioned Internet blogs . . . some animal sickness in Central China. Ya'll gotta' stop eatin' armadillos darlin'. They're roadkill for God's sake," he exclaimed.

Huiwei smiled. At least he would know where to place a surveillance device in her apartment. Jerome was a Commander in the British Royal Navy Air Fleet, often assigned as an *attache'* to Hong Kong. While Hong Kong was released from British control in 1997, with a limited independent government, China was always willing to assert its newborn sovereignty.

His Chinese father was raised in Hong Kong, a businessman holding several political offices. Jerome's mother was a British secondary school math teacher, teaching at a school for international students in Hong Kong, seeking to see the World in her youth.

Despite his cultural pedigree, even matriculating through Cambridge, and fluent in several languages, Jerome had the propensity to break into a Texas drawl, clouded by his British tongue. Given his handsome, athletic appearance, he could probably speak in any accent and be forgiven – at least she could.

Of course, his real job, not published at any newsstands, was his senior role in the Joint Intelligence Operations in association with the Secret Intelligence Services, and probably MI-6, 7, 8, or whatever number they are using. His flying ribbons indicated that he might have known how to operate the controls on a fighter aircraft, but his talents for the twelve years Huiwei knew him involved international, cyber intelligence.

They initially met during politically created joint operational exercises involving Hong Kong, China and the Brits – without doubt the Americans looking on. Their paths had crossed on several occasions over the past decade, in part, because of their independent sleuth abilities to create assignments that were miraculously in the same venue.

Huiwei's voice turned to a serious tone, "Jerome, before you make your next bad joke, I need your help. I got myself in trouble . . . don't say it . . . this is deadly serious, emphasis on the deadly."

"Thanks for the set up . . . but you've obviously got my attention Colonel," he replied, acknowledging that he knew she meant what she said.

"Your phone should show *this* number. George's brother is watching my apartment while I'm in Chengdu working at the Research Center," she said.

Huiwei knew he would understand her Orwellian reference, understand she is under surveillance, not to use any number for her in his contact list, and what her location is.

"Do you recall our days reading Ulysses' tales of the great pandas?"

"You always had a remarkable way to interpret the classics. Most certainly I do," he replied.

Somewhat out of necessity, but also with a flair of innocent teenage romance, they had playfully worked to create their own encrypted language, along with the program to decipher it. It was not terribly complicated to break the code for a cryptographer with average skills.

The uniqueness was being able to type in their coded language, with the program deciphering it into a garbled, nonsensical reading in Mandarin. Then, applying a second encryption application, that accurately read the message in English. Without knowing there was a second application, the message remained useless. There were obvious limits to the scope of vocabulary, but part of the fun were the attempts to come up with new code combinations to expand the conversation. She initially called it 'geek-speak.' Jerome, being the romantic, and knowing her too well, proposed 'Classical Panda.' That was a battle she did not mind losing.

"Perhaps, if I were to map Ulysses' path in escaping the great bears, you could provide more specific landmarks to the caves where he hid," Huiwei only hoped he understood.

Jerome paused to consider his words carefully, knowing the chances that the conversation might also have uninvited ears.

"Oh yes. While his path was far from the beasts roaming the Safari Park of Shenzhen, I believe I can assist. Knowing you, and how deathly serious you always are in your research, I presume you would like my input sooner than later."

Her shoulders relaxed some, knowing he understood with his clever response. Shenzhen was the city closest to the Hong Kong border and well known for its Safari Park zoo. She was glad the code name had an animal reference. He also covered for her opening remarks that she needed to get his attention.

"Yes, that would be perfect. I am hoping to look at Ulysses again day after next. I knew you would be the best person to help with my classical research. I'll be running *hot* until I finish," said Huiwei.

16

They ended their conversation. Jerome silently took his first and last swig from his bottle of Guinness. Standing up from his sofa, turning off the muted rugby game on his TV, and dumping the beer in the sink, he complacently said out loud, "Well panda-boy, showtime." As he walked to his bedroom to don his uniform and grab his pre-packed "go bag," he dialed his contacts, including the RAF Notholt airbase near London.

"Vice Marshal? Commander Xi here. I'm terribly sorry for the imposition. I need to get to Hong Kong . . . In rather a hurry, if I might."

After a brief discussion, he was able to secure the co-pilot seat on a Gulfstream 650-ER. An incredibly fast aircraft, capable of flying at 0.9 Mach, with civilian and diplomatic cover. Jerome indicated to the Vice Marshal it was best to avoid questions and assured him it was important.

Four hours later, the Gulfstream was rapidly picking up speed rolling down the Northolt runway, with four slightly perturbed, but young, Foreign and Commonwealth Office diplomats in the cabin – who were still trying to determine why they were hustled from home to take their flight to Hong Kong, eight hours early, and in the middle of the night. They acknowledged some compensation knowing they were aboard a luxury aircraft for use by others who were far above their pay grade.

Through the flight-check, the pilot, Lieutenant Commander Sloane Emery, was quite pleasant to her new first officer. She saw the ribbons on his coat before he hung it up in the cockpit – not needing to ask questions about his flying capabilities. Her only question was based on a presumption from the theatres of combat shown.

"Fighters and whirly-birds . . . impressive . . . which do prefer?" Sloane asked.

He smiled, "Depends on what our marines need. They see the whites of the enemies' eyes, not I."

"*Commando ops,*" Sloane thought, and pressed the thrust lever forward.

"Commander Xi?" said Sloane.

"Yes, Lieutenant Commander Emery."

"It seems our airline's flight schedule has not met the customer service expectations of our passengers," said Sloane. "Perhaps a flight bonus upon take off?"

"It only seems appropriate Lieutenant Commander," responded Jerome.

Shortly after the wheels left the runway, he saw the elated smile on her face as she thrust the engines, pulling back on the yoke, to a 30-degree climb.

"I do hope the flight attendant collected their cocktails before takeoff," smiled Jerome.

17

The local store owner immediately recognized Huan-Jun and welcomed him inside. Huan-Jun indicated he was taking his family on a hike and picnic.

He told the storekeeper he needed some non-perishable food items, a day-pack, set of hiking clothes, and perhaps some sports shoes - as he should not wear his uniform boots for a pleasure trip. Huan-Jun pulled a tissue from the box on the counter and coughed. "A travel-size first-aid kit if you have one, tongzhi," he added.

The owner rumbled around the potpourri of goods on the shelves around the store. If the store had any particular inventory organization, it was obvious that only the shopkeeper was aware of it. He placed a number of items on the counter for Huan-Jun to inspect.

Huan-Jun gave his approval, the shopkeeper looked pleased that his selections were satisfactory, and he carefully placed the items in paper bags he opened on the counter.

Huan-Jun breathed deep, then inquired, "By chance, do you have a decent camping knife. I do not want to use my military equipment for a family outing. You never know who might come along, even out in the woods."

The owner raised his eyebrow and looked at Huan-Jun a moment, then headed to the back of the store. Huan-Jun thought he might have tested his luck too far, fearing the storekeeper was calling some official. He felt the nervous sweat on his forehead, grabbing another tissue from the counter, coughed and cleared his nose. He let out a breath of relief when the man quickly returned holding two small, clear plastic packages.

One, a hunting knife with a colorful cardboard placard underneath, boasting a razor-sharp, fifteen-centimeter blade, with a hand holding up the knife to the wide-open jaws of an attacking bear. Not military quality, and unlikely to kill an angry bear in hand-to-hand combat, but sturdy. The second, a multi-tool folded up in a camouflage colored, nylon, belt-carrier with a graphic showing the ten different tool devices, from knives, to screwdriver heads and even a small pair of attached scissors. He nodded, and the shopkeeper placed both in a paper bag next to the others.

When he returned to the van, he saw Aiguo-Tao was in the back of the van waiting. He tossed him the bags of items through the metal grate door. Aiguo-Tao remained expressionless, quickly disrobing, using some of the sanitary wipes in the bag to wash off. He put on the new hiking clothes, the adjustable nylon belt, baseball cap, and tested the fit of the sports shoes.

He took a quick inventory of the food items and nodded, stuffing them in the day-pack. When he opened the bag with the knife and multi-tool, he finally found a slight smile. He nodded to his benefactor and somewhat ceremoniously returned the K-bar knife.

"What's in the bag in your hand?" asked Aiguo-Tao with some suspicion.

Huan-Jun looked at the bag and back to his passenger, "Some hiking clothes for my son, and a sun-scarf for my wife. I did not want the feed the shopkeeper's curiosity, and they will be useful when they leave Wuhan."

Aiguo-Tau instructed Huan-Jun to drive to the North side of Wuhan, avoiding routes with congested traffic when possible. He saw the Wuhan Tianhe International Airport in the distance and asked Huan-Jan to pull over.

Aiguo-Tao looked over at his driver, "I have likely overextended my trust to my regret; however, I need to find a quiet place to get to the tarmac. Are you familiar with the perimeter roads to the airport?"

Huan-Jun coughed into his shirtsleeve several times, then, reached to his long, pant pocket, pulling up the Velcro flap. He produced a plastic packet with a new cellphone displaying, "500 Minutes with Limited Data, Prepaid -Fully Charged." He handed the packet to his passenger. Finally, he saw the mysterious man grow a large, sincere smile.

"I told the shopkeeper I thought my son was ready to have a cellphone and I wanted to surprise him on our hiking trip." Huan-Jun returned the smile.

Aiguo-Tao looked at the GPS aerial map and studied the airport. The runways and tarmac were built like a large "H" diagonally sitting northeast to southwest. The public roads and terminal where at the southern end. He pointed to a service road wrapping around the southeastern perimeter and hooking back into the northern end of the "H". Huan-Jun nodded and headed toward the airport.

Aiguo-Tao signaled for the van to pull over near a copse of short trees. He got out of the van, followed by Huan-Jun.

Huan-Jun approached him with a grim face, "I have one more matter to address with you." He saw Aiguo-Tao reflexively reach for the Air Force Sergeant's pistol tucked in his belt. "Meiy'ou, meiy'ou! *no-no*, I need a favor before you leave."

"I cannot help you with your family, I hope you can keep them safe," responded Aiguo-Tao.

"I will take care of my family. I will pick them up on my way back, and hopefully get them to a hidden cabin in a rural area west of Jiujiang, where I have stocked it with some food and water. I will need to hurry and my body grows tired," said Huan-Jun.

Aiguo-Tao relaxed, "What is the favor?"

"I will need to return to the facility after a long absence. They may find me on the road before I return. Hopefully, I can take back roads to drop off my family. I am sure they are already searching." Aiguo-Tao nodded his understanding.

Huan-Jun continued, "You need to have disabled me in some way. They know you are more than capable, but I only have some bruises around my neck from the chain."

Aiguo-Tao looked at the man, with his glassy, red eyes, trying to hold his posture erect, "I have no need to disable you . . . I will keep my word to let you attempt to help your family."

Huan-Jun held his chin up, "You are a skilled fighter. I need you to hit me as you think, so they will know I had no choice and tried to fight back . . . I hope not to need serious medical attention, as I have a long drive still."

Aiguo-Tao, nodded. With a flash, his foot flew into Huan-Jun's ribs. Leaning over in pain, a fist washed across the side of his face below his eye. Finally, he felt a ripping kick across the small of his back, scrapping off the skin under his shirt. He fell to his knees unable to breathe.

It took less than two seconds.

Aiguo-Tao stood back as the man frantically tried to regain his breath. Huan-Jun reached up to his face seeing the blood left on his hand. He rotated his jaw, pressed his tongue to inventory his teeth and slowly stood. Holding his side to harness the lingering pain, he began coughing, doing his best to bow.

"Thank you," he said with a shortness of breath. He looked up adding, "If something goes wrong, you knocked me out near the Yangtze. I will tell them there was a dock where I think you stole a boat."

Aiguo-Tao nodded one more time, turned and jogged to the tree line, parallel to the southern runway, heading toward the hangers. Huan-Jun returned to the van, wiping the sweat from his forehead with his sleeve, still coughing from the blows, and drove back to Wuhan to find his family.

18

Huiwei called her office, telling her office assistant that she would not be in to work today. She had injured her knee while working out and may decide to go to the military infirmary at the base nearby – adding that she has no meetings scheduled, and unless someone asks, she would prefer for others not to know, 'after all it is embarrassing.'

She put a wrap around her knee underneath the hem of her uniform skirt. She grabbed three small packets of herbs she had mixed and dried the night before. She left her hair down, gathering the hair to expose her neck and ear on one side, using a clip with an artificial orchid attached to keep her hair pinned back.

On the elevator, she stopped on the second floor and slipped the keycard into the slot for room 201. She looked around the apartment. It was neat and orderly. Given the bottles on display, the kitchen looked like it was only used to pour a glass of wine or mix a drink.

Most of the cabinets were empty, and she placed a small backpack inside the one closest to the door. The backpack contained a used iPad, some clothes, new running shoes, toiletries, a reusable water bottle and some packets of food, all of which she had purchased quickly at the shops across from the apothecary the day before.

She wiped the few surfaces and knobs she touched, leaving the apartment and taking the elevator to the lobby.

When she walked out of the elevator, Wang lei's eyes widen like an anxious child being picked up at school by his mother.

"Colonel Lí! . . . Is your knee feeling better. . . Can I call a car for you?" he inquired.

Granted, she had taken a few steps, feigning a slight limp, but it was unlikely he had spotted the wrap around her knee.

She responded politely, "Thank you for asking. I am waiting to see how it feels. I may not need a car today." She saw some disappointment in his eyes. "May I ask who was caring enough to inform you about my knee?"

"Oh, . . . I believe it was one of the cleaning ladies, but I don't recall . . . uh . . . actually, I noticed you were limping some," he said, as Huiwei noticed the perspiration forming on his upper lip.

Huiwei was struggling to decide whether he was simply the worst liar to be promoted to a surveillance team, or whether she was missing some detail about his coy methods to get her to let her guard down. As for now, she concluded he was simply a bad liar.

Slipping on her khaki tan uniform gloves, she walked over to the tea service sitting in the lobby. She poured two cups of tea. Using her back as a shield, she sprinkled one packet into a teacup and dipped her fingers in another packet, running her fingers around the teacup and the edges of the saucer.

Holding a saucer in each hand, she turned and walked toward the desk attendant who was pretending not to be staring at a pretty girl in a bar. *"That could be the reason,"* hearing her vanity talk. *"Definitely, not,"* her rationality refocused.

"Wang lei, please share a cup of tea with me." She saw him shake his head and wave his hand in front of his chest, gesturing, *"no."*

"But, I insist. I would greatly enjoy your company as I contemplate testing my knee some more," she almost pouted like a spoil school girl.

She handed him the saucer, now standing inside the average person's, normal comfort zone.

"Well. . ." he nervously replied as she was not retreating. "If you insist . . . I . . ." seeing her take a sip of her tea, almost close enough to feel her breathe, with her looking up at his eyes.

He made a dry gulp, then, quickly swallowed the tea, and realizing his mistake as the hot tea burned down his throat. He coughed, and took a step back with an agonized face.

In a wheezing voice, he sputtered, "Sorry . . . sorry . . . it must have gone down the wrong pipe."

Huiwei's thoughts flashed, *"You still got it girl,"* as she compassionately reached for his shoulder to gesture that he will be fine.

She retreated from her *cat 'n mouse* game. She needed to keep him standing and talking for a few minutes – which she did. Huiwei finally detected the twinge of grogginess settling in his eyes.

Wang lei shook his head mid-sentence as he was babbling a bit by now, "Where was I? . . . I was talking about . . ."

Huiwei interrupted, "You were saying that when they changed the keypad code on the security room this morning, how funny you thought it was that it was the last digits in your phone number . . . that is quite a coincidence."

He shook his head, "No . . . they didn't change it . . . did they?"

Huiwei gently grabbed his elbow and prompted him to turn toward the corridor to the security room, "Oh, Wang lei . . . there's only one way to find out . . . you'd better check . . . you can't lose your job over something so silly."

With a befuddled look on his face, she helped him walk to the door as his urgent attempt to get there would have likely ended with a face-plant on the floor, passed out.

He slowed his motions down and stared at the keypad like a drunk putting the key in his locked car door thinking he can still drive. She believed she saw the numbers that he punched with his index finger and she certainly saw the pattern. The door lock clicked and he opened it. He started to walk in, then, he hesitated, stepped back, and pulled the door shut.

"Oh . . . I'm sorry miss, I can't let you in this room . . . maybe the break room." Wang lei suddenly closed his eyes, pushed his lips out and started to bend to Huiwei's face. With a gentle stiff-arm to the chest, she stopped his forward movement. His eyes opened, still confused, "but you . . . I think it's best if you leave now miss . . . I think I'm going to take my break," he said with a staggered speech.

Huiwei led him across the hall to the small, employee break room that had a small desk and chair, along with a small couch. She helped him on to the couch and watched his eyes blink to stay awake, before his eyelids finally submitted.

Returning to the security room, she removed her khaki gloves and snapped on a pair of latex gloves. Then, she pulled out a small UV flashlight. In trying to keep him from falling, she missed one of the numbers, but the UV light showed his fingerprints in a glowing purplish hue. She wiped off the herbal fingerprints, punched in the numbers and entered the room.

A somewhat basic security set-up – a multiline phone system, first-aid kit, CPR device, three fire extinguishers, a key rack for the golf cart and other vehicles, and a small, and one-way mirror seeing the lobby. Several monitors showed images from the cameras. A control board to bring different camera views on the screens and enlarge them or show picture-in-picture views. A standard desk computer tower controlling the functions.

Huiwei reached into her pocket and pulled out a flash drive. She could alter the program code if necessary, but thought it would work, as is.

Inserting the flash drive into the USB port on the tower, she saw the computer screen pull up her prompt. She entered the access code and downloaded her malware. The program would randomly run loops from the video cameras from the past several days, skipping today, coordinating with the same time of day. There were no significant weather changes to worry about. Images from today would be forever lost never making it to the digital recorder.

Unless there was full time monitoring, the loop would not be noticed immediately. At some point, the surveillance team will eventually review the digital recordings. If she needed that much time, her plans were doomed anyway. Tomorrow, her program would disconnect. A forensic data analyst could probably find it hiding out, but again, that takes time.

In the corner of the desk counter, she noticed a digital device with a small headset. Huiwei kicked herself for not thinking about it in advance. She let out a deep breath. Feeling violated, she wanted to go slap her sleeping beauty. Huiwei knew that his intent-listening was more than just professional curiosity.

She saw the model code on the device and started typing on the keyboard. Finding an applications menu, she spotted the model number and accessed the program. The screen showed the apartment numbers with the number either in *black* or *red*. Her apartment number was red – *active*, she presumed. It was tempting to switch it off, to black. However, she thought it could draw attention to the security system and her loop. Wang lei was sure to be back to his audio, peeping-tom mode soon enough. Apartment 201 was in *black*. If she could not avoid some discussions, she would simply retreat to that apartment. It was good to know it was not active.

Back in the break room she cocked her head to one side and looked at the young man lying there with an occasional reflexive twitch. She resisted the urge to slap him.

"Time to wake up my little super-spy," she said out loud.

She wiped off his fingers and wrapped his fingers around a half-full plastic water bottle, so he held it in his lap. Then, she reached into her pocket pulling out the third packet. Pulling his lower lip back, she sprinkled the contents on his lower gums. He flinched. While she did not have the benefit of a laboratory for accurate measurements, she presumed that he would be awake in five to ten minutes. Perhaps a slight headache, a confusing loss of some short-term memory covering the past few hours, but nothing more.

She left the room, wiped off the cup and saucer in the lobby placing them back on the service table, and went back to apartment 201. She had another call to make.

19

He hated feeling like a rat hiding behind the box-filled shelves and pallets stacked with everything from Yansing beer to aspirin. Aiguo-Tao mused that he could use both right now.

Once he carefully crossed into the active tarmac area, the cargo hanger was one of the first buildings he found. Workers had just pulled away with a forklift and a tractor pulling a wagon full of goods to place on some awaiting aircraft. No one was sitting at the supervisor's desk, with the inventory and shipping logs still sitting out.

Keeping his body close to the walls he maneuvered inside, grabbing a yellow and orange, reflective, safety vest, and a pair of noise-reduction earmuffs. He saw a somewhat grimy baseball cap dropped on the floor, with the cargo company's logo on the front. He snatched it up, replacing his own cap, stuffing it into his backpack.

He noticed a printed sheet with a flight timetable. Presuming it was the airport activity log for the day, to help coordinate logistics, he took the two-page document, copied it on a nearby photocopier, re-stapled the original and put it back in place.

There was a partial case of some flavored drink with the cellophane wrapping torn back – 'Brain Water, Raspberry,' *"People can be convinced of anything,"* he thought. He took a bottle, along with two small packs of cookies from a box that looked damaged from some part of the transportation process, 'Safari Animals, the Original Animal Cookie in the U.S.A. since 1935,' *"Leaving out the Made in China part,"* he chuckled.

Aiguo-Tao hoped his hiding place was sufficient while he planned his next move.

Western holidays were not celebrated in an official way, but still impacted the way people planned vacations, travelled for business, or to see relatives. Airports and train stations will be packed from mid-November through January and the Chinese New Year's holiday. Wuhan was not the biggest airport, but it will be full of travelers with a number of regional and international flights.

He pulled up the airport's passenger flight schedule information on his cellphone and cross-checked information with the logistics sheets. He had to decide, Hong Kong or Fuzhou.

Aiguo-Tao thought he had a better chance in coordinating with one of his two assets in Hong Kong. However, as a practical matter, Hong Kong was controlled by the People's Republic and the MSS openly operated there.

In Fuzhou, he would be relying on one contact, with the goal of getting across the straights of the East China Sea to Northern Taiwan. Operatives for the People's Republic were in Taiwan, yet they needed to operate more in the shadows – some of the same shadows he would be taking advantage of once he was there.

Time was limited. His escape from the interrogation facility was certainly gearing up for an investigation and manhunt by now.

His thoughts of getting back to the Virology Institute to review the operations status, or potentially clear up whatever injustice had occurred, was a waste of time. Escape and self-preservation was his only operation now.

The motor of the electric-powered forklift stopped and the rubber wheels on the smooth-finished concrete made a final squeak. Aiguo-Tao became a silent spider in the corner and listened.

"Flight schedules are getting all screwed up. I need to get out of here. My wife has a bad cold, and my son and daughter are probably breaking up the place," said the forklift driver.

"They're talking about forcing late shifts. Good luck with that," was the response from a gruff voice, probably the supervisor, he thought.

The supervisor continued, "It's the passenger flights getting held up with a bunch of added screening. Checking for fevers or something. They said new government protocol for holiday travels or something. Lots of delays, but the cargo planes are going out on time, so maybe we'll be okay."

"Maybe, but why work late if we can get done?" said the fork-lift driver.

"Shipments still go out on some passenger flights. Listen, I have to go to the mail hanger. The only Postal Airlines flight to Hong Kong is trying to get out early if possible with all of these backups. Get that China Cargo plane loaded. Try to get ahead of it. All of those Amazon boxes going international," said the supervisor.

The supervisor must have parked his tractor outside the hangar door. Aiguo-Tao heard the forklift start-up again, moving to stack more pallets on its tongues. A few minutes later, he heard the forklift leave.

He checked the flight sheets again and moved carefully toward the hangar door. About 100 meters away, he could see the China Postal Airlines plane being loaded for Hong Kong, from several wagons pulled by tarmac tractors. More concerning, were the airport police and PLA vehicles parked next to the plane with several soldiers carrying rifles, while inspectors were going through some inspection process for the bags and cargo.

Aiguo-Tao thought things through. Hong Kong was an on-going hotbed of social unrest where the residents still believed their corrupt capitalism, for over a century, should prevail over the benefits of control by the People's Republic. Obviously, added security was in place for a flight going there. Slipping onto a cargo plane seemed like his best option. The added security quickly diminished his odds of success.

He also realized that if there were active protests in Hong Kong, a passenger aircraft to Hong Kong would likely be subject to international travel protocols – screening social scores and passports. He didn't have a passport.

Aiguo-Tao, squatted down back against a wall inside the hanger. He reviewed the flights to Fuzhou Changle International Airport. There was a Xiamen Air flight to Fuzhou and also a West Air flight, both scheduled to leave within the hour.

He started going through the operational variables in his head. Xiamen Air flight was a Boeing 737-700. A pricier airline, typically with a business class section, reducing the seats to about 120, maybe 125. The West Air flight was an Airbus A319-100. About the same size, but as a bargain airline they packed the seats tight, all economy, closer to 150 seats.

Aiguo-Tao knew his plan depended on human elements as well. West was, and acted like, a cattle-cargo carrier. Efficiency and grumbling must be in the company's mission statement. Customer service was a minimal consideration – all passengers were second class – but there were more seats. Xiamen took pride in their customer service and catered to the business traveler. *"If you were not counting your Yuan, you took Xiamen,"* he thought. Fewer seats. Both were likely full flights.

Wearing the safety vest, company ballcap and the ear protectors hanging around his neck, he walked out on the tarmac. In one hand, he carried a small canvass tool bag and in the other a clipboard with his copy of the logistics sheets pinned down. He approached a driver on a tarmac tractor who had just detached the wagon he was pulling.

"Hey, any chance I can get a ride?" asked Aiguo-Tao, pointing to passenger terminal where the Xiamen 737 was waiting over 600 meters away.

"Sure thing. Got to make it quick if you can hang on. That would be a long walk," replied the driver.

"Things are all backed up. Everyone in the hanger is loading somewhere and left me stranded. Looks like a long night ahead," said Aiguo-Tao.

He jumped on the back end of the tractor, with only one seat for the driver, standing on the bumper, holding on to the safety bars. When they arrived at the plane, Aiguo-Tao waved to the driver as he sped off. He knelt down as if tying his shoes, with the tool bag and clipboard on the ground, and began to assess his next move.

Consciously or not, he seldom traveled to Fuzhou if avoidable. He preferred keeping any memories of growing up there scrambled in a foggy mist. To him, his childhood began at age 15, at the academy – he had no childhood. He wished he had not seen the side of Huan-Jun that cared so much for his wife and son. It was more comforting to remember him as his captor with a gun held to his head.

20

Huiwei sat on the sofa in apartment 201. She had pulled out the iPad from the hidden backpack to recheck the software, files and applications she had downloaded, testing her multi-layered encryption access.

She now focused on how to approach her next phone call. It was a long shot, but perhaps the most critical part of her plan. Plan B, was high risk and likely suicidal in the end. There was no Plan C.

Taking a deep breath, she dialed and heard the voice on the other end,

"Ni hao."

"Master Jun-Ling . . . this is Huiwei . . . Colonel Lí . . . if you recall, I . . ." she began.

Jun-Ling interrupted her, "Shi, *yes*, Huiwei, I remember you quite well. Given your last purchase, you are not one I would forget, nor one I would normally acquiesce to. Has there been a problem, and a healer's advice is needed?"

She regained her composure realizing Jun-Ling was acknowledging respect, yet still pursuing a slow inquiry, a game of wisdom in many ways, that only a master healer could know. "Actually, the herbs worked honorably for the purposes nature blessed them. I do, however, seek your advice . . . of sorts."

"You have a favor to ask of this old man, I see. Like a well shot arrow, a straight path is best to find its intended mark," Jun-Ling responded.

"I understand, and I promise to get to the point, if you will allow my confession first," she said.

"Huiwei, as you know, I am not a priest, but only a healer, yet I will be glad to entertain what you might wish to confide," he said with a soft tone.

Huiwei realized that the introductions were now over, but the game of wisdom would never end.

"What I told you about my family and my father is true. I left out many parts and did not tell you of my true home in Shenzhen." She paused to feel herself breathe, "I was taken from my parents when I was a young girl, to attend a government school. I have never seen my parents since the day the car drove away from my home."

He could sense that her recollection was something she never recounted out loud, certainly not to a stranger, and he sensed the swelling pressure behind her strong eyes in attempting not to let her tears emerge.

"Huiwei, it would normally pleasure me most to continue with my verbal *cuju* with one so astute, yet I believe my pleasure may not match your need for haste. Am I correct, Huiwei?"

"Thank you, Master Jun-Ling. If I said to you that, *laws control the lesser person and knowing right controls the great*, would that sound to political?"

"No, Huiwei, as I would rightfully tell you that, *to have principles, one must first have courage*."

"And if I replied my belief that, *without sorrows - no one becomes a saint*, would it offend you?" said Huiwei.

"Méiyõu, *no*, Huiwei. It would tell me your father taught you well and for such a young girl you had the wisdom to listen, as you know the masters' requisition for safe-harbor and escape."

"Can you help?" Huiwei solemnly asked.

"I do not know your situation, nor do I think it is of any importance to understand. I will do what I can, within the limits of my position. First, I must also confess a bit to you. In our brief time of acquaintance, my esteem for your knowledge has grown. Certainly, unusual for a person off the street to be so aware of the secrets nature holds. This old man also has use of the Internet in learning more about you and my suspicions. In piecing the puzzle together, I can tell you, I knew your father," said Jun-Ling.

He could hear Huiwei's slight gasp of surprise.

"Once you strike-out the entrepreneurs and charlatans, our *club*, so to speak, is not as great has you may think. Your knowledge of yourself is strong with intellect, but blind to many realities . . . and, one of those realities is that you need to get to me and I have no car," Jun-Ling whimsically ended.

"I'm working on that. Thank you." Huiwei hung up.

Huiwei sat on the sofa staring into space. The conversation certainly did not go as she had planned, but the outcome was better than expected. Her focus on her immediate circumstances wandered, as she saw the regenerated memories in her head from thinking about her father and mother. She wanted to curl up and look at the family photos she had downloaded to the iPad. Her senses shot back. Curling and winding her ball of emotions, she carefully rested it back deep inside.

Huiwei thought she might simply go to the security room, take the keys, find a car and drive off. She even knew there was an older car that sat idle in the parking lot, used by staff to run an occasional errand. Huiwei, being able to define, scramble and assess the variables, also knew that stealing a car and dumping it somewhere in Chengdu was risky and left a significant trail for an experienced agent. It was part of Plan B, but she wasn't there . . . yet.

She heard the young woman's voice answer after only two rings.

"Ni hao," she heard.

"Chén, this is Huiwei. Colonel Lí . . . at the apartments. You had left me your number and I had not seen you recently. I thought I should check on you."

They talked various pleasantries and Huiwei asked about her classes and her family. Chén was surprised with her sudden termination. The management company did provide a good recommendation for her when she found a job at a local hotel. It did not pay as well, but they let her fit her schedule around her college classes.

Huiwei intentionally, and systematically, led the conversation to her dilemma regarding transportation. She casually inserted comments that she needed to get to Chengdu, a car was not available and because of a hurt knee, she was less than excited about calling for a taxi and using the train, then the subway, especially at night.

Chén innocently took the bait. "Huiwei . . . I like calling you that. If you might allow me, I may be able to assist you with your transportation problem."

"I'm not sure what you could do. It was impolite of me to impose my worries on you. Please forgive me Chén. It was concern for you that caused me to call and not for my own woes," as Huiwei set the emotional trap.

Chén said, with a bit of excitement, "Méiyõu, méiyõu, it is no imposition at all. You have been so kind to assist with my school work asking for nothing in return. You are an excellent tutor. I am in your debt even if you do not seek it."

"That was an equal pleasure for me and certainly no debt was incurred. I'm not sure I could even borrow a car here to allow your assistance," she said.

"That is not a problem," said Chén.

"Really . . . I'm not sure you could help." Huiwei was beginning to think that Chén was perhaps devious enough to contemplate getting the keys to one of the vehicles at the apartments. She missed seeing that.

"I can come pick you up in my father's car. Not as fancy as you are accustomed to, however . . .," inserted Chén.

"I did not know you had a car," Huiwei truthfully said, reassessing her direction, but glad Chén had more honest thoughts.

"I do not. My father does. He is out of town visiting my aunt, his sister. While I would not normally use it to drive to school and pay the parking, I was actually wanting an excuse to. My classes will run quite late tonight and I do not always like using the subway and train so late," explained Chén.

Unexpectedly pleased, Huiwei responded, "Oh, that would be wonderful." She sincerely meant it.

"I will only accept your gracious offer if you allow me to pay you to refill the gas tank and pay the parking fees," Huiwei concluded.

"You do not need to. I was wanting to drive anyway, yet that would make it easier to explain to my father if he would ask. I told him about how wonderful you were in helping with my studies and he will understand," Chén sounded more excited about helping out.

"Okay then. We have a deal! I thank you for your kindness. I am meeting a friend near the Square. She will be pleased to know I can make it . . . Do you know the small park close to the apartments, the one with the children's playground?" asked Huiwei.

"Yes. It's only two streets away from your place. The one with the big panda that the children can climb," acknowledged Chén.

"I was hoping to test my knee some with a short walk without straining it much. Would it be possible for you to pick me up there?" explained Huiwei.

"Just a night out for dinner and so I will not be wearing my uniform," added Huiwei.

Chén thought, then asked, "Do you need a ride back with your knee and everything? I am not sure exactly when I will be finished at the college."

"No, that won't be a problem. I'm eating with an old university friend and her husband. I'll pack my clothes for work and probably spend the night at their apartment in the city. My biggest fear is that they will attempt to bring along a blind date for me. They've done that before and they know I am against it," Huiwei whimsically commented, realizing she had not thought-out her back-story for not needing a ride back to the apartments.

"I understand. I have friends like that too. What time?" said Chén.

They agreed on a time and Chén described her father's car, a blue Brilliance Tun.

Huiwei did not think Chén had access to a car. Her working plan was to identify the keys to the old car in the parking lot and have Chén return it, leaving the keys in the ignition as if a staff member forgot. Of course, she would tell Chén she had permission to use the car, later finding an excuse for not being able to return it herself. Chén's solution was much simpler and avoided the many things that could go wrong.

Huiwei went back to her third-floor apartment to leave things where she wanted and to make sure she had not forgotten anything. She had already flushed the herbs down the toilet in the other apartment and disposed of the bags. Everything would be left behind except the casual outfit she was wearing, her hidden backpack and her satchel carrying her laptop and a few items, including a uniform shirt and slacks. She would leave the laptop with Jun-Ling to keep hidden, or destroyed – a trust factor she had not calculated earlier.

She stood at the door looking back into the apartment. She had cleaned down the area around the sofa where the manufactured scuffle occurred, leaving the balcony door unlocked and slightly opened.

Hopefully, it would appear to be the work of a professional, with no useable evidence left behind. Some lowly desk attendant, perhaps Wang lei, missed the few moments of noise while Huiwei was knocked out with some injected chemical, or a cloth to her face. At least she thought the kidnapping scene would tell that story.

Going back to apartment 201, she wiped down surfaces she touched, then she packed up her belongings, strapped on her backpack and looked over the balcony to look for any activity that could create unwanted eyes. She only hoped that the kind man from the elevator, upon his return, would simply think he had forgotten to lock the balcony door. She wiped down the keycard tossed it on the floor by the sofa and shut the door.

There were no windows on the first-floor below her. Huiwei tossed her satchel in a bush below, hopefully for a soft landing. She crawled out over the balcony, hanging down while gripping the edge of the floor, then, dropped to the ground. Hanging down, she greatly reduced the distance of her fall to little more than two meters. She did not need a real knee injury at this point.

Huiwei retrieved her satchel and headed to meet up with Chén.

21

Aiguo-Tao slowly stood up and started walking toward the two baggage handlers who were pulling passenger bags off their wagon and loading them into the belly of the Boeing 737. One of the handlers was by the cargo bay door, stepping in and out, while the other fed him an assortment of luggage in a rainbow of colors and size.

Aiguo-Tao set his tool bag and clipboard on the tractor and approached the handler at the wagon, "Hey, looks like you could use some help." He had already grabbed a bag and was moving toward the other handler, before anyone could say, no.

"Sure. Why not. Cargo planes backed up as well?" the handler nodded at Aiguo-Tao's hat.

"No. The cargo planes are getting out fine. With the passenger delays, we've been trying to get ahead of it so our planes can work in for an early departure when there's a gap," responded Aiguo-Tao, as he grabbed a large, pink suitcase, carrying it to the cargo door.

"Makes sense. What brings you here?" the handler asked.

"I had to check on some freight going on a passenger flight. Trying to get ahead on their loading, they don't have anyone to come pick me up. So, I'm just in limbo for the moment," said Aiguo-Tao.

"Well . . . we appreciate your help. Thanks. It's really crazy in there and every plane is a full load. 'Customer first,' great company slogan until you meet some of the customers," the handler laughed.

"Where's this one headed, international? Asked Aiguo-Tao.

"Fuzhou. Regional. My brother used to work there," said the handler pointing at Aiguo-Tao's hat.

"He gave me his hat when he transferred to another job. Supervisor at a manufacturing plant in Wuhan. Lost it." The handler went on grabbing another bag.

"Lost his new job?" asked Aiguo-Tao.

"No. I lost the hat," responded the handler.

"You want this one? Not your brother's, but it should look the same," said Aiguo-Tao, wrestling with a set of golf clubs in a hard, traveling case.

"You mean it?" the handler suspiciously asked.

Aiguo-Tao took off his hat and tossed it to the handler. In turn, the handler tossed his Xiamen Airlines hat to Aiguo-Tao.

"Nice fit," said Aiguo-Tao. "I think I'll double check with the service agent to make sure they aren't waiting on any food or drink boxes from us," said Aiguo-Tao.

The handler nodded at Aiguo-Tao and he headed to the portable stairs leading up to the aircraft cabin entry.

Aiguo-Tao entered the aircraft door and heard the service agent talking to one of the pilots.

"Had to call-in a different cabin crew with all of the schedule changes. They're getting ready to board so we should be able to get the passengers loaded and get you on your way. We'll try to expedite getting the passengers on as much as possible," said the agent.

The agent nodded at Aiguo-Tao as he walked past him, carrying his tool bag and clipboard, then, walking back toward the aft. He passed a pilot sitting in the last row of the business-class, reading a magazine. No one looked up or seemed to notice him, despite the bright safety vest – just some anonymous repair guy doing his job.

He got to the back of the passenger aisle just as he noticed the first flight attendant boarding. Quickly slipping into one of the insanely small bathrooms, he locked the door. He pulled a disposable razor out of his backpack. He had a grateful flash of the Master Sergeant – he thought of everything. Aiguo-Tao shook his head slowly, then shook out any thoughts of his former captor.

He finished shaving, washed his face and used two more disposable wipes to clean his body. Then, he stuffed the vest, ear protectors and new hat into his backpack, along with the small canvass tool bag. He ripped up the sheets of paper from the clipboard and stuffed the pieces into the trash. He would figure out what to do with the clipboard later. He sat on the closed toilet lid and waited.

He finally heard two flight attendants outside his enclosure as they were scurrying to put their personal things away.

"What a crazy day. Glad we got this flight with all the changes or it would have seriously messed up my flights for the next week," said one of the flight attendants. Female, nice voice, he thought.

He heard a male flight attendant respond. "I'm off after tomorrow for three days, but this will work out for me."

"Safety first, but we've got to get the passengers on board and seated. No major shortcuts, but we don't want to lose our place in the taxi line," she directed.

"Sure-thing boss. I'll remind them up front," the male flight attendant replied.

Aiguo-Tao presumed the female must be the crew leader. He heard the on-going sounds of commotion as the passengers filed in to get seated, some smashing their oversized bags into the overhead carriers, a baby's cry, and then the intercom.

"Ladies and gentlemen. We have a full flight today and need you to store your bags and buckle in. Place small carry-on items under the seat in front of you. Your cooperation will be appreciated so we do not lose our spot in line which could create a further delay." Aiguo-Tao recognized the voice and could hear her talking into the intercom phone just outside his door.

The intercom squeaked again. "As the Captain, and on behalf of our veteran crew, welcome aboard to Xiamen flight 2343 where our customers come first. We hope you have accommodations in Fuzhou, because that's where this plane is headed." A pilot with a bad sense of humor, Aiguo-Tao thought, *'I don't like it,'* as he continued to listen.

"We have a full flight today. Please cooperate with our highly trained cabin crew. They are here for your safety first." The Captain paused and Aiguo-Tao whispered, "And to serve me my drinks with a bag of peanuts. I'm a comedian too."

"It looks like we are getting the final word from the service agent, and we'll be closing the aircraft door in just a second. Please listen to the flight attendant and watch the screen on the safety instructions and we will soon be on our way."

The pilot signed off and Aiguo-Tau took his cue, opening the door and looking down the aisle.

He squinted and scanned. He could not see an open seat nearby, or anywhere.

A realization hit him, like a slap to the face, things were about to get awkward very fast.

"My goodness . . . how did you sneak in there without me seeing. You need to take your seat sir." He recognized the familiar voice of the female flight attendant.

"I'm looking for my open seat. I forgot the exact seat number." Aiguo-Tao stated.

"Well, it's a full flight. Do you have your boarding pass?" she asked.

"I'm afraid I'm having difficulty finding it. My stomach was cramping and I needed to get to the bathroom. Ulcers. I tried not to block passengers boarding, to use the toilet in front. So, I hurried back here. I did not stop to find my seat and drop my bag. I looked in my pockets, and my bag, but I can't find my boarding pass," he said, intentionally trying to look innocent and confused.

"Oh my. Are you alright? Apparently, some bug going around in Wuhan and they have extra screening to make sure passengers are not ill. There are delays, but we want to make sure everyone remains safe. I'm sure the screening will be at all the airports soon since it's flu season." she said.

"Yes. I am fine. No fever for flu or anything like that. With my sensitive stomach I am used to it and it passes. I will spare you the details," he said, with pained look on his face. Not from any stomach pain, but from trying to figure out his next move in an extremely confined space with many security officers outside.

"Do you have the boarding pass downloaded on your phone perhaps?" She said as politely as possible.

"No. It has not been a good day. Hurrying to the airport, only to find the flight delayed. I believe I dropped my phone on the train. I had to purchase a temporary phone at the airport. Hopefully, my contacts are saved on my computer at home so I don't lose them," he said, with a look of remorse.

"Do you remember what section in the plane your seat is?" she said with a bit more urgency. He looked like he worked-out a lot, and seemed healthy. A bit serious, perhaps, but she thought he was rather cute.

"I know it was just behind business class. I paid extra for more leg room. I think the left side, if I remember the diagram when I bought the ticket," he said, knowing there were no seats in the back. But, maybe one he could not see further down the aisle.

"Oh . . . the comfort section. Let me see." She quickly walked down the aisle, stopped just before she got to business class. It looked like she was asking for some passengers on the left side to show her their boarding passes. Some were holding up their phones.

She looked back at Aiguo-Tao for a moment, and then walked to the pilot who he had noticed was sitting in business class. She bent over and spoke to him, while occasionally looking back at Aiguo-Tao.

The pilot stood up, took his hat from the overhead compartment and then walked to the cockpit. The flight attendant was watching the pilot.

Aiguo-Tao felt something in his throat, like a piece of food that would not swallow, with a slight burn. He held the backpack in front of him, double-checking that he had placed his pistol where he could quickly get to it and sensed the Velcro straps he fashioned in the cargo hangar, around his lower leg, holding the sheath with the hunting knife.

He went through his mental card-file of operational situations. Hostage or no hostages? Secure the cockpit, or get off the plane and run before any shots were fired? He felt confident that the airport security police were not very well trained for an active shooting situation, and their simulations and videotapes would not help once the first *real* bullet is fired. The PLA soldiers on site, that would quickly arrive, were a different set of calculations.

The flight attendant started walking toward him with an awkward smile. She had been nice to him and he did not want her to be his hostage, with him pressing the muzzle of his pistol in her ribs or holding the hunting knife across the front of her throat. Yet, she was leaving him very few options.

"Sir." She said politely. "Could you please come with me?'

He thought it would be tactically better to wait until they got to the front of the aircraft before he reached down to pull out the knife, grabbing her and pulling the flight attendant's back tightly against his chest, holding the knife against her throat.

Passing all of the rows, there was always a chance that some passenger played too many video games and thought he could be a hero. It would, of course, be a person who had never held a real gun or deadly weapon. Too many variables. He would wait.

He slowly followed her at a distance, closing the gap as she got closer to the front. With his peripheral vision, he tried to inventory the passengers to identify any potential wannabe superheroes.

He was less than a meter behind her when she suddenly stopped, turned towards him and held her palm open, pointing at the pilot's empty seat.

"Please. On behalf of Xiamen Airlines, I would like to apologize to you," said the flight attendant.

Aiguo-Tao was doing his best to control the look on his face so he didn't look like a deer in the headlights of truck. "Thank you," he said, not completely hiding his confusion.

"It appears the gate agent must have inadvertently issued two tickets for your seat. It was very hectic at the gate as you know. The passenger in 10-A had a boarding pass that was printed right at the gate while boarding. The flight was over booked. They must have given her your seat number without double-checking. It happens sometimes." She explained.

"So . . . I may sit here?" he asked

"Yes. Of course. We aren't going to delay the flight any longer to figure out something that doesn't matter." She said.

"But what about the pilot that was sitting here?" He responded. He was asking himself, is this a trick of some sort, so they can test his reactions to determine the level of threat?

"He was dead-heading to Fuzhou. He's stationed there and needs to be in place for his flight in the morning. When I explained the situation, he was glad to sit in the extra, jump-seat in the cockpit. Pilots often do that, especially with full flights."

"I see. Well, thank you again," he said. He sat down, putting his backpack and clipboard under the seat in front of him.

The flight attendant reached over and secured his seatbelt for him across his lap. Her action caught him off guard. "Thank you" he said in a somewhat stuttered voice. Aiguo-Tao did not think that was a normal practice, so he tried to show a smile of appreciation.

She smiled at him, "Customer first. Again, sorry for the mix up. Now, once we get in the air, what can I get you to drink. Anything you like in business class."

His first thought for a response would be completely inappropriate, especially as she just saved her own life, probably several others, and possibly his.

"A Bourbon and Coke please, then. I'd like to mix it, if that's okay," he said.

"Is Pepsi okay?" she asked with almost a school girl's smile.

"Yes . . . a Pepsi is fine."

Another flight attendant was finishing the safety announcements after the video screen went blank having played the safety instructions video, with several language options. He heard the turbines in the engines spooling up and then felt the speed of the plane rapidly increasing.

Aiguo-Tao felt the slight drop when the Boeing 737 left the runway, and heard the landing gears retracting.

The flight attendant brought him his Pepsi before serving the other passengers, along with two tiny bottles of bourbon. He reached down to tuck the bottles into a pocket on the backpack. Then, he sat back, pushing the seat back as far as it would go. Feeling cautiously safe, he drank the Pepsi in two gulps, then chewed the ice. He decided he should get at least one hour of sleep while he could. He knew he needed much more.

22

Huiwei stood up from the bench when she saw the small, blue car slowing down next to the park. To avoid any unnecessary attention, she did not want to wave or shout. Walking between two parked cars, she slightly stepped out so Chén would see her. Huiwei put one hand in front of her chest and gave a quick wave.

"Good timing," said Chén with the window rolled down. "I was afraid I would have to find a parking spot, which wasn't going to be easy."

Huiwei opened the backdoor and tossed in her backpack and satchel, then got in the front seat. "Thank you, so much. This really helps out and the new desk attendants are really no help. If you know them, don't tell them I said that."

"New management or something. They changed out all sorts of staff without any notice. It doesn't surprise me. They are the last people I would know . . . or ever want to. So, where are we going?" responded Chén as she drove off.

Huiwei was relieved that Chén did not have any contacts at the apartments. She hated having to interrogate her, even if Chén did not realize it.

"North of the Jinjiang, if you know where North and East Ma'an Road cross," said Huiwei.

"Oh yes, near Ganji's Pig restaurant," acknowledged Chén.

"Pig's intestines powder doesn't spark my appetite much. But, that's the district, yes," said Huiwei. She did not want Chén to take her all the way to the apothecary near Zhangjia Alley. The less Chén knew, the better, just in case.

Chén talked about her classes and discussed some of the theories her teacher had on statistical applications. Huiwei bit her tongue in wanting to explain some of the variables applications that would challenge her teacher, but she did not want to risk Chén somehow mentioning her name to others. A good investigator can often find the tidbits of information floating around and piece things together. Chén did not need to get dragged into her world, or her situation, any more than she was.

Huiwei asked Chén to pull over next to the Ma'an Post Office. She reached in the back seat to get her belongings, then, reached into her satchel pulling out a zippered clutch purse. She handed Chén six, 100 Yuan and three, 50 Yuan notes.

"Méiyõu, méiyõu! *no*. You do not owe me anything. This would more than pay for a parking pass at the college for the rest of the term . . . parking every day. It's too much," protested Chén.

"Then, please consider it a graduation gift . . . a year early. It is my honor. I'm afraid my work at the Research Center will be finished before then. Best, if you keep it between you and me . . . our little secret," responded Huiwei.

Huiwei got out of the car, put on her backpack, bringing her hand to her chest again, and gave a quick wave, then pretending to pull a zipper across her lips. Chén drove off. She was sincere about the gift, yet also knew Chén would now have a motive not to talk about her side trip.

She crossed the street and headed west on the Ma'an East Road. She smelled the aromas from the various restaurants, already serving dinners to the hungry crowds. It made her stomach grumble with hunger, but she knew there was no time to eat, not now. Seeing the sign on the Xiongshi Roast Duck Shop, she turned down Zhangjia Alley.

The apothecary shop was closed, but she saw Jun-Ling in the shadows through the window. The door to the shop opened before she could knock and she heard the little bell on the door ring to announce her arrival as she entered.

She noticed that Jun-Ling moved quickly, but in a manner that to-the-eye appeared only slow and graceful. She made a mental note to ask him about that skill if there was time.

Huiwei started to offer a bow to greet him, however, Jun-Ling had already turned slowly walking the back of the shop. He was already at the beaded curtain to the back by the time she even took her second step. She really needed to know how he did that, she again thought.

Pulling the beads back to invite her entry, Jun-Ling said, "Welcome Ji-Hehuanhua. We have many hours ahead of us."

Huiwei smiled, acknowledging his interesting combination of words – *my anxious flower seeking happiness*, of course, with an herbal remedy reference. She followed him around his work table, displaying several mortars and pestles, balancing scales and jars of herbs and powders. Behind the shelves, filled with boxes, jars and every miscellaneous item one might think of, she saw him standing next to another door leading to two stairways. One, to the basement cellar, the other to the rooms above the shop.

Jun-Ling politely held out his hand for her to walk up the stairs and led her to a small meditation room. Huiwei heard crickets singing, then, suddenly stop when he walked into the room and lit several, fat candles on a thin, lacquered table, and turned on a Coleman, LED camping lantern.

"A battery camping light? An ancient Zhiyú zhé, *healer*, tool I did not know?" mused Huiwei.

"Perhaps not traditional. This Zhiyú zhé has enough wisdom to appreciate some modern conveniences. I even succumbed to running water in my sink." He smiled, setting the lantern on the floor next to the sitting mats.

Huiwei's eyes focused on the small, window air conditioner. "The cool air calms the spirits of the soul. At least that's my excuse," said Jun-Ling, shrugging his shoulders.

"I'm sure it helps the Nanjing, medicine, in a most efficient manner Zhiyú zhé," replied Huiwei.

She looked around the room at the many rice paper paintings and decorations around the room, thinking the value of one, small one would more than pay for a badly needed coat of paint on the walls.

Jun-Ling carefully placed a small, opaque, rice paper tent over the ornately carved, jade cricket boxes, and the chirped singing resumed. No batteries required. He then placed a small brick of incense in a bronze Xunlu, formed as a dragon, with two large, emerald eyes. Those eyes alone must be worth a fortune, Huiwei thought.

Jun-Ling lit the end of a thin bamboo stick with a candle and carefully thrust the flame through the dragon to ignite the incense. The Cuibai, *cedar*, smell of the room, soon gave way to a unique and calming aroma.

"Bajiao and Dingxiang? A surprising combination," she said.

"Yes, the licorice root and cloves are a favorite of mine, and the smell, even when grinding, is also pleasant. Your quick senses are keen," he answered.

"I thank you for your patience and help Jun-Ling, but I think you must understand the urgency of my situation," Huiwei, respectfully pleaded.

"Perhaps I do not know the reason, yet I know your success will likely rely on your calm, inside, when your chi is balanced, body and spirit working as allies, not caught in a struggle to dominate your mind," he responded, in the most calming tone, yet with a sense there was no argument to be made.

"My father would say the same thing, and I understand, but I must leave as quickly as possible," she pleaded again.

"The need for your haste is acknowledged, yet there is much work to move forward. I do not even know your destination and I am not a travel agent with a wide variety of resources to plan your apparent long-term holiday," he logically explained. Huiwei looked at the whiffs of smoke rising from the dragon and realized the wisdom in his words.

Looking back at Jun-Ling, she said, "Hong Kong. I need to get to the border south of Shenzhen." Taking a breath, "by tomorrow night," she added.

Jun-Ling raised one eyebrow high and brought his fist to his chin, extending his index finger to his lips. "A most difficult booking using Alibaba or Orbitz. I presume you do not plan on needing your passport."

"Actually, through a friend, I have a Hong Kong passport with a British one showing dual citizenship. A Hong Kong driver's license and a credit card – all with a different name. However, if *they* are using their advanced facial-recognition monitoring, a different name will not help me," said Huiwei as she looked away.

"Given your position, I had presumed this, *they*, as you say. It is helpful to have verified this. I am honored by your trust in me. There is much for us to talk about that would likely interest you, yet I doubt your need for expediency will allow," he said.

"My father and mother?" Huiwei softly asked.

"More or less, mostly more. If you succeed in your journey, I am sure more will come to light for you," he responded.

"But if I . . ." started Huiwei before she was cut off.

"For now, you must meditate and find your chi. To stand and pace in anxiousness will not accelerate the calls I must make and unusual favors I must ask. Do you understand?" he concluded.

"I understand. I will hope to find some of your wisdom in my mediation," she said bowing her head.

As Jun-Ling walked out the door, he turned, saying, "You will." Then, he slowly headed for the stairs again, and Huiwei almost instantly heard the door at the bottom of the stairs close. "*I have to find out how he does that,*" she thought.

23

She looked around the room again with its dim lights casting against the walls. She sat on a mat facing the smoking dragon, with its gleaming, green eyes, and crossed her legs. By habit, through experience, Huiwei was not a trusting person. She really did not have a choice, yet felt an unusual sense of comfort relying on Jun-Ling's help.

Slowly, she placed her hands resting on each knee, touching the tips of her index fingers to her thumbs and closed her eyes, focusing on the pattern of the rhythm, hidden within the inconsistent notes of the crickets' songs.

Huiwei was quite familiar with her meditation experience and skills. She was able to quickly relax and find her zone of nothingness, shedding her conscious thoughts. It was not working! The harder she tried, the more she failed.

Making an audible sigh, she was about to give up and open her eyes. Suddenly, she heard a crashing sound in her head. It was the surging of waves on the shore of the sea.

She found herself looking at the beach from a distance as the waves pounded in synchronized series of the curling water. Two figures were on the beach. Walking closer, she could tell it was a young girl and her father as he kneeled with one knee on the sand and pointed to the horizon showing her the signs of the coming storm, then pointing to the waves as they crashed.

Walking closer, she could hear the girl giggle with delight as her father went on, and he laughed too, watching her throw a stone into the receding water from the last wave. Huiwei could feel her own smile deep inside her ball of emotion tucked safely away and starting to carefully unravel.

Struck by the scene, she could not help but to walk closer, yet she did not want to interfere. Still, she found herself at arms-length and reached to touch the young girl on the shoulder and not surprise her with the sound of the waves having silenced her approach.

Feeling the touch, the girl slowly turned her head and looked at Huiwei's face as Huiwei started to apologize and introduce herself. The girl turned back to look at her father, before Huiwei could speak. Then, Huiwei looked at the father, realizing she was seeing his strong chiseled jaws and compassionate eyes, through the eyes of the young girl, as her own, now staring at her father.

Huiwei heard her own voice, as a young girl, speaking, "Bàba . . . how is it that you know when the storm is coming and the waves are ready to grow?"

He looked softly into her eyes, with the wind blowing his hair across his forehead and eyes, "Huiwei, my beautiful seedling, there are many storms in life. Some wait for their ears to hear the sounds of the rumbling thunder, or remain unaware until the first hailstones begin to pelt them when it is too late to seek cover. Others open all of their senses to find the signs in plain sight, if they allow themselves to be aware. You, my daughter, have the gift to see the storm from afar and take heed."

"But why should I care to know, as I am safe on the beach, and you are with me Bàba?" asked young Huiwei.

"As the storm rises, the shifting tide will want to trick you into fighting, pulling you further to the sea. If you understand, you will know how not to fight, defeating it by finding the subtle currents to drift back to the shore. Knowing the storm, you will save your strength to battle the final waves seeking to crash you to the floor. This battle must be won, before you can find the safety of the sand beneath your feet," he said.

"But won't you be there to warn me Bàba?" said an innocent child's voice.

"I will not always be with you to jump into the waves. I will always be here . . . to help you," as he touched his finger to her heart. "This is why I want to show you the signs of the storm so you will safely reach the shore, on your own, knowing you must first face the tide and conquer the waves," he said, now pulling her close and hugging her tightly.

With a startled jolt, Huiwei opened her eyes, feeling the wet trickle of tears down her cheeks and the salty taste touching her lips. She wanted to quickly close her eyes and go back to feeling her father's strong arms holding her safe. Then, realizing it would not happen.

With her father's words, she knew what she must do to cleanse her spirit to reach a safe journey's end. She took a deep breath, smelling the licorice and cloves, closing her eyes and not fighting her mind, to take the path it needs to follow.

"Colonel Lí, why do you seem distressed from you geographic models? I thought you were pleased with the accuracy of your results," asked Major General, Lú Ho-sun, the MSS senior office in charge of strategic science division.

Huiwei, like most people, realized how young Ho-sun was for a Major General. Attractive in many ways, including his intellect, but too often knowing people better than they knew themselves, she realized his attractiveness was only his lure.

As a high functioning narcissist, he believed no one could escape his charm to attain whatever goal he set for himself. He succeeded with most. Huiwei was the exception, but she also knew how dangerous such a self-serving personality disorder could be. She pitied any woman who had fallen for his physical charm as she strongly suspected they encountered many serious bruises and bleeding noses and lips, or worse, from his thwarted sense of superior chivalry – leaving a threatening fear, should the woman believe there was any value in sharing the details of his amorous propensities.

"My calculations. The programmed variables into my predictive algorithms . . . yes, they are fine, perhaps over ninety-percent accurate," she replied.

"So . . . the issue?" he probed.

"Look at the maps and the predictive rings. You know what the colors mean. Yellow, infection spread, orange, long-term damage and hospitalization, red, deaths. I overlay it with coinciding economic predictive rings and you have a destroyed government infrastructure, economic collapse, inevitable rioting, especially in major urban areas, most likely regional or multi-regional wars, official or with overthrown military forces. You don't see reason for my distress?"

"I understand your point Colonel Lí . . . Huiwei . . . if I might, it fits you so well." Ho-sun said, while she rolled her eyes making sure not to look at him.

"But this is the purpose, and quite frankly, you are the best. Now, we can start to strategically plan for the political maneuvering and dedication of military and technology assets of our cyber infiltration capabilities, to keep it from happening."

"But, Major General . . . ," Huiwei began.

"Please, Ho-sun . . . Huiwei," he interrupted.

"Yes, Major General Lú, my concern . . . the People's Republic and much of Asia, likely into the Middle East and even Europe . . . China will be effectively destroyed and the remaining population, while perhaps sizable, will be a zombie-land with the leadership and economic structure gone," she said, realizing her emotions were now showing and she needed to focus her restraint.

"Exactly, this is why your work is so important. We know what the Americans are capable of, European allies, Japan or South Korea even. If we are ahead of it, we have effectively ended the threat, Huiwei, my dear," he continued.

Regaining some composure and attempting to ignore, *my dear*, she said, "I understand Major General. I apologize. It is simply a bit of a shock when I see it spelled out . . . the potential, I mean," she said calmly.

She knew he would hold it against her for calling him by his rank, but hopefully some of the rumors from her youth had reached his ears.

"Now, my understanding is that you also ran reverse-engineering modeling to contrast the data, correct?" he asked.

"Yes, I took the same variables provided to hypothetically determine what the same modeling would look like if it was the People's Republic strategically launching the virus. I can pull those up here," she said while typing on her keyboard to show different geographic mapping.

"And, your conclusion?" he asked.

"Using essentially the same variables and methods, it is a worse outcome. Not necessarily in mortality, because the same population ratios will remain subject to infection, but the economic and political fallout is more Global in many respects. China and Russia, along with some parts of South America would be impacted, but not in a devastating way. Manufacturing supply chains and communications networks crashed. Sungia's 5G would be the only choice and millions of circuit boards already in servers, electronics, cameras and hardware waiting to be tripped. In a sense, the People's Republic would be in a role to save the remnants of a civilized World.," she explained.

"Why the difference? Didn't you look at essentially the same variables?" he asked looking closely at the maps.

"The major difference has to do with greater ease of travel and movement and less restrictive immigration or customs control. I also factored in variables asked by the SCIO regarding media and cyber influences. Simply stated, our existing counter-intelligence media influence in the West makes it significantly easier for China to affect an outcome than the West could with us. But there are added factors." Huiwei said.

"What added factors. We gave you the parameters to consider." He said.

"Well . . . first, given the microbiology involved, we don't know what characteristics the Americans might insert into the coronavirus genome sequencing. Quite frankly, the potential danger of their research, as I understand it, should cause the U.N. Security Council, if they knew, to shut it down, even blow it up if necessary. Plus, presumably, once exposed, the nature of media and political influences would predictively cause them to shut it down on their own trying to erase the evidence. I have fairly accurate media-influence and organizational variable programs I can apply." Huiwei said, feeling more comfortable talking facts.

"And second." He asked.

"Again, we don't know exactly what their virus would look like. I am only using the parameters provided, with some predictability variables looking at SARS and even H1N1 outbreaks. Second, would be the points of insertion. Strategically, I took the liberty to analyze more effective targeting if you will – then the spread-patterns. It really gets bad at that point." Huiwei said looking up at him. She definitely had his attention and the flirtatious spirit seemed to have faded.

"Did you model those factors, outside your parameters?" he asked.

"Yes." Huiwei typed in some commands and other modeling maps appeared with bigger geographic circles especially in the death and disaster zones.

"The initial objective of the Americans, as I'm told, would be to insert the virus into our communities, causing a spread before it was apparent. A long infection lifespan, asymptomatic spread, no approved treatments and of course no vaccine to stop the ripple effect. Until a large enough portion of the population was infected in China, and survived, the virus would carry on until its mutating restrictions ran out of vulnerable hosts. China would have the best chance of a human intervening variable – vaccine or treatment – since we control the pharma production and research. Our economy would still be on the edge, but much better off than if China were the progenitor. If the genome information we have is close to accurate, we can simulate the virus, develop the treatment protocols and produce a vaccine that might only need modification. We can also expedite these factors without the longer regulatory restrictions in the United States and Europe. Basically, without the surprise factor, China would not even realize the impact of an annual influenza pattern. This strain would play out in the population and effectively disappear." She explained.

"But why so different?" he asked more intently looking at the maps.

"Well, *surprise* is the strategic factor, as the models show. And, more importantly, insertion without a viable trail of origin. Create the absence of a *patient zero*. Then, based on cultural factors, you do it differently in the U.S. I studied there you probably know." She commented.

"Go on. I'm listening. I didn't' know you were working on these alternative comparators, but I'm glad you have. Even more counter-intelligence information to work with." He said.

"Well, in China they would likely look at some tourist points of insertion – returning travelers - factories in major urban centers, perhaps, and things like that. But, definitely not aircraft in general, with containment issues given Global travel, or more traceable points of entry – maybe luggage. For example, the Americans might want to use a vacation cruise ship ending in China, with primarily Chinese residents, but China would not – too traceable to a China source with a contained environment – patient zero is on board. We also have more mobility of industrial access outside our borders. China investors own and control various operations, where Americans are primarily placing orders, despite any capital investment." Huiwei paused and pointed at two different screens.

"While Americans might have some access to factories in China, that's a population of the least impacted persons, at least age and family dynamics. We have access to their healthcare and literally own some of their flourishing elderly care facilities. The Americans will not be able to stop the overlapping media machine, as the SCIO would. Their politics are volatile, just like throwing a steak in the ring with two pit-bulls not seeing the spectators dying around them. We control the Global investment market and so many lobbyists, thus, we ultimately control the politicians, at least long enough, before they wake-up. Finally, the knockout punch – China controls over 90% of America's pharmaceuticals directly or indirectly, treatment drugs and vaccines, and even the technology components to medical devices and equipment. The American's plot would not have that kind of impact with their attack on us." She said, taking a deep breath. These models were based more on her curiosity, since it was the United States devising this evil – highly hypothetical she presumed.

"So hypothetically what would we do in designing an attack? I mean . . . as a comparison scenario." he asked.

"Social contact, letting the asymptomatic infection rate spread in anonymous or not easily traced origin sources, bars, restaurants, small business, retail stores, subways, congested immigration areas where healthcare might not be sought, and potentially elder care facilities or hospitals themselves. The infrastructure systems, especially hospitals, would be overwhelmed. Stay away from identifiable, isolated containment venues – cruises, aircraft, prisons, schools and things like that. Infected individuals will get there soon enough anonymously. Places like amusement parks, or ski resorts – lots of people, non-contained environments, no entertainment venues with reserved seating that could be traceable. We would slow pharmaceutical production and shipment, reduce exportable inventory, and even stop shipping technology components for medical use. We probably could even cause chaos by not shipping medical facemasks and hand sanitizer. We produce more US-FDA approved items than the Americans do – Europe, same thing. Then, the SCIO would come to the rescue with menial supplies after the damage is done, the heroes. Media influence would be a significant factor for China." She said now with a solemn look. "Add an intervening variable like a natural disaster, flooding or an out of control forest fire, and it just accelerates the collapse."

"How would the delivery system work? Too many things could go wrong with an infected asset, and they would be traceable," asked Ho-Sun.

"I don't know . . . maybe cheap flash drives left next to computers at Internet bars, or even a bunch of dollar bills left on tables. The Americans would likely have some sort of vaccine before they launched. It would be difficult to have controlled inoculations for the assets. That's how we would cut it off anyway by getting a vaccine prepared in advance." She responded.

"That's actually very fascinating. Why are you not more pleased with your assessment?" he kept probing.

"Quite frankly, it's just scary as hell. It would be hell. The only bright point in the whole assignment is knowing that it's the People's Republic with the best interests of the World in mind. Having the working knowledge in advance, such a viral attack by the United States could be largely cutoff, we could even have vaccines ready. It's the stealth factor and surprise, with an unknown viral genome, and no intervening variable that balloons the impact. It's not another flu variety," she said.

"Yes. I understand. From a counter-intelligence standpoint, I definitely want to get your independent modeling to study - for review and heightened planning . . . and I'd like you to spell out more in a supplemental report regarding these added factors on a reverse-scenario. It will be helpful," he said.

"Yes, Major General Lú. That shouldn't be a problem," she said.

"I have to admit Colonel Lí, you certainly impressed me, and I'm not easy to impress. Dare I say, I feel like you are the sister I never had," he commented, with a smile.

Huiwei felt relieved that at least her intellect somehow turned his course. While she would not want to ever have been his sister, with him likely ripping the head off of her dolls, convincing others she had done it, but he was back on a professional level in calling her by her rank.

"The sooner the better, if possible. I want to be able to take all of this analysis to Assistant Secretary Sun Jun-Lai at the SCIO. As a member of the Central Committee, I don't know where it might go. So, you might keep that in mind in drafting your supplemental report. And, rest assured, I will give you the credit. As brilliant as I might be, Secretary Sun would know this is not my work. Thank you again for your expanded tutorial Colonel." He concluded, and left the room.

Huiwei could feel the pangs of guilt and remorse running through her, even in a meditative state. She had been so egocentrically proud at that moment, because her work was so astute that it might reach the ears of the Chairman himself, and certainly the Central Committee.

24

He knew he had not slept for long, but it was still needed sleep. Aiguo-Tao could feel the subtle changes in the air speed and altitude knowing that the pilot or flight attendant would be announcing preparation instructions for the descent into Fuzhou.

"Can I get you something else to drink?" We'll be preparing to land soon." Said the flight attendant. He was glad she let him sleep and noticed his empty glass was gone.

"No . . . I mean . . . yes. Could I have a bottle of water please," he responded.

She smiled, walked to the front of the plane, then returned with two, small plastic water bottles. "Here you go. One for the road if you like."

"Thank you," said Aiguo-Tao.

She stood next to him in hesitation. He could tell she was contemplating whether to say something more.

"Thank you once again. I am sorry for any commotion I might have caused," he said.

She smiled appreciatively, "It was really no problem. I'm glad it worked out." Hesitating again.

"I do not have any business cards in my wallet. I must have run out. Perhaps you could give me your name so I can provide a good note to the airline," he said.

She pulled out a business card of her own, with the Xiamen Airline logo and her given name, "Hufar," on one side, rapidly writing her cellphone number on the back, with, *"call - I travel a lot."* She handed him the card. He quickly read it, nodded and tried to force a friendly smile. He liked her name, at least the way he interpreted it, *Tiger Lilly*, and raised one eyebrow in amusement.

She looked happy with herself – the social tension gone – as she walked down the aisle picking up wrappers and other trash from the passengers. Maybe an added sway to her hips knowing that he was probably looking, he pleasantly thought.

Aiguo-Tao stashed the water bottles in his backpack and sat back to enjoy a few more moments of relaxation. He reached up to touch the video screen on the back of the seat in front of him. It flashed on a map showing a little airplane graphic near the end of the dotted lines marking their path. He touched the screen again and selected a news site.

The official news agency was showing video of police and various municipal workers at a food market. He saw the abbreviated notes below indicating it was in Wuhan. The video showed municipal workers carrying cages with live animals and putting them in trucks. The verbiage at the bottom indicated the market was being closed, because of some illness from the animals.

"I guess some sort of outbreak from the wild animals sold in the wet-market there. Quite frankly, I'm glad to be getting home and out of Wuhan. People going to the hospital and all," said the passenger sitting next to Aiguo-Tao, gesturing to the video screen.

The man rolled his fingers pressing into his temples, then coughed into a drink napkin, clearing his throat. "Flying always gives me headaches. Pressure on the sinuses and all. Glad to get home."

"I've been tied up with my work the last few days. Haven't had time to catch up with the news." Said Aiguo-Tao.

"My Wuhan colleagues said it evidently isn't anything like the whole swine flu stuff that came out of Hong Kong, but it still puts everyone on edge. I guess a number of people going to the hospital. City officials say it's under control," the passenger said.

"My grandparents liked to eat all sorts of animals from the markets, but fortunately it was not passed down to me," the passenger continued, with a quick cough into the square, paper napkin.

Aiguo-Tao nodded, "If I didn't catch it and kill it, I won't eat it."

"You're a hunter then. Interesting. Any chance you might know my friend . . ." the passenger said, being interrupted by Aiguo-Tao.

"No. It's been a long time since I hunted a wild animal. It's just a saying I have. I wouldn't know your friend. If it's not packaged, inspected and labeled I won't eat it," Aiguo-Tao responded.

"Sounds reasonable to me," said the passenger.

The conversation of strangers ended. Aiguo-Tao certainly preferred it that way. He thought about the number, and somewhat strange variety, of wild creatures he had killed and eaten in the wild during survival training and even actual operations. Killing and surviving made sense to him. What he told to the passenger was also true. People may be crazy, but they are not wild animals.

The intercom clicked, "Ladies and Gentlemen, thank you for flying Xiamem Airlines and a special thank you to our frequent flyers. The pilot informs me that we are preparing to land at Changle International Airport in just a few minutes. Please raise your seats to their upright positions, make sure your food tables are secured and locked and please buckle your seatbelts. . ."

Aiguo-Tao listened as his new friend, Hufar, finished the announcements, then he settled in waiting for the plane to land.

"Pretty girl. Seemed to like you," the passenger said, raising his eyes to the ceiling indicating he was referencing the voice on the intercom.

Aiguo-Tao just nodded.

As the passengers started to exit the airplane at the front, Aiguo-Tao grabbed his backpack, put it over one shoulder and headed for the door. He saw the flight officer who had given up his seat, and nodded in appreciation. The officer gave a polite wave back.

Hufar stood near the exit. As he passed, she looked at him, quickly put her hand up to the side of her head, extending her thumb and little finger, gesturing, 'call me.' He was not good at smiling, but he did his best to return a polite smile.

Once he got inside the terminal door, he quickly turned, getting out of line, to stay close to the wall behind the gate podium. He pulled the cellphone out of his pocket and pretended to be talking to avoid suspicion. He was attempting to do a quick assessment of security cameras and security personnel.

Walking further down the wall and out of the way of bustling passengers and airline staff, he squatted down, pulling the Xiamem

Airline hat and safety vest out of his backpack along with the small canvass tool bag and empty clipboard. He put them on, grabbed the bag and clipboard, and stood up.

Hoping that the disguise was sufficient for the time being, he kept his face down to avoid a good view of his face. He saw a disposable facemask, with elastic straps, on a seat that a passenger must have left. He picked it up, rubbed the inside surface against his vest, then put it across his face. He felt better, now, about any facial recognition programs picking him out of the crowd, at least for a couple of days – if he needed more time, he had different problems.

He continued down the terminal until he found a gate where the aircraft had just left. The gate agents were packing up and he saw the door to the jetway still open. Walking through the door, no one made any attempt to stop him – just a faceless worker doing his job.

He heard the jetway door shut. Pulling out his cellphone, he powered it on and waited for the screen to light up. Then sat on the floor, letting his backpack slide down against the wall. He pulled his eyes tight and felt his eyes looking up under his eyelids as he searched his memory. He knew he did not have an extraordinary memory like some people he worked with. However, his years of training, forced skills to remember incredible details that the average person might miss, such as an address with just a glance or the make, model and tag number of a car.

Short-term, long-term memory, different beasts he knew. He could remember his locker combination from the academy at fifteen, but he did not even pay attention to the plate number on the van Huan-Jun drove. He tried to focus on the little tricks he learned, associations. He needed to recall the phone number. It was a long shot he realized, a long time since he dialed it, so repetition memory was not helping him. Fifty-fifty chance? Maybe.

He opened his eyes and quickly punched in the numbers he settled on. He stared at the phone, repeating the number in his head again, with some sense of false verification. He hit the call button.

"Hello . . . Bàba?" answered a young voice.

"Uh . . . duí bu qí, *sorry*, I must have dialed the wrong number." He said, quickly ending the call.

Aiguo-Tao, transposed the last two digits, and called again.

"Ni hao." He heard the direct but understanding voice he remembered.

Aiguo-Tao moved the phone away from his mouth for a moment, so his *sigh* of relief would not be heard.

"This is Aiguo-Tao. Can you talk?" he said.

"You must have a long contact list in your phone to remember my number, Aiguo-Tao. I'm retired from the People's Navy now, you know. If one can ever truly retire. How are you?" said Captain Lóng-Qing.

"May I ask if you still live near Fuzhou? I was thinking of stopping to see you if your schedule allows," said Aiguo-Tao cautiously. He was not sure where this conversation might go.

"That's very kind of you Aiguo-Tao. It is a surprise to hear from you. Yes, I still live in the province. I'm not there at the moment, but I am returning. Perhaps sooner than I thought," said Qing.

"I was hoping to see you tomorrow since I might be in the area. If you are not available, it is no problem for me to go on to Wuhan instead," Aiguo-Tao said.

"Wuhan? Don't eat any wild dog there I understand. No, no, I plan to be back tomorrow and it would be a pleasure to see you. I don't get many calls from past students. Too many untimely deaths in that list. Such is the nature of the business I suppose. But I always knew you were a survivor Aiguo-Tao." Qing said.

"That would be most kind of you. Can I use this number to call you?" asked Aiguo-Tao.

"Let's presume I will call you tomorrow at the number I see on my phone, if that's okay. My concern is that I can only think of three reasons you might call me so unexpectedly, especially since I have retired and no longer in direct service to our honorable Chairman." Qing said.

"Yes. This number will be fine, if you know about what time. What reasons do you think I would have to call you?" he responded.

"One, would be to invite me to your wedding. Two, would be to set up a meeting where the purpose of our reunion might result in my unanticipated funeral. The third, would be you are in need of a favor – likely a rather desperate one," Qing said with a slight smile, then continued.

"I highly doubt that some young woman has lasted a courtship with you to become your bride, and perhaps pity her if she has. The second reason most assuredly would delay my return, and thus I am left with the last option," she concluded.

"You are very wise and have always had my deepest respect. I look forward to your call," Aiguo-Tao said.

"It will be late afternoon, at the earliest. Maybe later," Qing said and ended the call.

Once an asset, always an asset, he thought. He had no other option in Fuzhou. Yet he also knew Qing had a long, independent streak that did not assure cooperation.

Captain Lóng-Qing was a teacher first, in addition to a remarkable career in clandestine operations. Unfortunately, the details of her noteworthy accomplishments were known to extremely few high-ranking officers and officials. Once she was in line for more prominent positions, crossing into the political realm, but the lack of her need for more widely known recognition, and her strength in operational execution, were fatal weaknesses in politics.

Captain Lóng-Qing did not have a specialty in anything, or, perhaps she was an expert in everything, depending how a person looked at her.

In training operatives on the workout mats, she almost always fought with Shaolin sticks. Her teaching point was that it is an unnecessary risk to allow an opponent to use potentially, superior strength or style in close-quarter combat, and to know the weapon or technique where you will not lose. She never lost, even when the sticks went away.

In covert techniques, she was a walking encyclopedia. Qing, more than any other person, made Aiguo-Tao the ghost that he was. She assessed his weaknesses and his strengths, always making him better.

Captain Lóng-Qing had worked as an asset in two of his covert operations involving penetration into Taiwan.

Right now, Aiguo-Tao needed to find a safe place until tomorrow. He had another call to make.

25

Huiwei remained in her meditation pose. Sometimes closing her eyes and sometimes wide open. Her meditation remained the same. As so many times before, she used her intellect to accomplish the task without using it to see the known and even the unintended consequences around her that others could not.

After Huiwei finished her report. Major General Lú copied her on the commendation letter he submitted. Zuìgāo jìmì, *Top Secret*, of course.

The signs of the storm were upon her. Yet, she was unwilling to see them, and with pride, she did not even try to look.

She was ordered to take an unheard of, month-long leave, with basically a blank check for travel within China or perhaps foreign bases. She ran the proposal up the chain of command, to perhaps go visit MIT. Some of her classmates were now professors. She recalled enjoying the night life surrounding Cambridge, runs along the Charles River, and, of course, nearby Boston.

Major General Lú himself came to her office to inform her that she deserves the extended leave. He did not want her to get Jīng pí lìjìn, *burned-out* – they needed her. He said that he feared events were happening too fast and it remained critical that she was available. The MIT request was a, méiyǒu fāshēngu, *no-go*.

She settled on starting her leave with at least two weeks at a PLA base far away from the political rat race in a crowded Beijing. It was not a vacation spot. The base served as a training center for special forces along with certain MSS personnel, depending on their role. The real reason was that her former, martial arts combat instructor was there.

Huiwei was a realist. Her brain did not let her think any other way. She knew the odds – all of them. Getting ready to turn forty years old tugged at her. Still more fit than most any twenty-year-old, it still seemed like some landmark she would need to deal with. She knew her body, bones, muscle and tendons were not twenty-five anymore.

The saying, *you are only as old as you think you are*, unfortunately rang hollow to a trained medical doctor. She had put her body through a lot, and survived. Of course, there were the associated injuries as well, including a badly dimpled scar from a bullet wound in the field. A quality plastic surgeon from Beijing was not available.

Her old trainer was somewhere in his sixties, still in top physical shape. He would understand and have the best knowledge – and he would actually give a damn. Basically, she had to learn to train like a forty-year-old and not a twenty-year-old, especially if she wanted to avoid injuries or re-injuries. Two-weeks in training classes would be well worth the time. Time she normally did not have.

After two weeks, she could feel the difference and was grateful. She ended up staying a third week helping to train new, cocky arrivals. Whatever black belt degrees they won in their *duì lain* sparring at their Wushau, kwoons, were soon discovered as almost useless when facing Huiwei's more practical, and lethal, skills.

Her trainer often had to hold his laughs against his serious exterior when the almost middle-aged female, computer programmer, seeking to enhance her self-defense skills, felled her young opponent, typically in seconds. The trainer enjoyed introducing Huiwei in that manner, leaving out her lengthy resume.

Then, she travelled to some vacation spots along the East China Sea coast for another week, or so. She always had trouble being able to simply relax. Walking on remote sandy beaches or climbing up the rocks along the shoreline to find a perch, felt transformative to her. The wind blowing her hair and feeling the mist of the smashing waves gave her a sense of safety in the midst of chaos.

When she returned from her leave, she realized that her modeling files were not accessible to her. She backed-up a lot of her early data and other programs on a private storage device. She had learned to never trust a server she did not control. It saved her on many occasions when even sophisticated servers crashed or had glitches.

Huiwei knew that the science director and others would know that she discovered she no longer had access. Yet, intuitively, she felt the tug of the tide trying to pull her. Instead of taking an obvious risk to inquire, she quickly devised a research project on enhanced effects of covert communications intrusion.

Popular tactics carried out in the United States and Europe from military war rooms thousands of miles away in China where the infantry was a room full of highly talented hackers recruited from the colleges. They wore their uniforms and ranks, but would not know which end of the gun was lethal. Of course, Huiwei could make either end lethal. The SCIO would be glad she had moved on with a project that benefited their operations.

After all, her modeling on the potential virus spread was purely hypothetical. Her access being denied was likely Major General Lú Ho-Sun deciding to go against his word and take credit for her research. Perhaps, the counter-intelligence channels with the Americans forewarned them that the MSS was aware of any devious plan, thus stopping it in its tracks.

For over a year, she moved on with her other research projects. Working quite late one evening, Huiwei was looking at various SCIO databases to derive certain data-points. She happened to notice a reference to, "SARS-CoV2."

Using her own covert, computer skills she piggy-backed on her footprint access to the SCIO and MSS databases. She was now digging into "deep" files and knew she had to be careful.

Once she had reviewed some basic information, her heart sank. She retraced her thinking process over and over again trying to figure out why she had not thought to do this in the first place. In hindsight, it seemed so logical, and it was nothing new to her with other project assignments.

Huiwei read the profiles on the Wuhan Institute of Virology. Studied the technical research data on the corona virus genome sequencing and the Institute's genome intron and exon splicing protocols.

The historical records kept reaching a dead end. That's when she accessed old personnel data files and found contacts from prior researchers and technicians. In a hit-and-miss fashion, she was able to reach enough individuals so that she could start putting the pieces together. A seemingly innocuous set of viruses out in the wild that could be successfully altered to be potentially lethal to humans–depending on the host.

Feeling the tender, but firm hands of *Matsu* grabbing her ankles from under the sea and pulling her further from the shore, Huiwei pushed on – operational files. She knew accessing operational data was a point of no return. If her footprint did not belong there, it was more likely an execution without interrogation.

She did not need to dig too deep into the files. She just needed to understand the operation objective. Huiwei would be in and out before any crumbs of her cyber-trail were known.

SARS-2 in its early reference, then SARS-CoV2, now simply CoV-2. The strategic objective was embedding the virus in a general population to create economic disruption.

The operational objective was two-fold, insertion and plausible deniability – *a sneak attack where I know nothing – and you can't prove otherwise.*

The MSS covert operative in charge of strategic field operations was a Major Zhu Aiguo-Tao. She made a mental note to later access his personnel records – probably highly classified.

Next, the protocol operation method – the instruction manual. She froze when she saw the multiple references to her long, coded file names. She did not need to risk opening them up. Huiwei already knew what was there.

Part of the design in her report was the need to develop a treatment protocol and vaccine. She presumed the Americans would, before launching a potential pandemic. With prior knowledge, China's vaccine would be the saving grace for the Chinese population. She presumed the vaccine was there. Her concern was the cryptic information in the operations plan. If she understood it, the assets were given a placebo and told it was a vaccine. She was not sure why they would not just give them the vaccine. Maybe local assets and the MSS did not want the vaccine to leave China's borders. Maybe she could find a database, later on, about the vaccine.

As she gracefully had drifted against the tide, starting to see the shoreline within grasp, reaching to touch her big toe to the sand, she felt the blast of the first wave crash over her head, pulling her underwater, feeling her knees and legs smashed into the rocks and coral of the sea floor, and wanting to pull her back out into the tide again. The waves would only increase in danger as she moved closer to shore, with more shallow waters, for her whole body to be pounded to the floor or a rocky shoal.

The Peoples Republic, her people, made the virus, the plan, and now the resources and methodology to deploy it – and Huiwei had been the key to unlocking the front door, and every window in the house. The operation was *"ACTIVE."*

She was on the short list of those with critical knowledge on an active operation. A super-computer database program, one she improved, was filtering the names on that list, 24/7 looking for any anomalies. In some instances, the recommended command would be custody, interrogation or even elimination, simply because of being the wrong person with that much knowledge.

Huiwei scurried out of cyberspace, slightly shaking, nervously retracing her steps and erasing them.

She did not sleep that night. At least she could not recall falling asleep despite burying herself under the covers and stuffing her face in the pillow deciding whether to cry or scream. Maybe it was best. Sleeping meant dreams and the only dreams she was capable of that night were nightmares beyond Dante's imagination – only hers would be a real canvass of bodies around the World.

The next morning, she went through her routine. She dressed and arrived at the MSS Science Division offices on time. After impatiently wasting time, she set-off down the hallways.

She ran into a military scientist she had met several times. He seemed to be rushing with a very strange smile mixed with confusion. He haphazardly bumped into Huiwei.

"Oh, I'm so sorry Colonel Lí, so sorry . . . my baby . . . I mean my wife . . . she's having our baby. I have to be there. She's almost fully dilated. I have to hurry."

Huiwei bent down to pick up some folders he dropped, "Major . . . she will be fine and so will the baby . . . you, I'm not so sure about. She needs you to be strong. Women have been doing this successfully for thousands of years."

"Yes, Colonel, you're right. I know, but it's our first child. Oh no . . ." he exclaimed.

"Those files. I didn't mean to bring them. I need to get them back in the office." He went on panicking.

"I can put them back in your office. I just need the access card and I can leave the card in an envelope with an assistant. Security can let you in the main door when you get back," said Huiwei, thinking quickly.

"Yes. Oh, would you. Thank you. I've got to get going," he said, unsnapping his keycard from his shirt.

Huiwei walked to his office, opened the door and laid the files on his desk covered with stacks of reference books, reports and other files. She was looking for an empty office where her phone call would not receive any attention. There's no such thing as coincidence she thought, but she was hedging on the existence of a little fate.

For the past sixteen hours she kept trying to think of who she could talk to. She had lots of acquaintances, but not in in the realm of, *'mind if I tell you about the end of the world as we know it, or the crash of the worldwide economy and the deaths of hundreds of millions, because I caused it . . . and by the way, any suggestions on what I should do . . . since my boss is the Chairman of the Communist Party and may not want to provide any fatherly advice, or just buy me an ice cream cone.'*

In the middle of the night, it came to her. Susan Kilmer. Susan was a colleague at Princeton working on her post-doctorate in mathematics. Something about calculating gravitational densities and nuances in geological strata – evidently, Sir Isaac Newton never tossed an apple in the air below the Earth's mantle. She was now a professor at MIT.

Huiwei picked up the desk phone and sat on the floor behind the desk. She spoke to Susan maybe once or twice a year, just to stay in touch and visited her several times, without going into the different reasons she was in the States. Susan was always a wonderful friend as far as high functioning post-doctorate professionals go.

Huiwei pulled her pink, tampon case out of her pocket and scanned the desk area. She found the listening device under the lip of the desk. She did not know if it was active. She saw a stress-ball the Major had on his desk and a foil sandwich wrapper in the trashcan. Huiwei ripped a small crease in the ball and covered the devise, then covered the ball with the foil. She saw a tape dispenser on a side table and taped the foil in place. Not perfect, but it should be enough to muffle the call or interfere with the reception.

The phone records would log a call to MIT from the Major. In his field of study, there would be no reason to question it. She dialed.

"Hello. This is Dr. Kilmer. Can I help you," Susan said.

"Well, I don't know that I need a doctor, can I speak to your wife, Susan?" said Huiwei.

"Huiwei! Oh my God! How wonderful. Are you coming to the States? I'd love it," exclaimed Susan.

"No. It's a professional question . . . I was hoping you might help out," said Huiwei.

"Usually, you don't have a question, you have the answer. But, of course, what's up," said Susan.

"I'm working on some statistical modeling for our health agency. Kind of like your CDC. I had a question about where things were left in developing vaccines and treatments for SARS from back in 2003 or *four*. Can you think of anyone?" Huiwei said with a little less luster knowing it was a remote chance.

"Well . . . actually, I do. Whether he's available of not, I have no idea. I can call him. Maybe give him your number, have him call you. At least its early in the day here compared to your time zone," she said.

"Again, I know it's strange Suz, but besides the time difference, I really need to figure this information out. I have a deadline for my preliminary report and, shall we say, the bosses here are not as forgiving as they are at MIT," Huiwei pleaded.

"Sure. It's Eric Thomas. A brilliant microbiologist who works with some virologists as well. He even worked with some committee of my father's when Dad was in the U.S. Senate. I think he believes he owes me favors for that being on his resume," Susan explained.

"Is he available . . . I mean available to speak with?" asked Huiwei.

"Well, actually a John Hopkins professor, but he's working on something here at MIT. I ran into him just yesterday. Different building and all. Can I put you on hold and try to conference him in?" asked Susan.

"Sure . . . if the music's any good on hold?" Huiwei joked, heard Susan laugh, and went on hold. A panicky thirty seconds with some bad electronic version of a Mozart piece playing in the background. Then, she heard the click reconnecting.

"Eric. This is my dear friend Lí Huiwei. We studied together at Princeton and have stayed in touch. As I was telling you, she's smarter than both of us put together with a lot more initials after her name, so don't try to dumb her down or dazzle her, Eric," said Susan.

"Thanks for the introduction Susan. I'll try to behave. So, Susan tells me you have a SARS vaccine question or something. I don't work on SARS specifically, actually no one does, but I've advised the CDC on related issues. What's the question?" Eric asked.

"Do you have a vaccine in the United States?" Huiwei asked.

"Simple question, simple answer, *no*. Unless you count a colleague's freezer somewhere in Houston, probably next to the frozen pizzas. Long story made short, SARS hit North America in about 2004. A lot of panic. Folks tended to show symptoms before passing it around on a platter. So, it was cut-off fairly well. Then the little guy pretty much disappeared. A mystery in itself. Plenty of frozen samples sitting around in labs." Eric expounded.

"So, there is a vaccine. In Texas?" Asked Huiwei.

"Not really. One team down at Baylor Children's in Houston finally came up with something, but it wasn't until maybe 2014-15 . . . trying to get it to human testing. We survived the H1N1 by then. No money, no interest, no testing, no vaccine. A group in France, I believe, came up with something, but it seemed the cure was potentially worse than the disease, same thing, no funds, no vaccine," He said.

"So, the United States is no further along than China with a vaccine?" asked Huiwei, not wanting to say the wrong thing.

"Evidently not. If there's more interest in China, that's great. You basically own the vaccine market. If it crops up again it could be nasty, especially if it mutated allowing for something like asymptomatic transmission. But again, nobody is sick, the little germ went away, so I don't think any vaccine sample will get thawed out any time soon. Does that help?" Eric asked.

"Greatly. Maybe my statistical modeling will convince others to show more interest, especially financial interest. You've been very helpful. Nice to meet you Eric. Maybe I can meet you next time I'm visiting Susan." said Huiwei.

"Eric, don't get ideas. Not only is she awfully pretty, she'll kick your ass. Kung fu black belt Huiwei?" said Susan.

"That's correct Suz, self-defense classes growing up. Sometimes you have too good of a memory. Right now, I need to kick some ass, as you say it, on this report. Thank you so much," ended Huiwei.

As the memories began to fade, Huiwei stared at the dragon, with smoke rising through the vents around its body and mouth. She had an eerie sense that the dragon had seen all of her thoughts while she meditated, yet made no judgments.

26

Eric Thomas and Susan Kilmer just pulled up from their run along a trail next to the Charles River. Susan had told him that she needed to try to get in better shape and probably needed to find a running partner to help motivate her. Eric volunteered to help her get started.

"Heard from your friend, Huiwei lately?" asked Eric.

"No. Sorry, if you're looking for a date this weekend. I don't think she'll be in town. Why?" asked Susan.

"No reason. Just a sixth-sense. Wandering thoughts while I'm running I suppose," Eric said.

As they walked to cool down their muscles, Eric was thinking about why his instincts were suddenly signaled, thinking back to his conversation at least a month ago. He tended to trust his instincts. Maybe he should put in another call to Assistant Director Lewis at Langley.

Weeks ago, Professor Thomas sat back in his chair at his temporary office on the MIT campus. He steepled his fingers against his chin, thinking about the phone call he had just had with Susan and her friend Huiwei.

He reached for his laptop backpack, pulling out a black zippered case and retrieved his sat-phone. He stared at the phone for a moment and dialed a series of numbers.

"Alan Lewis here. From whom do I have the pleasure?" said Lewis.

"Eric Thomas, director. I was hoping you might be able to answer a question for me that just came up," responded Eric.

"Eric! You still carry a sat-phone I see. Anyway, is it Commander, Professor or Doctor today? asked Lewis.

"Probably Commander. Faculty and students, as they are these days, might balk at me wearing my uniform on campus. A dry-cleaning bill to get a milk shake Molotov cocktail off seems unnecessary. Let's just go with Eric," he said with a chuckle.

"So, what's the mysterious question Command . . . Eric?" asked Lewis.

"I just had an interesting three-way . . . conference call . . . with a colleague here at MIT and her old friend from Princeton days. Huiwei. Chinese. Government computer person. Statistical modeling if I understand correctly," said Eric.

"Didn't happen to get a surname did you, and I'm ignoring the *ménage* à *trois* reference, just so you know I caught it," said Lewis.

"Lí, if I recall. She said she was working on some project for their CDC and wanted to know the status of SARS vaccine development in the U.S.," Eric said, still smiling.

"What'd you tell her?" asked Lewis.

"That to my knowledge, there wasn't one, here or anywhere that I know of," replied Eric.

"The name actually rings a bell. Let me call up a file here. I hate all of these passwords . . . *three-way*, really?" said Lewis. Eric waited.

"Yep. Thought it sounded familiar. Colonel Lí Huiwei, People's Liberation Army. Lots of initials after her name. Must like school a lot. She's a unicorn," said Lewis.

"A what?" asked Eric.

"Unicorn. We know she has to be affiliated with their secret service, MSS, but she's a professor when she's in the U.S. Even has quite a resume as a medical doctor, psychiatry. Not a diplomat. Comes in from time to time working with this or that university on different projects, even lectures sometimes. Participated in some China-U.S. coop exercise out at Pendleton a while back. Martial arts evidently. That's how we tied down her PLA rank. A Major then. Nice looking woman from her photo here," added Lewis.

"That's what my friend said. Don't get any ideas or she would kick my ass. But what's the unicorn thing?" asked Eric.

"Well . . . she comes and goes. Always a good cover. By all appearances plays by the rules, but coincidentally, various classified information gets pirated. Never been able to tie it to her. We've tried. She flies away undetected, into the clouds, like a magical unicorn – thus, the tag," explained Lewis.

"Should I be concerned?" asked Eric.

"You should always be concerned. I might do some digging. Anything unusual on the vaccine issue?" asked Lewis.

"Not really. Just that it's not something on anybody's radar in virology. SARS went away. No funding to worry about a vaccine.

Most efforts are in trying to predict what strain of influenza is coming about to make the right cocktail for next year's flu shot. Hope you got yours this year. We do the same thing here helping the CDC with modeling information," said Eric.

"Sure. I got my shot. Required to. They even come to my office with the plunger in their hand. Don't really have much of a choice. Let me know if anything else comes up Command . . . Eric."

"Aye, aye sir," Eric said with a smile and ended the call.

27

Aiguo-Tao pulled the business card out of his pocket, looked at Hufar's name, flipped the card over, and dialed the phone number. He did not know where she lived, but presumed she had either left the airport or was already headed off on her next flight. She answered.

"Hufar. This is Delun. We met on your flight and you gave me your card," said Aiguo-Tao.

"Delun . . . I don't think I even got your name. Hey, just so you know, I've never done that before . . . you know, giving out my card like that . . . just so you know . . . but I'm glad you called," responded Hufar, being sincere in what she said. She still felt a little bit foolish.

"Unusual for me too. I understand," said Aiguo-Tao.

"So, what's going on? I just checked in to the hotel. I have a one-day layover, two nights," she said.

"Well . . . I just found out my meetings are cancelled, but I won't fly out again until tomorrow sometime. I didn't know if you lived in Fuzhou or not. Since I'm stranded here, I thought I'd call," he said.

"I already ate a meal on the flight, but maybe you could meet me at the hotel for a drink or something," she suggested.

"Where is the hotel?" he asked.

"The Sheraton. There's nothing really close to the airport, but they have a shuttle bus," she replied.

"Nice hotel, if I recall," he said trying to place the location and landmarks in his head.

"It is, but the airline negotiates a crew rate. Plus, I think the hotel likes the guests seeing the crew here, especially the flight attendants. Although the truth is, we don't leave our rooms much. Catch up on sleep, order room service, make-up on and leave. A one-day layover is great to catch up on my sleep," she explained.

They ended the conversation. Aiguo-Tao headed down the ramp stairs to the tarmac wanting to avoid security cameras in the terminal. He worked his way through the work areas, past the baggage handling area and found the route to the passenger baggage carrousels, where he knew the shuttle bus station would be nearby.

The shuttle driver asked for his name to confirm his hotel reservation. He pulled out his airline hat from his backpack.

"I'm with the airline. They flew me in for a maintenance issue and said they'd put me up at the Sheraton. Said they have a special crew rate and I just need to show up," said Aiguo-Tao.

The driver looked down at the hat, and waved him to go sit down. Once he arrived at the hotel lobby, he called Hufar.

"Where are you Delun?" she answered. She must have recognized the number showing on her caller I.D.

"I'm in the hotel lobby. Very nice place," he responded.

"I'll be ready in a minute. Why don't you just come up to my room, 1008. Just jump on the elevator after someone swipes their room-key card," she said.

"That sounds fine." He responded.

The elevator required the swipe of a room-key. He waited until a guest with two children entered the elevator and swiped her card, then he stepped in without any questions. Aiguo-Tao knocked on Hufar's door and she answered wearing a casual, silk, rose colored blouse and black slacks with black high-heels.

"Thanks for coming up so I could get ready. I don't pack many street clothes, so you get what you get," she said, stepping back and flinging her arms in the air to show her outfit.

"It looks good on you. Actually, better than your flight uniform, no offense," he said.

"None taken. So, where's your bag?" she asked, only seeing him holding his backpack in his hand.

"Long story, or maybe a short one - they lost my bag and said they would send it to my hotel for tomorrow night. It was a carry on, but they were asking for volunteers to check bags, because of the full flight. I left my travel wallet in my bag not thinking about it. So, I only had my I.D. in my pocket for the plane and won't have my credit cards until tomorrow night. No extra clothes either," he explained.

Hufar's face showed a scowl as she crossed her arms across her stomach.

"So, you thought you could just hit me up for a room? Not very romantic," she said forming a pouting face, and then a smile.

"I'm sorry. I should have said something. I wanted to call you anyway and it seemed like a good idea at the time. I thought I could come see you and figure out my next move. Maybe call a friend to reserve a room some place for me over the phone with their credit card," he explained.

"No, that's fine. I understand. Traveling creates all sorts of inconveniences. You almost lost your seat after all. I tell you what. You can sleep on the sofa over there, it may fold out, and then you'll be able to clean up in the morning," she offered.

"That would be great. I promise to use my manners and lift the seat." He paused and scratched his head, "Sorry, I don't have a credit card or cash to take you for drinks," he said.

"We can't drink alcohol anyway within twenty-four hours of a flight and I don't like to risk it anyway. Truthfully, I wasn't planning to go out and they have a tea and coffee brewer over by the sink. I can order room service and the airline will pay for it, within my per diem expense," she said, kicking off her high-heeled shoes toward the closet.

"Tea sounds good. I had some snacks to eat and I'm fine," he replied.

Aiguo-Tao woke up and looked at the clock by the bed, shining, 6:45. The sun was just starting to rise. He silently folded the sheet and cover away from his body and glanced at Hufar's naked shoulders and angel wings.

Walking like a sniper in the woods, which he was at times, he closed the bathroom door, used the toilet and washed off his body with a hotel wash cloth and soap. He stared at the mirror, not seeing his face, but rather, his thoughts.

What to do with Hufar? In many ways she had been his guardian angel the past 14 hours. He knew he was not a romantic person in any way. Most women responded quite happily with him in bed, not worrying about whether he was a good lover. He felt better and it seemed they did as well.

Unless an operation called for it, he did not flirt, nor did he like to. He knew he was attracted to good looking women with sleek and shaped bodies. He certainly had no interest in a relationship of any kind. He presumed the same was true for women who slept with him. His body was fit, with hard, shaped muscles. For the women, it was probably a desired break from their out of shape boyfriends with fat-rolls of varying degrees.

The sofa was a fine option to him. However, he strongly predicted that the sipping of tea would eventually lead to the comfortable, queen-sized mattress. He was not much of a conversationalist when it came to small talk. Thus, things tended to either evolve rather quickly, or, not at all.

Hufar gave him her card. She invited him to the hotel. She offered her room without hesitation. She cried out her pleasure, several times, and satisfied his mind and body, bringing him a sense of peace, if only for a short time.

His face finally came into focus in the mirror. *No*, he concluded. He would not kill her. Aiguo-Tao realized how easy he could. Then, cover his tracks, and move on without a witness left behind, and without remorse. He needed to stay away from public view, security cameras, the police or even a wandering agent. Hufar could provide him safety for now. If she became overly suspicious, or inquisitive, he could still change his mind.

When he walked back to the bed, she rolled toward him, pulling the sheets down to expose the hard nipples rising from her breasts, then kicking the sheets over to show her bare hip and leg.

She reached her arms in the air, beckoning him back to bed. He willingly complied.

It was mid-morning before their bodies finally rolled away from each other. Short naps between each dance of their lips and flesh. She showered first, coming out of a steaming bathroom with a white hotel robe wrapped around her and her hands working to dry her hair with a towel.

"Your turn. I'm afraid that if we don't get dressed, I might break you and you have another flight to catch today," Hufar said with a sultry smile.

"I think it's me who has already broken you - you will never find another lover to make you smile like that again," he responded, thinking maybe he heard the line in a movie.

He got out of bed and walked to the bathroom. Hufar lightly passed her hand across his naked buttocks, "Maybe you have Delun."

Aiguo-Tao grabbed his backpack, with all of his belongings and closed the door of the bathroom behind him. He hung his clothes up to cleanse in the steam and took a long shower.

When he emerged, with his still-damp clothes on, he saw a breakfast tray set out on the sofa table. Hufar still had her robe on and made subtle movements as she ate, that were obviously intended to draw his eyes to the fleshy slopes leading to her breasts and her bare leg fully exposed through the break in the robe.

"I went ahead and ordered some food. I hope it's okay. I was rather hungry," as she bit down on a strawberry looking up at him, "I just don't know where this appetite came from," continuing with a smile full of false innocence. "I didn't want to get dressed with my hair still wet and the blow dryer was in the bathroom," she finished.

Aiguo-Tao sat next to her on the sofa, stroked her smooth leg and reached for the glass of orange juice to drink.

He explained that he was waiting for a call from the home office to make sure they are taking care of things for his flight and to find out about his agenda for the next day. After Hufar finished eating, and being done with her flirtatious performance, she dried her hair, dressed and said she wanted to go shopping for a while. Aiguo-Tao insisted it was best if he stayed to wait for his calls. He also thought it might be good for her to be seen in the hotel, carefree and alone.

His phone finally rang. Of course, it was Qing. He had already deleted his phone number from the memory on Hufar's phone.

"Ni hao," answered Aiguo-Tao.

"Ni hao, Major Zhú. If you remembered my phone number, I suppose you can remember some simple directions without having to write them down," said Qing, in a no-nonsense voice.

"Shi," said Aiguo-Tao.

"Do you know where Chibiaodao is?" Qing asked.

"Yes. You know we have met there before. I will have to arrange transportation," he said

"Will six work for you then. If not, it's still at six. Don't be late," Qing ended the call.

When Hufar returned, she had some shopping bags. She pulled out a pair of blue chinos, holding them up to her legs, "I thought I might want something more casual."

She handed Aiguo-Tao another bag, "Here, these are for you. Who knows if your bag will be there at the hotel. They lost it once."

He pulled the pair cargo pants, shirt, underwear and socks out of the bag, "Thank you Hufar. Thank you." He reached to embrace her and found her lips for a long and grateful kiss.

"Did you receive your call. I hope you didn't. Because then you have to go," she said.

Then, Hufar reached in a bag and pulled out a small ball of black lace and satin, now dangling from her index finger, "I don't know what I'll do with this if you go," she said casting the best sensuous look of innocence she could muster with her eyes.

"I certainly would like to see you model that . . . at least for the short duration it would be on, if I did. But I have to meet a business associate at six and then take a late flight out. I have to figure out transportation," he said.

"Where? asked Hufar.

"South, toward the island coast," he replied.

"Let me take you. I was wanting to rent a car and drive to the coast anyway," she said.

Hufar continued, "You must. For me. The obvious is that I would need to give you money for a taxi or train. I know you would repay it, but it would make me feel like . . . well. . .that I hired you. I don't want that to be the way you leave."

He thought a moment. It would be much easier, provided she would let me tell her where to drop him off and be on her way.

"Okay. Deal. Provided you understand that I won't be able to invite you to my business meeting," he said.

"That's not a problem. I love finding a nice restaurant on the shoreline and eating while the surf splashes away. That's what I was going to do. I just wish it was with you, but I understand," she said.

"In that case, why don't you see if that wad of lace can really fit on your body. I don't see how it can," he said.

Hufar gave a little happy squeak, kissed him on the cheek and pranced to the bathroom. A few minutes later, she walked out, wearing the white bathrobe. She saw Aiguo-Tao's naked body partially covered with the sheet, propped on its side with his cocked elbow raising his hand to brace his head.

She slowly walked toward the bed, exaggerating the movement of her hips, then reached up to let the robe fall off of her shoulders and slowly drape off her body.

"Worth the wait Dulan?" she asked.

Ninety minutes later, Aiguo-Tao anxiously looked at the clock waiting for Hufar to come out of the bath and finish dressing. He did not regret the detour, when Hufar convinced him that it would be worth it to hear her song of elation repeated once more.

Hufar knew he was in a hurry . . . because of her. She also knew he did not have any regrets – he wasn't always the silent type. She hustled to dress, called the front desk to arrange for a rental car and was almost ready to leave.

"You finish up and I'll go down to make sure the car is there, okay?" he said.

"Sure," she responded and gave him another quick kiss, "See you at the valet."

Aiguo-Tao wanted to avoid security cameras picking up the two of them together, if possible. He thought that Dulan fellow must be a great guy, but that wasn't him, he was a ghost.

They drove south to Chibiaodao.

"Can I ask you about your finger? It still looks hurt," said Hufar trying to keep her eyes on the road.

"Cut-off during a secret intelligence interrogation," he responded looking straight ahead.

"Seriously . . . what happened? And, you have scars on your body . . . a little bit sexy even," she continued.

"Military . . . once upon a time . . . things happen . . . finger was lost consulting on a machine repair . . . I prefer not to talk about it if that's okay," he said still staring straight ahead. *I tried to be honest,* he thought.

"Sure. No more questions," said Hufar.

He knew where Qing would want to meet. He asked Hufar to pull over, so he could get out and walk the added block down a narrow side street. He kissed her, reaching across the seats. She wrapped her hands around his neck, keeping his mouth pulled to hers for a long kiss. Then, he opened the passenger door to get out and walk to the backdoor on the other side to get his bag.

"Thank you for the new clothes. That was really wonderful of you," he said, truly meaning it.

"You're leaving me for who knows how long, maybe forever for all I know, and it's the clothes you that you think are *wonderful*," she spouted.

He knew she was mostly joking, but he took the hint, walking to the driver's window. He reached his head in and gave her another long kiss.

"That was rude of me. The breakfast was wonderful too," he said, with perhaps his first, unforced smile in a long time.

Hufar lovingly hit him on his arm as he turned to open the rear door to grab his backpack. Suddenly, he heard a whiffing sound he had heard too many times before. He dropped to the pavement, having looked to see Hufar's lifeless eyes, wide open, with a nine-millimeter hole in the center of her forehead.

In his push-up position, he threw his head looking to the left, seeing the black leather boots with his eyes flowing up to see the suppressed pistol returning to cover beneath a cape-like coat and then the face of Captain Lóng-Qing. She was holding a smirk on her face, walking toward him. He quickly pushed up and stood.

"Aiguo-Tao. Lovely girl. I presume you granted her, her last wishes," said Qing.

"What did you do? She was helping me!" he was almost shouting.

"And here, I thought I trained you better. A prime witness. A person you probably know very little about, except that she could satisfy your erection for one night. If you want my help, there isn't going to be a trail that leads to you

. . . or me. Do you understand Major?"

Aiguo-Tao did not respond, but only stared at Qing like he wanted to collapse her trachea with one quick kick, which he could do.

"I take that as a, *Yes*. We need to go. I have someone who will deal with your girlfriend," Qing said.

Aiguo-Tao followed her to a car parked in a nearby alley. He realized Qing knew he would probably have a driver drop him off so he could walk to meet her. He did not think that if it was a taxi driver, she would have shot the person.

This was personal Aiguo-Tao knew. He met Qing as an instructor. As his skills became more noticed, Qing was the director of covert training, providing advanced classroom and simulated field training. More than a decade older than he was, he still recognized her attractiveness, despite her ice-cold exterior. Somewhere in her mid-fifties now, her subtle beauty would still command looks from the straying eyes of men or interested women.

She would make flirtatious hints to him. He was not interested. Maybe because he respected her as his mentor. Maybe because he did not see her as vulnerable. Maybe he liked vulnerable women. It did not matter. If he played into her sensuality, he might be a dead man in the morning, or at least out of the MSS. If he did not, he would either gain her respect or wrath. He never knew the answer for sure - until just now.

"We are driving over the bridge to Zhonglouxiang island, then south to the coast and the small islands near Dafucun. I think you may remember the area. I have a small boat there that will get us to Donglongao Island where we can catch a ride to Hsinchu on the coast of Taiwan. I hope this meets with your approval . . . if it doesn't, too bad," said Qing.

Aiguo-Tao stared straight ahead. He was afraid to speak, not knowing what words would come out. He was even afraid to nod, not knowing if he could stop one movement from leading to another causing one more, dead chauffer. Right now, his operational objective required Qing's assistance.

Aiguo-Tao closed his eyes and tightened his jaw in anger. Qing certainly knew that Dafucun was where he last saw his parents . . . many years ago.

28

Jun-Ling stood in the doorway looking at Huiwei sitting on the mat.

"Do you believe that if you stare hard enough at the dragon that she will answer your questions?" he asked.

Still looking at the emerald eyes, Huiwei replied, "No . . . but I think she helped guide me to ask the right questions." She finally turned her head and shoulders to see Jun-Ling standing there.

"Then, you have perhaps found the wisdom you seek. You have been in meditation for quite some time now. If you are ready, we must prepare for the next step of your journey," he said.

Huiwei followed Jun-Ling down the stairs to the back room of the shop. *How does he do that?* she thought again. He pulled a set of shelves back from the wall, where the shelves were a hinged door to a room about five meters square. There were more shelves strewn with books, scrolls and other objects.

Against one wall was a long, rectangle, work table, close to the floor, with a sitting cushion. The table was the only area that had some semblance of organization in the room. Paint pots, brushes and quilled pens with rice paper for shûfâ writing, and a variety of carving knifes and detail tools next to several pieces of soapstone and jade. One scroll was a work in progress with many, fine characters already painted and detailed pen drawings along the margins. A piece of soapstone had finished carvings and the jade was beginning to take shape in a finely crafted, jumping goldfish.

A square *bā xiān zhuō* table sat toward the center of the room away from the worktable. It also had several scrolls laying on top, along with several documents of typing paper and information printed on them. The more obvious feature was an older man, also of a nondescript age, sitting at one side of the table.

Jun-Ling closed the hinged, shelf-door and went to sit on the cushion between the two tables.

"Please sit Huiwei. Let me introduce you to your new ally in your journey, Master Yáng Longwei," said Jun-Ling. Longwei looked at Huiwei and bowed his head.

Huiwei sat opposite to Jun-Ling, making eye contact with both masters.

"Huiwei, Longwei has a long history, but for now, his ability to provide you travel south is the only important skill at hand," said Jun-Ling.

"You can get me to Shenzhen . . . by tonight?" blurted Huiwei anxiously.

"Huiwei, please, I thought your meditation would have calmed your anxiousness. Listen, and do not fight your tide," Jun-Ling admonished.

How would Jun-Ling know about her visions of the tide, she thought. She wanted to blurt out, *'did you know my father too Longwei,'* but she breathed to slow her pulse and heed Jun-Ling's admonition.

"I have acquired many allies in my years, most are unaware in their roles in my drama. Allies are often more valuable than your closest friend, and their colors will never change in your relationship. There are many, even those in powerful positions, that correctly believe in the traditional arts of the Zhiyú zhé and *Nan Jing*, as even Western medicine is beginning to understand. There are many who desire the elements and knowledge of tinctures and herbs that I uniquely can provide. The desire of man, especially in need, opens many doors," said Longwei.

"Yes, Huiwei, Longwei may be able to transport you to your destination . . . by tonight . . . but the journey is not without risk," added Jun-Ling.

"Jun-Ling has informed me of your dilemma as best he understands. Stealth in travel seems the most important issue," Longwei said, and Huiwei bowed her head.

"I can acquire access to cargo transport on a bullet-train. It will not be comfortable, and your body and mind must be strong. An anxious or nervous man would not succeed. Jun-Ling assures me you are up to the journey," forewarned Longwei.

"The quickness of your moves or the power in your blows from kung fu will not help you. It is the training of your mind to succeed in the *dui bu' qi* that must be your weapon. I hope your Wushu trainers were competent in passing these skills as well," said Longwei.

After they stood up, Jun-Ling went to a shelf and lifted a small stack of clothing, handing it to Huiwei.

"The black slippers are light, yet strong and will make your feet agile. The dark pants will move with your body and the cloth is treated with a potion that will provide warmth, coolness and keep you dry. The cloth also plays tricks with camera images, although I've never figured out how," said Jun-Ling, as Huiwei noticed the small, cloth tag, *"GORE-TEX®."*

"The *changsang* blouse is much the same. You will find that it is supple so that the embroidered black side can be quickly reversed to a shimmering green as your appearance may need to change. The head piece is a folded scarf around the neck, that can be pulled to cover your head, your face, and even a mesh that will hide your eyes, yet let you see. It's features to conceal can be arranged as the situation might demand. Practice, once you have them on, so you will understand," explained Longwei.

The masters left the room and she quickly changed. She moved around and did various Wushu dances that created her muscle memory long ago. She practiced, fashioning the headpiece into different configurations, and flipped the traditional blouse inside-out, incorporating these movements with her *Shaolin Taolu*. She only had a few minutes to experiment, but understood what Longwei had described.

Jun-Ling returned and she followed him back to the stairs. They went down to the dimly lit stone cellar. The collection of items, large glass jars, trunks and open boxes full of herbs, vegetation and what she presumed where bugs and parts of animals. There was no time to explore as Jun-Ling was already at the door to the cellar entrance leading to the alley. *'How does he do that?'* she thought, once more.

"An old Huizhou farmer's pull cart?" asked Huiwei, with some skepticism.

"Yes, the ancient and the new," said Longwei, looking at the wooden, spoked-wheel, cart. It was loaded on a small trailer attached to a three-wheeled, Goody Van.

"For now, you may ride in the back of the van," he continued, pointing to the back of the small cargo hold on the van.

"My calling-card for many is a bit of theatre I suppose, but it soothes the mind for those in want of medicinal magic. The eyes see only what the mind wants to see," said Longwei.

"Longwei has a diverse, but interesting clientele. The cargo master at many train stations know him, and they have been satisfied by others, cash, promotions of family or favors, such that he is often just waived on to cargo cars. They are limited on the high-speed trains, yet with notice, Longwei can often secure some precious space – but only the wagon . . . not the trailer or van," explained Jun-Ling.

I will have a passenger seat near the cargo car. Definitely, not first-class. Sometimes there are private security or even military guards sitting with me related to whatever cargo they are entrusted with. A little-known aspect of our transportation system," said Longwei.

"I'm to ride in a passenger area potentially next to military guards? I think that would be more than high-risk, as you described," Huiwei queried with a tone of frustration.

"Oh no . . . as I understand your situation, that would not be appropriate. You

. . . will be tucked away in the cart, my dear. As I mentioned, if comfort is your goal, you have chosen the wrong travel guide," Longwei said, grinning slightly.

"The cart is far too small, especially presuming you have to put something on the cart," she said.

"More theater if you will. There is a fiberglass box built into the front end, veneered to be of ancient timber. The cart has a deceiving lower edge so that if not looking closely the small chamber does not exist," said Longwei.

Huiwei stood with her hands on her hips. Her confused face transformed to one with confidence, "Then let's do it."

Longwei drove off to the train station with Huiwei in the small cargo hold of the tiny van. She had to leave most of her belongings behind, including her laptop. She explained to Jun-Ling how important it was that no one find her laptop. He promised he knew exactly where to safely secure it.

She was limited to a small, black, waterproof pack, a little bigger than a tourist's fanny-pack. It was barely large enough for her re-programmed iPad Mini, phone, a short connecting cord, a small ice-cube charger, three flash drives, a mini-back-up drive that she jacked to one-terabyte, and her pink tampon case. Jun-Ling also provided a small make-up compact with small pads of lipstick, rouge, powder, eye shadow, and a tiny liner pencil, should she need to alter appearance. Of course, he provided a small pouch of separated herbal concoctions knowing she would understand what the hànzi character labels meant. She also stuffed in her false passports, I.D. card and credit card.

Fidgeting in the dark, she pulled out her iPad and turned it on. There was a weak 5G signal, but she knew she had to try to get a message out before she got on the train. She started typing in the address, Fly_boy#333, and reached into her memory to remember, the best that she could, the code language they created years ago.

When the van door opened, Huiwei saw they were in a non-pas-senger area near the train. Longwei was talking to two transportation employees, having detached the trailer and unloaded the pull cart.

Longwei motioned to Huiwei to wait as he loaded his various sacks and containers on to the cart. The train employees finally left the immediate area. Longwei waved his hand quickly, motioning her to exit the van and jump in the cart.

He had pushed back some items, revealing the open compart-ment. It looked like an open, full-size Samsonite suitcase she saw in a thrift shop in Boston. It was maybe a meter long and thirty centime-ters deep. She took a deep breath and started contorting her body to fit inside. Longwei started to attach the cover seeing Huiwei's squint-ing eyes.

"I made it out of an old piece of luggage," said Longwei, proudly.

"Gee . . . who would of thought," replied Huiwei, as he secured the lid.

Huiwei heard him move his goods back on top. She settled in the darkness, focusing on her chi as she felt Longwei lift the handles to the cart and pull it into the train car, cargo hold.

29

Jerome had his work cut out for him during the flight. Too many things had to fall into place and one never knows they are missing the last piece of the puzzle – until it is too late.

Glancing only occasionally, he saw that Lieutenant Commander Emery had the flight soundly under control. He was impressed with her ability to adjust altitude and make slight flight pattern changes to take full advantage of the atmospheric variables, increasing flight speed without burning fuel. He knew this was a pilot with innate skills, beyond what you learned in flight school. Jerome thought she could probably fly any bird with the avionics completely shorted-out – she probably has before.

"How's it going over there, Commander?" asked Sloane. She could hear his end of some of his sat-phone conversations, but could not tell what he was typing out on the computer mini-pad wired to his phone.

"Need any help Lieutenant Commander. Sorry for being such a bad conversationalist for a long flight. Seems like you're making good time," he responded.

"Too bad this flight is probably off-the-books. I might be setting a record for a civilian bird. Ninety-seven hundred kilometers with a twelve-thousand-kilometer fuel range at normal cruise speed. Found some good currents up here. Thought we might make the *boom* a couple of times – not good over foreign terrain. We'll make it, with some fuel to spare. Surprise myself sometimes," said Sloane with a little pride.

Jerome was trying to figure out the best exfiltration point – and how to make it happen. Acquiring resources takes time – time he did not have.

He settled on *Mai Po Nature Reserve*. He thought he still had contacts in the Hong Kong conservation department.

The first several kilometers of the northern Hong Kong border had been a *closed zone* since 1951. Mao Zedong took over China with his Communist regime in 1949, as Kim Il-sung was taking control over North Korea. The Korean War was reaching full-bloom.

To stop the flow of Chinese immigrants and illegal arms trade, the British erected a chain-linked fence along the *Sham Chun* river separating Hong Kong from China. Special permits were required and only a few government buildings were allowed to be constructed in the zone. Stronger fencing was later built to control the heavy flow of unauthorized Chinese immigrants into the 1970's, who were fleeing Communist China.

As the Brits scaled down their control, the heavy patrolling of the lonely road along the river was left to intermittent skeleton crews.

Since 1997, when China gained sovereignty, immigration was monitored, but the prospect of permanent freedom was largely diminished. The bigger concern for China, was illegal drug-smuggling. The Central Committee members, and their *associates*, heavily frowned on any competition with its profitable monopoly in the trade. Nonetheless, the Northern border area remained with its *closed zone* status.

Dry-suits, rebreather scuba-gear, cutting-torch, drone, and transport, on such short notice, seemed impossible. *"Was that the right list?"* Jerome was not sure. They could get the few weapons they had through diplomatic customs, but if any heavy artillery was needed, the operation was already doomed. If his contacts were no longer available, including those with knowledge of the area, it might be hopeless.

Jerome had a back-up plan, but he did not like it, since he had no time to make sure his Will was in order before he left.

Despite the movies, and best-selling books, he knew that successful covert operations seldom involved a rain of bullets or high-speed chases. In many respects, the difficult training and skills for close-quarter combat, were more about fitness, body hardening, and building confidence. If a gun was fired, the target was less than three meters away, with fewer than three bullets fired. A single bullet hit anywhere, or even a sprained ankle in a fight, more than likely meant capture, or worse. Missions often times abort over the smallest reason – retreat, and be alive for another day, another mission.

Just over eight hours in flight, the Gulfstream lightly touched down at Hong Kong International Airport. Sloane radioed the diplomat terminal wing and taxied over.

"Nice landing Lieutenant Commander," said Jerome, complimenting Sloane.

"It was the least I could do for our passengers after our take off," she replied.

Sloane opened the cockpit door, put on her uniform jacket and went to assist with getting the passengers off the plane. Jerome heard the bustling of the young diplomatic wannabes gathering their belongings and making their departure without paying any gleeful homage to their pilot, ignorant to their unofficial, record-breaking role in history. Jerome made one last call and got up to retreat from the cockpit.

"You're the flight attendant?" asked Jerome.

"Yes, Commander. I'm yours for the duration, Sir," responded the flight attendant.

"You're relieved of duty miss . . . Petty Officer . . . or, whatever rank you are," he said.

"Civilian, Commander Xi. Stephanie Reid. Nice to meet you, Sir," she replied.

"Pardon me for noticing, Miss . . . Reid, but despite your accent, you look more Chinese than I am. You're dismissed, Royal Navy or civilian," he retorted.

"Genetically, I probably am Commander . . . more Chinese, I mean . . . but born and bred in Dartford, Kent. Stephanie's my given name, but the family name had too many "x's" and "z'" for the kindergarten teacher. Parents changed it to Reid," Stephanie responded.

"Evidently, Commander, during our brief conversations . . . it appears Miss Reid knows a bit about aircraft herself. I surmise she is not moonlighting from Virgin Airlines," interjected Sloane.

"Aeronautical engineering, Imperial College, Sir, post-doctorate. I do know how to pour a bottle of wine and drop an olive into a martini, by the way," Stephanie added.

"A bit young for the initials, it seems, Miss Reid . . . Stephanie. . . please call me Jerome since we are not waiving salutes around . . . the same, please. . . Sloane," said Jerome.

"Partly good genes . . . Jerome . . . Steph, is fine . . . Masters in metallurgical engineering at Edinburgh when I was twenty-one, but I'm thirty-seven . . . even if I still have to show I.D. at some pubs," Stephanie said, now with a bit of a smile.

"Okay, you've established you paid more attention in the classroom than I did, but I'm not sure you understand the nature of my diplomatic assignment here. I am not in need of a civilian protégé. You're free to go to Disneyland on the island here if you like, or perhaps the excellent shopping in the city, before you return," said Jerome.

The airport is on Lantau Island, as is Disneyland Hong Kong. It is thirty-five kilometers to downtown Hong Kong and another forty kilometers north to the Sham Chun river. Jerome did not have time for idle chat with a flight attendant, whomever she may be, or the quality of her martinis. Time was running out and he had a lot of logistics to take care of, including uncertain assets.

"Sir . . . Jerome . . . I think I do understand. That's why I'm here," said Stephanie.

"You're still here? How could you possibly know why I'm here? I'm sorry, but I really need to get going. I'm on a rather tight time schedule here . . . Steph," said Jerome.

"You spoke with Sir Harold Hoover to get clearance for the op and to get the Gulfstream from the Vice Marshall. Sir Harold called me. I'm here. I agree we don't have a lot of time to pursue introductions," said Stephanie.

Jerome looked at his pilot, "Sloane, please tell me, that you have some level of security clearance to overhear this conversation."

"Level five, Jerome, I think you're safe," Sloane responded, gesturing the turning of a key to her closed lips and tossing it away.

"Steph . . . are you telling me you're MI-6?" asked Jerome.

"Seven . . . but of course we don't exist, except in the movies. Sir Harold is really a fine chap. He gave me the impression you knew him better. Shall we go now. You're in charge of the mission, but I'm known to . . . shall we say . . . improve one's perceived agenda. I need you to brief me in the car on where you are," said Stephanie.

"Please, tell me you have *some* field experience. Have you ever been in China or Hong Kong . . . Miss Dartford" Jerome said, with a worrisome, acquiescence.

"Typically, consulting role . . . but let's just say, I've disqualified more than a few Special Boat Squadron candidates for not keeping up. Hong Kong, a little, China, less. Family reunions aren't real popular there once you leave," Stephanie said, with a tone of innocent pride.

"Why ya' little whipper-snapper! If ya'd knew anything 'bout the mission . . . well now. . . it's a bit touchy without much room fer error . . . and that error factor may already be in stampede mode," said Jerome.

"So now you're a Chinese, Texas Ranger from Whitehall? Sorry, Davey Crockett . . . Colonel Lí . . . she's my sister, Commander. There won't be any errors on my part," confessed Stephanie.

Jerome was doing his best to hold back the shock of her words.

"Miss Reid . . . my trust in you is 'bout ta' fall of the cliff . . . I know Colonel Lí . . . personally, if you will . . . she ain't got no sister and her parents were kilt' or died in a re-education camp when she were twelve . . . "Lí" don't have a lot of 'z's and x's', neither," Jerome said, taking on a suspicious tone and not realizing his faux-Texas accent, that would probably get him kicked out of most bars in Waco.

"My father escaped to Hong Kong with his wife. She died. He moved to England courtesy of Her Majesty's Secret Services. Remarried and here I am. Sir Harold, a young agent from the RAF then, straight out of Oxford, changed his name when he arrived. Too risky to contact Huiwei. He died, hoping I might meet her some-day. I plan to honor my father's wish . . . please, Commander . . . we don't have time for history lessons . . . can we get moving?" Stephanie emphatically said.

"My middle name is Lee, L-E-E, by the way," she added, with a huff.

"I suppose you're a black belt in Kung fu, too," said Jerome, try-ing to climb out of the crater left in his thoughts by the revelations.

"Karate, Taekwondo, and Jujitsu, different skills, same result. Please don't make me knock you on your sorry Chuck Norris ass to prove it Commander," said Stephanie.

"Evidently . . . you are Huiwei's sister . . . knocking me on my ass seems to be a genetic trait," he said, and his Cambridge drawl returned.

"Let's go find your sister. We don't want her late to the cotillion. I owe Sir Harold a long visit if . . . when, we return," said Jerome.

"Any idea on Huiwei's sit-rep?" asked Stephanie.

"Long story . . . encrypted code from Huiwei while we were in the air. The code is not perfect, but it appears she's somehow traveling by train from Chengdu to Shenzhen," he said, pausing and looking down.

"Something about a medicine man who knew her father. My guess, it's going to take magic more than medicine for her to get here once the MSS realizes she's on the run," said Jerome.

"That may make some sense. I don't know. Huiwei knew our father as an apothecary . . . a master, zhiyú zhé . . . she never knew he had been a respected biochemist . . . disavowed in a re-education camp shortly after Huiwei was born. Secrecy was a way of life with the *Party* watching you. He had friends though," said Stephanie.

"Well, the rabbit hole keeps getting deeper here . . . good to know . . . Sloane, it's been a pleasure. Do have a more relaxed journey home . . . at normal cruising speed, perhaps," said Jerome, as he grabbed his duffle bags and turned to go.

"Sorry to break it to you Commander. The plane stays here . . . at least for twenty-four hours, hopefully less, and I'm your ops backup," Sloane said

"So now I have two operatives, with unknown skills or experience . . . at least to me. Are there more hiding in the closet," said Jerome, with intended sarcasm.

"I've dropped a few Marine commandos in action, too - Afghanistan, Zimbabwe, Ethiopia, and other tourist resorts. Aikido and Judo if we're taking inventory here, Sir," Sloane, chimed back.

"Well . . . I guess I'm the coach for Her Majesty's new martial arts team," he finally submitted to the situation.

They all grabbed their duffels from the cargo hold next to the cockpit and went down the ramp stairs. Jerome felt a sigh of relief when he saw Hong drive up in the forest green, utility van with the

Hong Kong, Department of Agriculture, Fisheries and Conservation, decal on the sides. Now, he hoped that Hong truly was his father's son.

30

Huiwei concentrated, trying to relax in the inhumanely cramped space. *"How long will I last before I start banging on the lid to get out.,"* she was thinking. She also knew that somebody's private security guard remained in the cargo hold.

After an hour, she felt the jarring of the train as it stopped in Chongqing. There would be no more stops for over seven hours to Shenzhen's North Station near the financial district.

"Relax . . . find your chi Huiwei," she told herself, over and over again.

Eventually drifting into stillness, Huiwei felt herself sitting on a crop of jagged, slippery rocks, dangerously watching the crashing waves below her and feeling the residual mist. The noise of the waves seemed to block out all other sounds.

Pacing around her apartment, her emotions seemed to change by the minute, from focus, anger, fear, anxiety to sorrow. Then, the entire cycle again.

"Millions may die," she kept thinking, *". . . because of me."*

She did not care about the nameless faces, the nationalities, or her loyalty to the conquests of the Party. This was purely a matter of humanity and evil.

"Why didn't I see this . . . it was right in front of me."

Using a secure program on her laptop, she could see the spreading circles of death and harm, with the layers of economic upheaval swallowing nations like the suddenly expanding crevices in a massive earthquake. People would survive, but to an alien world.

Adding variables to her program, she saw the answer. Without any forewarning, it was annihilation. It would not be a perfect solution or even a good one. People in China would also suffer. Innocent people, her people. Yet, it was the only hope the numbers showed her. She always trusted her numbers.

She had already seen the files on Major Zhu Aiguo-Tao. From the incomplete information of her hurried search, she gleaned some details of the operational plan.

Recruits in various locales around the World targeting restaurants, bars, and anonymous social gathering places with tainted flash drives and local currency. The assets were told to inject themselves with the enclosed hypodermic containing the vaccine solution to protect them. However, it was only a placebo, or more accurately a common influenza vaccine – now prepared to carry out their directives with confidence from a false cure. The assets were told to leave the infected area as soon as possible.

"So, they would fall ill a week or two later, either seen as a victim of community spread, or, if traced, they would have traveled from an already infected area, like any common traveler. They don't want the real vaccine to leave China," she whispered out loud to herself.

The only cure she realized was to cause a controlled outbreak in Wuhan. Not immediately suspecting it, many people will get sick, old ones may die, but it will be contained. She overlaid her calculations with media variables, concluding that there would be enough spread so that the outbreak cannot be totally hidden from international attention. Enough warning to prepare, to warn the population, maybe unfreeze the vaccine in Texas.

It will still be devastating around the World, but not the total vision of hell planned. China may be seen as the epicenter, yet it will contain the information, shut down the Internet if needed, and make sure those who held any knowledge, before or after the outbreak, were appropriately dealt with.

"I will be on that list," she said out loud.

If she made any attempt to warn anyone in China, she would be killed and the plan would still go forward. If she reached out to colleagues outside of China, it would never reach the right people - those who could take action. Even if it did, the first step would not be to confront Chinese officials. She knew the variables and the chances. The political and diplomatic risks were far too great to level a totally unsubstantiated and outlandish allegation.

"Hey, this is the Chancellor of Germany. Mr. Chairman, we believe you are about to unleash a virus around the World that that will be the first-cousin to the apocalypse. I hope this allegation, based on conspiracy theory, will not interfere with our trade agreements," she play acted the conversation out loud, then shook her head.

She identified an asset in Wuhan. A Chinese businessman and a minor member of the Party. He was to travel to Tehran to unleash his venom.

Hacking into the communications system, she piggybacked on to Aiguo-Tao's email, sending messages he would never see in his *sent* file, or any responses. She had pulled up his background records and felt comfortable with his inevitable demise.

She sent an email to one of the two laboratory assistants, instructing her to send the local asset two containers, but only log that he was sent one. With an added note, *"Please do not ask questions."* He would be on the list and it would not raise any suspicion to her.

Next, Huiwei sent an email to the asset informing him that he would receive two containers. He is to use one to distribute the infected items in the wet-shop area and surrounding gathering places, then plant one of the flash drives in the cafeteria at the Virology Institute. The message included the same admonition not to reply, adding, *"don't worry about the currency being Rial and not Yuan."* She also instructed him to fully bathe, change clothes and not hesitate to take his flight to Tehran that day.

As infections grew, the sick would seek medical help. Samples would be taken and not fully identified. Logically, the samples would be sent down the street to the Wuhan Virology Institute and the virus will be identified. With the prominent Institute being local, and having infected staff, it would be a fast discovery, with fewer infected, as opposed to the virus first spreading in another city.

She knew from the protocols that the Health Ministry would consult with the MSS. The MSS would not trust anyone, except, perhaps, Major General Lú Ho-Sun. MSS computer forensic specialists would investigate and quickly find Aiguo-Tao's emails. They would put the pieces together without much imagination.

Huiwei thought about Ho-Sun as the target. However, she also knew that he had enough connections, along with a thwarted personality. He would delay action, or cause further digging, allowing some Dorrito-munching analyst to see her hidden fingerprints, even if they could not associate it with her. Again, more delays and risk.

Her final coup was to provide a motive. She called an acquaintance who worked in international finance at the People's Bank of China. Huiwei was assigned to model some potential economic outcomes with trading practices and tariffs for Russia. The woman was helpful and they shared lunch one or two times.

Huiwei told her that she was looking at another international finance issue and was wanting her input on what the best sources would be to create a hidden account. She proposed a small, private bank in Brazil and one in Panama.

Huiwei used the one in Panama to set up Aiguo-Tao's ghost account. She kept the name of the Sao Paulo bank for herself, if ever needed.

The account only existed in cyberspace. The bank would not have a record. If asked, it would likely deny it, at least for a while. The investigation of the money trail would not go there, because it would show that the money was deposited, laundered through a fictitious company as loans, then the money was withdrawn, without a marker to where the money went next. A dead end.

How the money got to Aiguo-Tao would start with an anonymous, laundered, account in Ukraine, without any traceable identification. Deposited in an account for Aiguo-Tao, and electronically transferred in a micro-second to Panama. It is similar to what she would do if she established her own account. Bank robbery of an

Eastern European bank with poorly designed firewalls, however, was not her motive at the moment.

The national news service and underground blogs verified that her plot had been successful, at least in part. Animals and poor sanitary practices would be blamed.

Her only lingering concern had been the small amount of information she could see about the containment plan she had put in her report. China would ultimately be the hero, miraculously processing a vaccine, overnight, that they were giving to people in Wuhan.

It was early in the process, still, enough information was reaching the media and Internet channels that suspicions and attention would grow.

The World, unknowingly, already infected, would have a chance to take preemptive actions. If the politicians in countries like France, England and the United States could avoid ripping each other apart for political gain during a crisis, and focus on the common interests – they had a chance.

Her body sensed the train slowing to a glide and her reality returning, hearing the electric motors of the train spinning down. She was about to arrive in Shenzhen.

31

As the bird flies, the Dafucun coastline was only eighteen kilometers from Chibiaodao. However, much of the rocky island, especially as it went south to the East China Sea and the Taiwan Straight, was not inviting to human habitation or development. Traveling by car, it would be at least forty kilometers of concrete and gravel roads.

Aiguo-Tao looked out his side of the front window. He could see the waters of the Haitan Straight. While the conditions could be vastly different on the reefs at the south end of the island, the waters looked fairly tame.

There had been little conversation during the ride. Aiguo-Tao was able to center himself and wash any anger or emotions aside. His only concern was a confusion that he reacted as he did to Hufar's assassination – much more than the reference to his parents. His focus returned.

"I have a row boat that should be tied up near a beach inlet south of Dafucun. You're rowing by the way. I'm retired," Qing said, with a little amusement.

"I could use the exercise, I'm sure," he responded.

"A pilot will be waiting in his boat on the west side of Donglongao. Presumably, it is sea-worthy to get us across the straight to Hsinchu," she explained.

"I still don't know why I agreed to help you. Teacher's pet syndrome, perhaps, if there is such a thing. It does surprise me to see you in such trouble. It's rather obvious that you're not running away from a jealous boyfriend," Qing said.

Aiguo-Tao knew Qing was trying to get him to talk. He had witnessed her ability to gain government secrets from her methods of small-talk. The unwitting target never blurted out things. Rather, bits of information and clues rolled out of her polite interrogation, where she assembled the pieces.

"Thank you for your help," he simply said.

"Oh . . . my dear boy . . . please don't make me prolong this tedious chit-chat. Whatever trouble you're in has me already knee-deep in it, maybe up to my neck, for all I know. Please, do not make me pull over and stop this car. Childish as you may be at times, you're no longer a boy," Qing admonished.

"I suppose that's fair. There are only three relevant points to my *trouble*, as you call it," he said.

"Interesting . . . and those would be . . ." she led him on.

"First, the MSS is trying to *recapture* me, and I don't think it's because I missed a meeting . . . although, in a sense, I did," he said.

"Recapture? You certainly have my attention. The second," she interjected.

"Second . . . I truly have no idea why," he said.

"You, of all people, I can imagine escaping from a group of incompetent guards. Having no idea as to why they commanded your attendance, is a bit more than I can stomach. But, please go on," Qing said.

She had long ago learned, if she did not write the book, that keeping a target engaged in the conversation, a mutual dialogue, eventually led to the critical information.

"Last . . . the reason does not matter, and escape, for now, is my only option," he calmly said, still staring at the intermittent view of the waters as the car drove along the narrow coastal road.

"Surely, they gave you some clue. If a bullet to the brain was not the first method of interrogation, someone must have said something," Qing said, continuing her own interrogation.

"If you are in to your knees, or your neck, the less you know might play to your own benefit. Consider my reluctance as a favor, not a discourtesy," he replied.

"Very well. You make an excellent point, although you are surely aware that I don't even put my toe in the water, until I know a crocodile is not lurking below the surface. Tit-for-tat, then. Agreed? she said.

She glanced at Aiguo-Tao and he remained motionless, staring in the distance.

"Again, I will take that as a, *Yes.* From the little I know, in such a short amount of time from your call . . . and I am flattered that you remembered my number

. . . my understanding is that you were recently working in Wuhan. Given your status, I must presume your task was not to be advising on community relations between the residents and law enforcement," she said.

"How would you know I was in Wuhan?" Aiguo-Tao said suspiciously.

"Well . . . first, if there was any doubt, you just confirmed it . . . but when you called, you said you might move on to Wuhan. Please trust me on this, when a person is in distress, despite your superior training, their mind doesn't just pull meaningless references out of the air. You said, Wuhan, intentionally or not, and the calculus is really not that amazing. Satisfied?" she responded.

"Very well. You've made your point. I still don't know why this situation is happening," he said.

"I suppose there may be some truth to that. As you are surely aware from the media, there has been some sort of an outbreak in Wuhan. The SCIO is in full regalia, explaining that things are under control. Just some bad food from the wet-market – bat soup of all things. I've never tried it and certainly, now, do not plan to. In any event, we both know that if the SCIO is involved, the likely reality is something much different. I would guess another virus . . . not in Hong Kong this time . . . and that things are less than, *under control,*" she said.

"I hope it does not surprise you that for the past several days, I have not been occupying my time watching the news from my sofa, or reading stories on the Internet. I heard a stranger comment on people becoming ill in Wuhan. That is all I know," he responded.

"That's correct. Excuse me. Of course, you've not been following the media lately, have you. That said, something is going on in Wuhan . . . it's more serious than they say . . . and you were there. Please understand that despite your ability to avoid being the center of attention, I also know that if bad things happen, and you were there, that the connection is not far behind," she smiled, glancing over at her passenger.

"I do not know . . . I simply . . . do not know what happened. When my life is on the line . . . I know that my primary objective is to survive," he said a slight tone of anger, or maybe frustration.

"Emotion is not your strong card Aiguo-Tao. That's what makes you so, shall we say, *special*, to those who need you. Early on in your training, at least after showing you the deceptive grace of my Shaoulin stick, I taught you, or, at least intended to, that when confronted with a problem, do not fight the resistance to see that the simplest answer is most likely the correct one. The dogs of the West would call it Occam's razor. You are trying to figure out your perception of the correct factual circumstances. Yet you know, especially in China, the facts and the truth are often different species. So . . . my prize student . . . the man who feels no pain . . . who had no emotions to act upon . . . throw the facts in the trash can . . . what do *they* believe . . . those who want to harm you. This is also a truth that you will serve yourself to know."

"I was in charge of a highly classified operation. Perhaps the most significant in the history of the World's warfare. Battles for show may be fought by the Youxia, yet modern war is fought with our surrogate allies, artificial intelligence, social media modification, tariffs and sanctions. The belt-and-road is a tactical strategy that allows our conquering while drinking Baijiu at the same table. Cyber military wings do their part. They may break the enemy line, yet they are not able to win the battle, or, the war," he said

"A philosopher. I did not know your level of wisdom had advanced so. Your rank, certainly does not reflect the breadth of you potential and worth. Is that the problem, promotion? . . . that would cause such action," she said, knowing that intuitively, Aiguo-Tao, the perfection of a loner, needed a person to talk to – a mother, a sister, a wife, perhaps a lover – but, now, he has none of those.

"My operation objective will change the World. China will no longer need to care about the capitalistic evils that it endures, in the false name of diplomatic relations. China's superiority will be known, not by bullets and fallen heads, but by the rationale of its earned place in the World," he said.

"I'm sorry. I would love to talk political science with you all night long, especially in more comfortable accommodations, but the issue remains why you have become a terminal target for the MSS," she said. She spun the web bigger trying to transition his positional thoughts of cultural value, to workable interests based on the solvable issues.

"The reality is that something happened. Your fingerprints are on it . . . and whether right or wrong in some cosmic sense, your life is in jeopardy, as you have said. Let's say we focus on the thing you did, right or wrong, and determine why your head on a pike is so important, despite your loyalty to the Chairman and the Party," she said. Qing knew her *fly* had passed a point where cleaver denial or even silence would allow any credibility.

"The operation design was next to perfect. It was being executed without any setbacks or errors, no warning flags. Even anticipated problems never occurred. There simply was nothing wrong," he said.

"Yet something did go wrong, Aiguo-Tao. I'm presuming people getting sick relates to that something. Did you allow all of these people to become ill?" she asked.

"No . . . if anything, I planned for people in Wuhan not to get sick, not in China, minimal at worst," he responded.

"So, your mission involved some sort of chemical or germ weapon. That's a violation of all sorts of international treaties you know," Qing gloated a bit.

"I can tell you no more. I would not want to place you in more danger. My goal is to escape. Perhaps, in time, I can create channels to clear things up," said Aiguo-Tao.

"If I recall . . . you were not in the Chess Club at the academy. Used any extra time in the gym. That may be the factor that leads to your demise," she told him.

"What do you mean? My record is impeccable," he responded

"Yes. I see I am going to have to bring things to your level . . . um . . . If you see a soccer field only from the player's perspective, it is an incredible view. If you see the game from above the ground, you see the whole game – every player, the location of the ball, and the pattern of the play. This is why coaches sit up high in the stadium. The coaches on the ground see much, but not enough. The player on the field, the one who actually executes the operation on the field, perhaps the one least able to see the bigger picture of the game, he feels he is controlling it," she said.

"Now, you are the one spouting philosophy," Aiguo-Tao said.

"Very good. You caught me . . . did you learn anything?" she asked.

"There's a bigger picture I may not be seeing, because of my limited view. . . but I don't think that is the reason that I do not know why this is happening," he concluded.

Aiguo-Tao saw that they were coming to the end of an industrial road. She slowed the car down and he saw a sandy beach at the head of an inlet.

They got out of the car. Qing saw Aiguo-Tao scanning the area. She presumed he was absorbing some set of emotions thinking of his parents. Looking closer, she could tell that his mind was far away from that experience. She planned on giving him some time to deal with any memories – create a weak point. It seemed she had over calculated the breadth of his sense of humanity.

"I see the boat. Tied up by those rocks along the east edge, high on the beach," Aiguo-Tao yelled over the sounds of the splashing waters.

Qing grabbed her all-weather satchel, throwing the strap over her shoulder and a 40-liter, dry-bag duffel. She had not seen any signs that Aiguo-Tao was armed. He did not pullout a weapon when confronted with Hufar's demise. When he reached for his backpack, she thought she saw what might be a knife harness strapped to his leg, but maybe not.

"Give me your backpack to throw into the dry bag. I think there's room. No reason to risk things getting wet," said Qing.

"I'm good. Let's get the boat," he said, throwing his backpack on.

"Very well. Remember, you're rowing," Qing responded, *"Definitely armed,"* she said to herself.

Aiguo-Tao untied the rope wrapped around a rock and dragged the small, Zodiac inflatable boat to a small crop of rocks to avoid having to wade in the water to get in. He shook his head a little bit, when he saw the Yadao 1200 watt, 5hp, motor attached.

Donglongao Island was basically a series of large, uninhabitable rocks, stretching about one kilometer long. The distance to the tip of the island was only a little more than a kilometer. Aiguo-Tao presumed there was a small dock somewhere along the western, leeward side.

"Please, don't be too disappointed. You still have some rowing to do, to clear the rocks, as well as when we approach the boat on the island. Do you need directions or a map?" Qing asked, with a sarcastic tone.

"I think I've got it covered," he responded.

The water was not smooth. It never was in this area with the confluence of the merging waters of the East China Sea, into the Taiwan Straight and then the Haitan Straight, but it was still much smoother than normal. The electric outboard plowed the water without much sound as the boat bounced against the small waves.

"Was it for the money Aiguo-Tao?" Qing almost shouted to be heard above the sounds of the sea.

"That question cannot be answered *yes* or *no*, Qing. You know that much," Aiguo-Tao shouted back.

Aiguo-Tao's focus zeroed in on Qing. He instinctively went through his options in less than a second of thought. Inflatable boat and knifes don't mix, distance of reach, unsure body movements in the raft, and ability to reach his pack to find his 9mm. *"She knows more than she has said,"* his mind screamed like a warning siren.

"Qing! My dear friend and respected teacher . . . should I be asking whether this is a rescue . . . or a set-up," he shouted.

32

Huiwei felt some relief once they had arrived in Futain Station and felt the motions of Longwei lifting the cart and rolling it from the train's cargo hold. She did not know where the cart was, but the sounds of street noise were growing louder.

Longwei moved the items covering the panel to Huiwei's compartment and began lifting it. He smiled seeing that she appeared to have survived the journey as she was blinking to adjust her eyes to the light and unfolding her body.

"Where are we?" asked Huiwei.

"Near the doorway that leads to the street. You can stretch for a few minutes, then, we must continue your journey," said Longwei.

Huiwei tried her best to block out her anxiety from thinking about having to cram herself back inside the hidden, suitcase compartment.

"I'm booting up my iPad . . . and transcribing. You'll have to wait a couple of minutes," demanded Huiwei

Encrypting the message left by Jerome, she double-checked to assure herself that she understood what the incomplete phrasing meant. Fortunately, single letters and numbers were easy to send and translate through the code, and coordinates were nothing but numbers with a letter for the compass direction.

"Longwei, do you know where Mai Po Nature Reserve is . . . in Hong Kong? asked Huiwei.

"Generally, speaking. The closed zone, I believe. Is it your plan to walk across the customs stations into Hong Kong? I may not agree to continue as your tour guide at some point," he responded.

"No. But I need to get close it appears. Down Yitian Road to the river. The problem is that it's almost ten kilometers to get where I need to. I don't see how that's possible with you pulling an antique, farm cart, especially with my added weight," she said.

"Please, do not be fooled by what you may think you see in an old man. Plus, it's mostly downhill toward the river," he said.

Longwei pulled out a small, tinted glass bottle from his coat. He removed the cork, swallowing the contents, then making a satisfying sigh.

"Are you telling me you have some magical elixir that gives you the strength of an ox to pull this cart. Unless I see muscles suddenly bulging and ripping through your clothes, I think I may be safer risking the subway," Huiwei said, with a voice filled with a mix of frustration and fear.

"Perhaps, your knowledge of science clouds your mind to what is possible from ancient knowledge. Despite your lack of wisdom, however . . . ," Longwei stopped, and turned his head with a glance for Huiwei to follow his eyes.

Huiwei sighed, and even let out a small laugh of relief, when she saw him looking at a similar, tricycle van and trailer parked near the wall.

"The elixir, is a wonderful, spiced rum concoction of my own. Tastes a bit like Dr. Pepper . . . very good. My body may not receive any super-human strength, but even I am susceptible to the emotions of a stressful situation. I feel the warmth comforting my chi already," he said with a small 'gotcha' smile, lifting the bottle above his head, then recorking it and returning it to his pocket.

"I suppose I'm supposed to applaud your performance, now, so you can take your bow," she said with a bit of sarcasm.

"Not necessary. I suggest you hurry to the van, before some bored security agent notices us or sees you on a video camera," he said, already lifting the tongue-handles of the cart and rolling it to the van.

There was a small hole cover between the cramped cargo hold and the driver. Once they were settled, Longwei knocked with his knuckles against the cargo hold. Huiwei swung the cover from the five-centimeter hole and saw Longwei and the limited view she had.

"Good. You found the peep-hole. You are not the first person to have had the pleasure. It would be useful if I knew where we are going. An old healer and his cart full of magical wonders, can attract unwanted attention, especially if I'm seen floundering around," he said.

"Wait just a few seconds, please," she responded.

"From looking at a Google street map, we need to go south on Yitan. It goes almost to the river's edge. There's a cross street going west, Shihua Road. My target point is the area at the end of Guanglan Road, at the river bank, dock, or whatever is there," said Huiwei.

"I think I know the area you are describing. Does your magical treasure map also happen to show an area called the Jiuce Science and Technology Park, it's a business park, industrial buildings?" he asked.

"Yes. I see it. The west end of the industrial park has a parking area right along Guanglan," she responded.

"Well then, while I may not be the expert you are in such matters as are these, might I intrude upon your plan?" he asked.

"Go for it. I'm not really sure that I have a plan. I only have a place I need to get to," she said.

"In that case, I will need to make a call. There is a laboratory in Jiuce park, Shihua Chemicals. I have some contacts there. A member of the board who appreciates the arts of the Zhiyu' zhe', and a couple of chemists who like to tinker with my tinctures and teas, seeking to perhaps unravel the components . . . more likely hoping to synthesize them. It disturbs me some, but there is quite a market for herbal remedies these days, if they come in a labeled bottle . . . and they pay me well, I admit," he explained.

"We have a plan then . . . I guess . . . let's at least get there," Huiwei exclaimed.

Longwei headed away from the train station. Huiwei went back to her iPad, and struggled typing in the jostling cargo hold.

33

Jerome had reached out to one of his contacts in Hong Kong. It had been a few years since they last spoke. Jerome gave some vague indications of his needs.

His contact explained that he had suffered an accident. The injuries to his right knee and arm have left him unable to work. Jerome was emailing from the Gulfstream, with several breaks in reception, as the contact explained, that he may still be able to help.

Cryptically, he acknowledged his presumption that the nature of Jerome's request for assistance was something the local authorities might frown upon. He indicated that he had been able to secure a job for his son, Hong, with the conservation department. After his accident, Hong had largely assumed many of his duties in the Mai Po Reserve.

While his contact emphasized that Hong was a Hongkonger first, Jerome remained more than a bit concerned. The father had worked with the British military since the 1970's. After the change in control, he became a valuable asset for British intelligence in a number of covert missions. Hong did not have a trusted background that Jerome could confirm. The chances that he would understand the logistics needed for a covert operation made Jerome feel like he was being slapped in the face, back-to-back. At this point, he really did not have a choice.

Jerome, Stephanie and Sloane were in the van headed away from the plane. Jerome wanted to inventory the supplies that Hong may or may not have picked up. He was not sure that the diplomatic terminal area was the best place. Jerome was in a hurry and knew they still had to go through the diplomatic customs process. Sometimes a Chinese customs officer enjoyed making the process as harassing and uncomfortable as possible, even though there was not much they could do, unless you said, *"Please, don't look in that bag of weapons. It's not the droid you're looking for."*

"Nice to meet you Jerome. My father said to call you *Jerome* and not use any military rank. We are friends and should look natural together," said Hong.

"Nice to meet you as well, Hong. I presume your father has told you a bit about my situation, at least the urgency. The first thing is for me and my friends to get into Hong Kong without much fanfare . . . and you're driving the opposite direction from the diplomatic customs building, so we can get through that process," said Jerome, thinking he had already made a very big mistake.

"No worries, Jerome. I have already processed you through customs when the other college students went through. Here, you need to use this stamp on your passports, perhaps," smiled Hong, handing Jerome the small Hong Kong custom's stamp.

"Those were members of our diplomatic contingent, not college students, although I could understand the mistake. How could you process us without even having our passports. You didn't even know about Lieutenant . . . Sloane or Stephanie here? By the way, please let me introduce you to my martial arts team , Sloane and Stephanie," said Jerome, a bit perplexed.

"No worries, Jerome. I found the names on the manifest and you are marked approved. I thought it would make it easier if I went ahead and approved the pilot and the flight attendant . . . make it easier for them when they came in. Good luck then, since they are with you Jerome. Hello Sloane and Stephanie. I am Hong," he explained.

"You are a mystery, Hong . . . thank you. I don't presume you have any experience with, shall we say, unauthorized activities with the China border?" asked Jerome.

"My father tells me he thinks you need to get someone across the border, correct Jerome?" said Hong.

"Perhaps a bit more complicated than that . . . but, yes, that is our mission in a nutshell. I'm not sure you fully understand the seriousness of the situation. You see the person involved may already have a target on their back . . . coming in *hot*, as we might say," said Jerome, hoping to slap some reality into Hong.

"Some Like it Hot . . . Marilyn Monroe . . . I would like to help save her. Jerome, as my friends would say, Hong is a little bit crazy, but he is not stupid. I understand your concerns," he said.

"Very well, then. I'm listening. You've done this sort of thing before?" asked Jerome.

"I was a student before my father was injured. Now, I work full time. I helped with the Falun Gong in many things, especially our student protests. Sometimes they also need help with border and customs situations. To help my family, since my father cannot work, I also help with drug smugglers. Fentanyl, narcotics, even antibiotics and blood pressure medicines. Big black-markets in many countries. Human organs sometimes. I know they are harvested from prisoners in re-education camps – it makes me want to stop, but I must help where I can and swallow hard. Everybody knows Party leaders are the ones making the money. They clear many hurdles with officials and even the PLA officers guarding the river. Working with the smugglers gives me access to also help Falun Gong without the officials knowing. They already have their pay-offs to look the other way," explained Hong.

"And your official duties in the conservation department at the Reserve . . . is your calling card," said Jerome, looking at the road ahead, re-calculating his early assessment of Hong.

"Well, hot damn, pardner. Looks like we got a rodeo to git to, saddle-up," said Jerome.

"You're from Texas? My father said you were British . . . Cambridge man," said Hong.

"No. You're correct. I am British. Sometimes I talk with a Texas drawl is all," responded Jerome, smiling.

"No, you don't. I watch American movies," Hong smiled.

Sloane and Stephanie listening from the backseat, could not contain their laughter with Hong's accurate slight to Jerome's Texas drawl. It was one of those laughs that grew more infectious and loud the harder they tried to stop.

"Okay, okay . . . enough with the laughter. Hong has evidently proved himself competent, so far, as an unofficial customs agent and an amateur comedian," barked Jerome, as he immediately joined in with the laughter.

Once they got to the lonely road in the Mai Po Reserve, leading to the northeast part of the security road running along the riverfront, they stopped the van. Jerome pulled open the rear doors and began to take inventory.

In flight, he had contacted another asset in Hong Kong, who had access to a black-market cache of military gear. He saw that Hong was able to connect with the asset and pick up the items – one scuba rebreather, one customary scuba tank, fins, masks and two dry suits, plus a small acetylene torch. Two canvas bags of some assorted tools and supplies were there. Not a perfect match to his list, but a few extra things thrown in. A Norinco Type-56, with a pull-out stock and three magazines was a bonus from his wish list. The Chinese knock-off of the Soviet AK-47 was good enough, but hopefully not needed. The small brick of PE-8 plastic explosive, with digital blasting-caps and a remote control device, might also come in handy.

He needed two rebreathers for his plan to work. The regular tank was of no use. Many parts of the river were shallow at the banks, until they reached the dredged-out channels for the cargo barges and boats. The bubbles floating to the surface would raise a flag to any half-savvy security soldier – especially, if they already had a security alert.

Jerome was reviewing his escape plan with Sloane and Stephanie. Stephanie was quickly trying to figure out if the right tools and items were available to create an extension splice allowing two divers to use one rebreather.

"I know it's not any of my business, but then again, I guess it is, since I'm here," said Hong.

"Go ahead. It will take less time to hear what you have to say . . . I'm sure . . . than the time it will take asking you to let us concentrate," responded Jerome, with some signs of stress in his voice.

"This is a very good plan for a bad French movie. All very unusual devices, outfits and methods of travel. One, out of place thing is noticed, you don't even have bullet proof jackets to stop the hundreds of bullets firing at you, not that it would help," said Hong.

"And . . . I suppose you would have us cross the river in a Venetian gondola with a gondolier singing opera. I'm sure our lovely escapee would enjoy her ride," Jerome retorted with a bit of frustrated anger.

"Close, but I really don't like opera music, and recommend against it," said Hong.

"Please . . . enlighten us with your wisdom, Sir Hong," said Jerome.

"Well . . . your point of extraction is excellent. There are several companies there who make pharmaceuticals, and easy access to docks nearby. I would go by boat, to pick up this lovely person, you say. If she has the ability to look like a carrier for a smuggler, I can hide her on the boat, and return here," suggested Hong.

"Walk her right on a boat, in the open," said Jerome, still somewhere between wanting to slap or listen to Hong.

"Basically . . . yes. If you were going to use scuba gear, I'm presuming she is agile to some extent. I do not know her resources or looks. She must be able to look like a courier, and carry items that look like pharmaceuticals from a manufacturer – not real, just enough so a person already turning the other way won't take a second look," explained Hong.

"Let me talk this over with my martial arts team. If we go with your plan, you're not going alone. I'll be there. Things can go wrong and despite the many surprises you seem to have, weapons and close combat training do not seem to be in the mix," said Jerome.

"It will be me Jerome . . . not you," inserted Stephanie. "I know you feel like you have some personal stake in this, according to Sir Harold, but mine is bigger."

"Too many cooks in the kitchen. One person. No weapons. No coms, except my clean cell phone. They will search us and they know the couriers do not carry weapons. No offense Jerome, I would pick Stephanie. She looks more Chinese than you do. Also, they will be less suspicious of a female, just like it will be easier to transport a female escapee," said Hong.

"Huiwei," said Jerome.

"What?" replied Hong.

"Our escapee . . . her name is Huiwei . . . Stephanie Lee . . . how is your Chinese these days? Looks like you're taking the proverbial, slow boat to China today," said Jerome.

"Very little talk Stephanie. You may look like my cousin, but with your British tongue, no matter how hard you try, you will not sound Chinese," instructed Hong.

"Okay. Then, let's figure this out, team. Hong, I presume you have some calls to make for our Uber-boat. Sloane, you need to test the drone from my gear, and find the best set up point. I still want to have eyes on the operation where we can. Stephanie, I hope you have something more traditional to wear besides your flight attendant uniform," said Jerome, going into operation leader mode.

"In fact, I do. I was going to figure this out on my own if I had to. Abort was not an order I planned to follow. Sorry, Jerome," said Stephanie.

"How did you know I can operate a combat drone?" asked Sloane.

"After seeing your flying skills, I seriously doubt if there's anything you can't fly. Time to move team," ordered Jerome.

Jerome watched the team break-up to work on their tasks. He opened up his iPad to send more information to Huiwei. He only hoped she was able to receive it and let him know something about her status.

34

Huiwei saw a message from Jerome. He was set up at the Reserve and would send more information soon. He asked if she had her "fins on". She interpreted the message as an underwater exfiltration – scuba. She knew how to use scuba equipment, but it was not a skill set she enjoyed to work on.

She wanted to just pick up her phone and call Jerome, but she knew there was a 90% chance she is being considered as, "on the run," and if so, a 100% probability that a super-computer, monitoring communications, has already been fed a directive to find the clues to find her. The Hong Kong border would be high on the hit-list of geographic areas for focus, along with airports and transportation centers.

She put a message together hoping that the translation would be close enough "Jiuce park," "Shihua Chemical," "near," "Guanglan." She gave the coordinates of the train station, indicating the coordinates for Shihua, indicating thirty minutes.

When Longwei pulled into a secluded place near the Shihua parking lot, she saw that Jerome got her message, "Sushi," "chemical," "good," "boat," "illegal" "drug smoker" "you" "fake box" "Honker +1" "friends" and a coordinate that she presumed was a dock on the river. The message ended, "2" "tick-tock," their term for 'hours.' She had to hide for two more hours and figure out what Jerome was trying to say.

"Longwei . . . can we stay hidden for two more hours and get me to a dock?" said Huiwei, pointing toward the river.

"It would be difficult to sit still and not receive notice, but simple distractions may work. You may have noticed . . . my flair of theatrics . . . serves its purpose. How do you know to be at the dock in two hours?" he responded.

"I have a code language with my contact. A game, at first. The messages require interpretation. Quite honestly, I'm not sure what to do with his last message," she confided.

"Where is the confusion? You must focus and let your emotions stay in the shadows," he advised.

"Easier to say, no offense. His prior message seemed clear that he was using scuba gear to go across the river. Dangerous, but possible. The river is probably less than 100 meters wide, but shallow at the banks. Now . . . he mentions a boat and a fake box. I think he wants me to do something, but I can't figure out what it is," she admitted.

"May I see these code words," he asked, and Huiwei handed him the iPad.

Huiwei watched him as he studied the words, of the several messages, then holding up the iPad and turning it in different directions, watching the screen rotate the message with his actions. Her frustration was growing and she wanted to grab the iPad back. She calmly reached asking to reclaim it. Longwei pulled it back to his chest, indicated he was not returning it, yet, then, held it out so they could look at it together.

"Ancient scrolls often times hold the mixtures and methods of prior masters. It is a habit that they not be read like a cookie recipe in the kitchen. Wise guesses, trial and error, often unlock the secrets to another master. I do not know your code and I doubt we have room to experiment, but I might offer some practical observations. A child's eyes sometimes see more than the fox," he said, as Huiwei moved to look at the screen in his hands.

"Your friend seems to be sending two strangers, he wants you to trust. I presume they are on a boat, but maybe underwater near a boat. I do not know," he said.

"I get that part, but the problem is putting it together. I don't see it," she said in a voice of concern.

"Your code, obviously spells the company name differently, but he knows where you are, but not who you are with, if anybody. This area, near medical factories and the free-trade zone will likely have illegal smuggling. Officials in the Party largely control these activities, and eyes may be watching the flocks in the sky without concern to the squirrels gathering nuts on the ground," he said.

"I'm sorry . . . I know you speak wisely, but we really do not have time to place riddle upon riddle. What does it say?" she emphatically exclaimed.

Longwei pursed his lips with a look of some disappointment, then, shrugged his shoulders.

"You need to look like the courier for a drug smuggler. It is dangerous business and there will be those you can trust and those you cannot. It seems you will not be kissing any fish in the water, unless things would go badly," he said.

Huiwei let out a sigh. "Okay . . . that actually makes sense . . . but how do I look like a drug smuggler?" she sighed.

"That is where I may be of further help. I already called a friend at the lab to provide a reason for our presence," he nodded.

Longwei handed Huiwei a small, pocket mirror and directed her to the van's cargo hold, while he unloaded his cart and put some items in it. He pointed out where he thought security cameras might be, noting he parked in an area he thought would not as likely be seen.

Following his directions, Huiwei reversed her female-styled changsang, in shimmering green, and worked to put make-up on from the small compact Jun-Ling gave her. Using the light of her iPad was less than optimal.

She saw another message from Jerome checking on her status. She responded where the message should show, "ready" "yes" "??" "working." He also asked if she had contacted anyone, besides him, outside of China, concerning her situation. At least, that was her interpretation. Names could be tricky, but she responded with, *Susan Kilmer, Eric Thomas, MIT, vaccines, questions.* The code breaker, ending up in English did better with Western names, as opposed to Chinese. "MIT" would certainly show up.

Huiwei nervously heard Longwei whisper he had returned and was opening the door. When she saw him, she blinked in surprise and pulled her head back. He had neatly combed back his hair, and trimmed-up his bearded chin. He was wearing a silk, tang suit that neatly trimmed his physique, highlighted by a pair of round, John Lennon sunglasses. She thought he looked more like the twin brother who took up entertainment promotions instead of the healing arts.

"Say what you like young flower, yet I am a man who plays many roles," he said, expecting some shock, if not wisecracks.

"You are the drug smuggler . . . not me," she said.

"Perhaps a team. I've come this far in your journey," he responded.

He handed her a cardboard shipping box marked in the *Shihua Chemical* labels, *Pharma – Division*, in English and Chinese, and a red, plastic six-pack cooler with a handle built into the white folding top.

"Are we having a party?" she asked.

Longwei smiled, "The company makes various generic drugs, including some opiates and antibiotics, along with herbal remedies, bottled and marked for the unwise. I asked my contact for a small box of herbal samples so I could reverse the trend and experiment with their concoctions. If we are dealing with smugglers, they will not question the box. If they open the box, I am hopeful they will presume they are false labels for transport. I do not know for sure," he explained.

"And the cold beer?" she asked.

"While I do not think this company is involved, unfortunately, part of the smuggler's trade in China involves human organs for transplant . . . unlikely from willing donors. There are ice packs inside and you will need a place to conceal your belongings to avoid a search. Knowing the sensitivity and prices involved, I would predict that they will not open the cooler once we attach a taped seal . . . I told my contact I needed to keep some elixirs cooled for my return journey after picking them up from a fellow healer. He was happy to help," said Longwei. He handed her a *bio-hazard* sticker to stick to the cooler.

They drove the van and trailer down to a street along the river's edge and parked it where they thought it would not be obvious. She thought a passerby, or security guard, would think somebody was buying an old farmer's cart for a yard ornament. They sat on a rock wall shaded by trees, keeping an eye on the docks nearby.

Huiwei thought she heard a buzzing noise high up in the sky, and looked, but could not see anything. A strange sounding insect in the tree, she thought. They looked toward the docks and saw a small, fishing boat pulling in. Perhaps nine meters long with a pilot's deck and perhaps a small cabin below.

Huiwei pulled her head piece off of her head and left the face mask part up, covering her face from her nose down.

"Showtime . . . my young thespian," said Longwei, standing up.

"*All the world's a stage, and all the men and women merely play-ers,*" she said picking up the box and cooler.

". . . *they have their exits and their entrances; and one man in his time plays many parts, his acts being seven ages,*" he finished the Shakespearian quote, smiling at Huiwei, as she cast a surprising stare back.

"King's College, biochemistry, seventy-six . . . you're not the only one with a foreign diploma, my dear. Perhaps once you have settled after your odyssey, we can talk of your father's grand laugh after a glass of baijiu," he said.

Huiwei suddenly stopped, looked at his eyes, took a breath, and keep walking.

"Yes . . . that would be good . . . after this is over. I loved my father greatly, even if it appears I did not know the whole of his life," she said.

35

Aiguo-Tao stopped the small motor and pulled the propeller out of the water. He grabbed the oars, maneuvering the raft around the rocks and pulling up to the dock. Qing stayed seated as Aiguo-Tao grabbed the nylon rope, reaching to the dock to tie it off on a cleat. There was a metal pole-ladder. He looked at Qing and she gestured for him to climb up. Qing was then able to confirm the knife strapped to his calf. At a safe distance, she threw her satchel over her shoulder and tossed the dry-bag to Aiguo-Tao on the dock.

The boat was tied up on the opposite side of the weather-worn, wooden dock. It was a more modern fishing boat, almost a small yacht, but for the long forward deck. Sleek fiberglass about twelve meters long, it looked like it could adequately travel the sixty-five kilometers to Hsinchu across the Taiwan Straight.

One man, with a three-day beard, stood on the boat, about thirty-five, guessed Aiguo-Tao. He was wearing clean, but somewhat disheveled, tan pants, white shirt and short, blue wool jacket, with a blue-knitted skull cap. He looked at the pair coming across the dock, but did not wave them on board or assist.

Qing tossed her gear on the boat and climbed in, waiting for Aiguo-Tao to follow. As he stepped on to the boat deck, he saw Qing quickly reach in her satchel and pull out a pistol. The entire, practiced move took less than a few seconds, when he saw the flash of the barrel and the pilot drop to the deck. A bleeding hole at the bottom of his left eye. *"Her aim is off,"* thought Aiguo-Tao.

Her gun swiftly turned to Aiguo-Tau.

"Please . . . do not reach for the knife on your leg or the pistol in your backpack. I don't intend to spend a bullet on you, unless you decide to dance," she said sternly.

Aiguo-Tao slowly raised his hands.

"The knife first . . . slowly . . . two-fingers, please, you don't want to lose more

. . . unstrap it . . . leave it in the sheath . . .slide it on deck toward me," she ordered, and he complied.

"Backpack . . . slide it toward me . . . slow movements, please," she continued. He complied.

"Thank you for answering my question Qing . . . a set-up or an assassination . . . perhaps both for the Captain. You are too young to retire, afterall," he said.

"Oh, I'm retired from the Navy. I still have many contacts and the occasional requests for my talents . . . from private business, pays quite a bit better. Of course, separating the Party officials from the so-called capitalists is really not possible. Please sit," she ordered.

He sat and she reached with one hand to unzip his backpack and blindly fumble her hand inside until she pulled out the Air Force

Sergeant's 9mm pistol. She opened her dry-bag and tossed it inside. Her gun sights never left a straight line to Aiguo-Tao's head.

"After your call, you had to know I would make some calls of my own. A nasty virus contamination in Wuhan. Evidently, you orchestrated it. They have your emails to the asset with your attempt to cover it up. Nothing really can be erased from the Internet I'm told. It's all in a server somewhere, if you know where to look. You have no family to threaten. A bank account . . . in Panama, I believe . . . but you were able to transfer the money and keep it hidden. Several million U.S. Dollars is what I was told," she told him.

"Again, as I tried to explain to a Colonel Zhào . . . a while back, I do not know anything of these fictions. Why the boat pilot Qing?" he asked.

"While it would be difficult to connect any dots to you . . . I am here on my own. It is not totally unusual for me to request such things as a boat to stealthily sail to Taiwan. I've even arranged such for you before, I believe. Given the nature of my *clients*, if you will, few questions are asked. Most likely he was a mildly competent, chief petty officer. I don't like witnesses as you know," she responded.

"Who will pilot the boat? My competence on the sea likely ends at a five-horse- power outboard," he said.

"My first commissions were gun boats, then surveillance patrol boats, before other talents emerged. I believe I will be able to coach you at the wheel . . . at a safe distance of course. I will notice if you decide to play any games," she replied.

"Why?" asked Aiguo-Tao.

"You are slow on the uptake. Your physical skills were always your strong suit. The money, Aiguo-Tao. No one knows what I'm up to. There's no association to you, and if I should be lost at sea . . . it would raise only a few eyebrows . . . perhaps some disappointed frowns . . . people prefer not to talk about the reasons for my associations with them. It's up to you. Do you want to sail away and get lost together, or feed the sharks," she explained.

"This is a most interesting way to propose, Qing," he said.

"Perhaps, but I don't think you would trust it any other way. So . . . happily ever after, or not my beloved," she pronounced.

"Are you serious?" he asked.

"Only half so. Once I have secured the money, depending on your attitude, I might find it interesting to have a travel buddy I don't need to profile. A danger? Perhaps, but a day-at-a-time I suppose. I would make sure your needs were met . . . in several ways . . . and a reasonable allowance. You wouldn't have to look over your shoulder nearly as much either," she said.

Aiguo-Tao tried to process these new revelations. He could not see a favorable ending. Most importantly, there is no hidden bank account, and it is unlikely Qing would ever accept that reality, before he was permanently maimed, or dead.

"The pilot's station. Now, please. We need to get going. The waters should be in our favor for the next few hours," she said, flicking her gun to have him move.

"Your interrogation . . . some abandoned dock house in Taiwan?" he said.

"Oh . . . Aiguo-Tao . . . don't spoil the honeymoon before it's started. I'm hoping your wisdom will bloom and any interrogation will not be necessary . . . I think you know that the results would be quite different than with Colonel Zhào . . . excellent credentials. A most deathly sore throat I understand . . . to the wheel, please . . . the

open sea, I always found, is a good place to think through any difficult questions," she added.

36

Jerome hesitated several times. He also needed to keep a close eye on the operations. The smuggler boat would be arriving soon to pick up Hong and Steph. He decided to make the call. He hoped the encryption on his sat-phone was sufficient to avoid any communications detection deep within China's sovereign territory. He still thought he should use his words carefully.

"Hello . . . what an unexpected surprise Commander. Please tell me you have not encountered any serious problems," said Sir Harold Hoover.

"Speaking of surprises, my trusted friend . . . you are quite fortunate that Emery is a more splendid pilot than I am. But . . . seriously . . . her sister! And, no heads up? We need to have a long talk," exclaimed Jerome.

"I'm glad you are pleased Commander . . ." responded Sir Harold.

"The operation is in motion. I'll spare you the details. In my somewhat cryptic communications with our target, I ventured to inquire if she might have reached out to anyone else, about anything. Of all things, I believe she identified an Eric Thomas at MIT. If I recall, a bit more than teaching freshman biology," he said.

"There is a lot that has happened, even in the short time since you were wheels up Commander. Simply stated, there is a virus on the loose. It's even in Europe, Italy mostly, perhaps the States, even Iran, but new case reports by the minute," he said.

"I thought there was some illness issue in a Central China," responded Jerome.

"Yes . . . the presumed epicenter. The Chairman and his henchmen have their hands full. Difficult to rely on information there. They're shutting down all communications basically. Suspicious arrests all around," he said. "Of course, global health officials and politicians playing it down . . . nothing worse than a cold . . . but it is . . . much worse," he added.

"I don't have much time. I need the bird's eye view, please," pleaded Jerome.

"Yes . . . of course. Virus started in Wuhan. New corona virus, worse than SARS or MERS. Maybe asymptomatic transmission. No known vaccine unless China is holding out on us . . . and they might. I trust the WHO like I do my second ex-wife. Development stopped once SARS went into hibernation. China's national virology lab happens to be in Wuhan . . . but that's another set of issues. Your target had some critical involvement with whatever was going on. Some senior officer, from the sketch we have . . . our contacts are drying up . . . he released the damn thing in China. Only good news is that it gives the rest of us a head's up for what's coming. China's saying it's under control, but it's not," reported Sir Harold.

"What does this have to do with our target? I'm not here to save the World right now," interjected Jerome.

"Protocols . . . the Party . . . MSS . . . communications services, SCIO. First, round up those who might know anything. Tie 'em up. Gag 'em, and write the script they want," said Sir Harold.

"Sounds like you've been watching American Westerns lately. Go on," Jerome said.

"The euphemisms certainly fit . . . yes . . .well, your target seems to have an invitation to a command performance, and she's in the wind. As is this Major who is suspect. Although, if you listen to the worst-case scenario, to the little information we have, the Major may have saved thousands of lives, maybe millions. Again, this is not swine flu. Your target's off their map and they're working very hard to get her back on it. I'm sure it won't end well. She knows things they don't want us to know. It would be wonderful to know what that is," said Sir Harold.

"Is this Thomas fellow, the Naval scientist, went field ops CIA?" asked Jerome.

"That's the one. Excellent boxer at their Naval Academy. I even believe his boxing coach was the famous Oliver North . . . Light Colonel Marine. The whole Iran-contra fiasco. Black-ops to television personality. Only in America, they say . . . but, yes. Captain Thomas is a key bioweapons consultant with the CIA and even our office. . . likes to still get his gloves in the ring and not be an advisor ringside," said Sir Harold.

"Let me finish. Sorry . . . I know you're in a terrible hurry . . . our target called a professor friend who put her in touch with Thomas.

Strange questions about vaccine capabilities for corona viruses. Some early reports what was coming out of China, so he ran it up the flagpole. With this illness spreading, he and some colleagues are even talking of a pandemic. If we did not have this knowledge, it appears it could be Moses' plague. And, there's already a locust problem in Africa," Sir Harold rambled on.

"Relevance Sir . . . please . . ." pleaded Jerome.

"Americans are on board. We are keeping the status of our target off the books, but they read between the lines . . . know we are up to something. The potential International fallout of things is simply unpredictable. Too many unknowns. It will be a political mess at home and in the States, then the pencil- necked diplomats pointing fingers like a broken windmill," he continued.

"Politics are really not my tea, Sir . . . anything else," Jerome injected.

"Bottom line . . . anything she has to add to our base of knowledge will be critical. Thomas has already said he's ready to provide any assistance. He has a pre-approved, blank check from the Yanks and us. My U.S. counterpart, Alan Lewis, he's full, onboard. I'm sure he's put more than two-plus-two together. He knows we have a Gulfstream in your parking lot . . . loquacious, diplomatic groundlings, need their tongues cutout. My guess . . . Thomas is headed to the China Sea, Philippines perhaps, as we speak. Chinese agents everywhere and the billionaires with the politicians grease the wheels. We can't keep up," said Sir Harold.

"Good to know. Let me make sure we secure our target. Enemy lines on both sides of the front. A lot can go wrong. Get his contact for me, if you can," concluded Jerome.

"Very well Commander. God's speed my friend. I plan to have that long talk," ended Sir Harold.

37

As they approached the boat being tied up to the dock, Huiwei saw four people.

One man in a working man's charcoal shirt and pants, with a black merchant cap. Given his gruff demeanor and age, she presumed he was the pilot in charge. Another, scruffy, skinny, young man in three-quarter length pants was busy with the ropes taking directions from the pilot.

Another Chinese man and woman were standing toward the aft deck, in dark colored, business casual attire, looking up behind their sunglasses. Probably, combination, night-vision lens like Longwei had – her new *friends*, she surmised, as she sized up her situation.

The Chinese woman looked like she was in her early twenties, extremely fit, with a confident demeanor beyond her years. Her partner looked about 170 centimeters tall, over 75 kilograms, maybe late twenties, at best a fourteen second 100-meter dash – obviously, the drug smuggler in charge. From the draping of his shirt, she could tell the pilot had a pistol stuffed in his belt. The young woman, a likely threat, Huiwei hoped she understood the definition of *friendly* the same way she did.

As they stood next to the boat, the pilot gave a polite gesture to board. Huiwei stepped on the deck carrying the box and cooler. Longwei remained on the dock. The pilot told Huiwei to put the packages on the deck and raise her hands so he could pat her down. She complied. He was a bit rough and brisk, but he was only there for business.

"I believe my associate, Daiyu, will be able to take it from here. She is not a conversationalist, per my instructions, so please do not take her to be rude. My colleagues and myself would be disappointed to learn she could not follow orders," said Longwei. Huiwei, liked her new name, *black jade.*

The pilot nodded his acknowledgement and stepped back, signaling his mate to grab the cooler and package to inspect. As the mate reached down, Huiwei's body flashed, striking the mate, rolling him facedown, with her knee in his back, and her arm cocked to deliver a blow to his neck.

"I don't' think that will be necessary Daiyu," Longwei calmly barked at Huiwei, noticing that the pilot was a bit stunned, and started to reach for a pistol in his belt.

"Please, please . . . and I thought our introductions were going so well . . . put the gun away, before you find the barrel pointing in your direction," said Longwei.

"I need to inspect the packages, or we do not leave the dock," said the pilot.

"That would be unfortunate for all of us . . . but mostly for you captain. Our cargo is most sensitive, and time is of the essence," said Longwei.

The pilot stared at what looked like an organ-donor container, took his hand off the pistol grip, and gave another nod. Longwei felt the perspiration growing under his suit, yet was enjoying the youthful rush of adrenaline.

The smuggler approached Huiwei, "I think you can let him up now. Everybody understands the rules. Please, grab your packages and you can go below in the cabin for the short journey," said Hong.

Hong looked at the pilot and Longwei, receiving nods of agreement. Huiwei picked up her contraband and went below deck to the cramped, one-man berth.

Longwei retreated from the dock, to avoid drawing any more attention, and stood under a secluded tree on the shore to watch the boat back out, turn, and slowly head to back into the river channel. He silently wished her well, feeling like a father watching his daughter leave home for the first time, but knew there was nothing more he could do for her.

The river was only 80 meters wide, at that point. The boat went west, down the channel about two kilometers, until it hooked back along the south shore line, heading east for another 100 meters, making a careful shore landing on a small beach of river gravel.

Jerome moved into position staying out of sight, watching the boat land. Hong had Huiwei jump down to the ankle-high water first and handed her the box of herbal supplements and the cooler. Hong and Steph, then, followed.

Jerome felt his chest heave in relief when he saw they had safely made it to land.

"Leader 1. You have a single bogey at your four o'clock, 50 meters, fire-stick in hand. Blind to the shore, just a walk in the park for now. I'm pulling Tweetie-pie from the air, 200 meters downwind," said Sloane over her ear-com, into Jerome's earpiece.

"Copy bird's-eye," he responded.

Jerome all too well understood the message. Things could get out of hand very quickly if he suddenly appeared to warn Hong and the others. Of course, a surprised Private on patrol would be impossible to predict once he stumbled on the smugglers, with a rifle he may or may not know how to shoot.

Jerome scrambled away from his hidden spot. At a safe distance, hidden by foliage, he grabbed a sizeable stone hoping to distract the patrolman in another direction. He saw the patrolman approaching from about 30 meters away. He tossed the stone. As expected, the patrolman looked up, turned, and took several cautious steps away from the river walk path toward the sound.

The pilot's mate was trying to start the boat engine, without immediate success. As the sound of the noise from the cranking starter reached the rise, the patrolman turned to look toward the river and began to move in that direction.

Jerome saw Hong's head peek over the embankment. The patrolman was already back on the path, surely having seen the travelers hiking up to the same path.

Jerome pulled his pistol as the patrolman raised his Norinco CQ rifle. The distance was too far for a sure shot. The sound of the shot would alert the boat pilot and who knows whom else with the echo-chamber of the river banks. There was no choice. He began to squeeze the trigger.

The drone landed, Sloane quickly threw the drone and controller in the bag. She could get it later. Running as quickly as she could, she saw the scene unfolding in front of her. Sloane crossed her fingers in full-stride hoping that the patrolman was too nervously focused on what he was seeing to hear her feet gracefully pounding down the path. She knew she could run only so silently.

When she got as close as she thought she could, to avoid his peripheral vision, she leaped into the brush off of the path, belly crawling with incredible speed like a hidden mountain lion on the hunt.

Jerome suddenly saw a figure pop out of the brush behind the patrolman. The figure was fully kneeling like a Kozak dancer, pirouetting in several rapid spins across the path, with her leg smashing the back of the guard's knees, as he collapsed backwards, releasing his rifle with a surprised grunt. In one orchestrated move, he saw Sloane's elbow smash down on the guard's throat. The patrolman's movements stopped in complete silence.

Jerome hurried over to Sloane to assist. There was no need. The patrolman was dead and Sloane was wiping the sweat from her forehead, still standing on her knees.

"Unusual move . . . I think I won't cut you from our martial arts team, after all," said Jerome, eliciting a smile from Sloane who was still catching her breath. He knew taking a life was never pleasant, attempting to distract Sloane's thoughts.

"Thanks Coach," she responded.

Introductions and greetings could wait. Stephanie motioned Hong and Huiwei to separate and move across the path into the foliage, while she ran to the small funeral gathering.

"We have an added problem," said Jerome looking at Stephanie.

Stephanie and Sloane stripped the patrolman down to his underwear and wrapped the bundle with his belt, also grabbing his rifle. They were glad to see it was a low-level, routine patrol where he did not even carry a walkie-talkie – just a cell phone in his pant pocket.

Hong was not sure about Jerome's plan. He had run jobs with this pilot before and thought he was all business. Nothing was certain in this line of work.

Hong scurried back down the embankment, waiving at the boat, hearing the engine finally starting and the water-pump gurgling at the back. The pilot jumped down to the gravel beach.

Hong, as artfully as he could, explained that his benefactor in Hong Kong had a recent problem with a disloyal drug dealer who thought he was entitled to an added commission on his sales.

At first, the pilot seemed hesitant to deal with a corpse, to go down the river and dump it in Deep Bay. Hong pulled out a wad of folded Yuan bills that Jerome had stuffed in his hand. After a brief, back-and-forth negotiation, a price was agreed on. Hong retained a small portion of the bills. If he did not insist, the pilot would have been suspicious.

Hong whistled toward the rise. Stephanie appeared at the crest with a body poised on the back of her shoulders. Hong waived, and Stephanie let the body roll down the embankment with its own gravity. The pilot waived to his mate who jumped off the boat, dragged the body to the boat, awkwardly pushing the patrolman over the gunnel rail. Then, he lifted two large rocks to put onboard. Hong helped push the bow off of the gravel, and watched the boat slowly back up to the channel, and accelerate west toward Deep Bay.

When Hong returned to the group, they had all just mustered back together, having gathered their gear, and trying to clean the area of any trace, as much as possible.

"What's next boss?" said Hong to Jerome.

"Well . . . I wish I could say Disneyland . . . but we have a plane to catch," replied Jerome.

"Since I'm driving, any idea where we're our bird is heading?" asked Sloane.

"No . . . actually. Seems the World has been falling apart a bit while we've been vacationing. We need to get back to the hangar and I need to make some calls. Huiwei . . . you can't imagine how wonderful it is to see you. I trust you will not hate me if I keep things in operational mode. We are literally, far from out of the woods," said Jerome.

Huiwei nodded, said, "thank you," but as her emotions of relief started to rise, she threw herself at Jerome in a hug, pressing the side of her head against his chest, holding him tight, "Thank you . . . I knew I called the right person . . . this is as professional as it gets, right now."

Stephanie felt her eyes wanting to well-up and join the hug, but she knew this was not the time for anymore shock-n-awe.

Hong led the way back to the van and they loaded up to leave.

38

Traveling at eighteen to twenty knots, depending on the waves and the wind, Aiguo-Tao thought it would take about two and one-half hours to cross the sixty-five kilometers to Hsinchu, maybe a little longer. It appeared the boat was built to make the crossing, and he saw the switch for the auxiliary fuel tank, if it was needed.

He looked at the GPS locator on the pilot dashboard, calculating that they had been cruising for about an hour.

The pilothouse, was a three-sided structure with glass windows providing a full view forward and to the sides, fixed in the center of the boat. The pilot stood at the dashboard, and the helm with a chrome steering wheel and throttle.

The aft deck was the same level as the boat house deck. The forward deck was about stomach-high from the aft deck, and covered the berth-cabin below. Two narrow beds, a small kitchen and a bolted-down table with two simple chairs that could be latched to the table when not in use.

When they started out, Qing took a black, insulated, water-proof coat out of her bag, along with a fashionable, black, floppy beret-shaped knit hat. She would occasionally walk to the aft deck and sit, then return closer to the opening to the pilothouse, always keeping a safe distance from Aiguo-Tao and never letting her gun leave her hand.

"Why are you slowing down? We don't want the weather catching up with us out here, especially in this small boat," said Qing.

"The fuel. It seems like we are burning through it faster than we should, and the RPM gauge seems to be erratic . . . I'm concerned one of the propellers might be slipping," he responded.

"The boat is in fine shape. It seems like it's well maintained and I haven't heard anything unusual in the engine. Do not lie to me," she barked.

"I don't think we are in any position to make repairs out here, especially if I had to get in the water. Even if I could determine the prop is slipping, I don't know that I could fix it," he said.

"If your plan is to escape in the water and swim away, I don't think even you could make a thirty-kilometer swim . . . not in these waters," she replied.

"No escape. I want to get to Taiwan more than you do. Remember . . . you said I was a new millionaire . . . I think we need to take it easy on the throttle for now and see if it makes a difference. If one prop strips out, I'm concerned the prop-shaft might burnout, spinning without the prop drag. If one goes, I don't know if that will affect the other. You're the Naval officer," he said.

When Qing would retreat to the aft deck, Aiguo-Tao had been fumbling with the multi-tool in his cargo pant pocket. It was one move at a time. The bagginess of the pants must have avoided Qing's detection of the tool pouch, or maybe she thought it was only his wallet . . . that he did not have.

Acting on blind feel, inside his pocket, with one hand, he removed the tool from the nylon pouch. Then, he pinched the release buttons moving the pointed end of the plier's piece forward a few millimeters with each sliding push. Next, he spread the handles and was able to flip open the knife blade tucked inside the handle, closing the handles back together, with the pointed plier-head at one end and the knife blade at the other. He tried to block another image of Huan-Jun from his grateful thoughts.

"Then, let me see the gauges . . . I need you back at the stern . . . on your knees," she commanded, pointing her gun and waving the barrel to show him the direction.

"So . . . you do know boats. That is good. I'm not a Naval mechanic," he said, as he slowed the boat more.

"I'm not a mechanic, but I don't believe you. Sorry, my dear. I would hate to change your level of comfort for the rest of our romantic cruise," Qing said, waiting for him to step out of the pilothouse.

Qing stepped to the starboard rail as far as she could, giving Aiguo-Tao a safe area to move to the stern. Finally, Aiguo-Tao saw what he wanted. The boat, traveling at almost a crawl, began to turn more parallel to the small waves, but he saw a series of slightly larger wave lines approaching.

He put his hands in the air, turning to walk out of the pilothouse, as the boat increased its rocking motion. When the sudden jolt of the bigger waves hit, he caught Qing shifting her feet attempting to balance.

Grabbing the wrist of her right hand holding the gun, he twisted her arm in on her. He hoped she would drop the gun, but at least take the direction away from him.

As he predicted, she moved toward him and tried to kick his ankles out from under him. He flung his body to the side, swinging his legs out and hitting them on the short starboard wall. He turned his torso into her back, to keep his lower shoulder below the edge of the gunwale, so he would not go into the sea.

The combined momentum of his turning body and Qing's momentum forward, with his arm wrapped around her, brought Qing's chest down to the deck with a slipping, slam. He saw her right arm splayed on the deck, but still gripping her weapon.

Her body acted on trained reflex, quickly turning over and attempting to slap him in the head with her gun. Instead of rearing his head back, he knew to follow the momentum pressing his head toward her shoulder blades, now suddenly her breasts. With her missed swing only grazing him, he rolled with her momentum, a full turn, and was once again on top of her.

He felt a stinging scratch across his face from her fingernails or the brush of the pistol grip from her attempted knockout swing, and the sensation that the multi-tool, in his pocket had cut into his leg. He quickly reached to grab the multi-tool. He did not care which end, as he brought it down into her throat.

Qing suddenly gasped sensing the nicking of her cardioid artery. She dropped the gun bringing her hand to her throat, slapping Aiguo-Tao again with her hand.

He could feel the fight quickly going out of Qing, continuing to pin her down.

"I do not have any money! You are going to die for nothing," he yelled, watching the blood slowly flowing out of the cut on her neck, with a small, pulsing spurt each time her heart beat.

"A young girl's delusion for an old woman's sense of romance. I suppose neither of us will enjoy your new-found wealth," she struggled to say.

"There is no money. I don't know what this is all about. If I have been set-up, I will find the people responsible. Their fate will be certain," he said.

"Unfortunately, you will never enjoy that goal, or the money you say you do not have. I tried to give you . . . us . . . a chance," she said with a bit of delirium setting in.

"I could have used your help. Instead, you turned on me . . . for money. You will die a fool, and I will find my enemies," he pronounced.

"No . . . you won't Aiguo-Tao, I'm sorry . . . you won't," she said.

"Why would I not?" he asked, feeling a twinge of remorse as his former teacher lay dying beneath him.

"My rings . . . on my hands . . . your face is cut badly, although the painless man does not feel it. Retractable, poison pin-needles . . . very strong," she slowly finished, unable to keep her eyes open to see his face.

He felt her body going limp. Not dead, but dying. He stood up and picked up her gun, holding it down at his side. Then, he tucked it in his belt and reached down grabbing her under her arms, dragging her to the back of the aft deck. He did not want to risk any chance of a last, feeble attempt to attack him. He looked at the smear of blood across the deck as he set her head down.

"Perhaps a sailor's burial, but I will let you finish your life above water," he softly said.

Qing, did not respond.

He walked back to the pilothouse and threw the throttle forward, directing the boat back on course to Taiwan.

A few minutes later, he found himself staring at the GPS screen as the sharp, backlit lines began to fuss, and slightly wiggle. He slapped the GPS with his hand hoping it would correct whatever circuit was failing.

When he arrived at the reefs, that he had never navigated, he would need the electronic map to guide him. The images on the screen did not improve. He looked up at the horizon and saw the sky and sea moving in visual contortions, beyond what the motion of the sea would cause.

He fought the sensations, just as he had learned to fight any pain so many years ago. "*Scorpion venom was stronger,*" he said to himself. In his mind he continued to view the sea's horizon and the little whitecaps topping each wave. It took a while for him to realize, that those visions were false, as his only view was the ceiling of pilot's house and glimpses of the sky. The neuro-toxin would not allow his limbs to move and each breath was becoming a bit more shallow.

He grinned, "I feel no pain . . . I never feel the pain," he tried to yell, and he let his eyes close.

39

Hong drove down a utility road on the perimeter of the airport, pulling the van up to a small, obscure gate near the diplomatic terminal hangar. He stepped out and spoke to an armed PLA guard. Jerome, in the passenger seat, looked the other direction, overhearing some laughter between Hong and the guard. He presumed there was an unceremonious, but customary exchange of cash, as Hong got back behind the wheel and started the engine.

Pulling up to a vehicle door at the semi-private hangar, Hong got out, entered a combination to the electronic keypad and the door went up. He drove the van in and went back to close the door.

"Clear," said Hong.

Jerome directed the others to get out of the van.

"Try to relax some, as best you can. I need to make some calls and figure out where the next exhibition match is for our martial arts team," said Jerome, with a smile.

They all looked up seeing a relatively large, man, maybe thirty-ish, wearing mechanics overalls, approaching them.

"Can I help you, young man?" asked Jerome, suspiciously.

"Are ya' Commander Xi by chance?" said the mechanic.

"And . . . to whom do I have the pleasure?" responded a surprised Jerome.

"Aw, I love it when ya'll talk with that British accent an' all," the mechanic said reaching out his hand to shake with Jerome's.

"I'm Raymond Ludwikosky . . . Chief Warrant Officer, Seventh Fleet, USS Gerald Ford, if you're in ta' ranks and such. Got put in the back of an F-35 Panther, in the middle of the Pacific to the Philippines . . . and a puddle-jumper to here," he explained.

"Very well Chief Warrant Officer Lud-wa-what-ski . . . but," responded Jerome.

"Smith . . . everybody calls me Smith . . . a whole lot easier, just don't tell my daddy," said Smith.

"Very well . . . Smith . . . who exactly made you the flight attendant on an F-35, and why are you here . . . from Texas, I presume," said Jerome.

"Cleburne . . . yes sir . . . I brought some extra parts for ya'll," said Smith.

"Extra parts?" replied Jerome.

"Yeah . . . evidently, we gottta' land that Gulfstream over there on the Ford. Been looking at it for a while, trying to figure it out . . . Commander Eric Thomas . . . said you might want to call," said Smith.

Sloane suddenly stepped forward with an excited voice, "You want me to land that bird on an aircraft carrier . . . its designed for

1,800 meters and as good as I am, I still need a minimum of 600 meters with a good headwind and a lot of luck. That whole boat is only . . . what . . . a little over 300 meters long," chimed in Sloane.

"Lieutenant Commander Emery, by the way . . . I'm the one flying that bird," added Sloane.

"Well . . . I guess that's why I need to figure out how ta' git that tail-hook lying on the ground by the Gulfstream, somehow attached, Lieutenant Commander

. . . got any good ideas?" replied Smith.

Stephanie reached up to put a calming hand on Sloane's upper arm, "Smith . . . if you have some schematics of the Gulfstream and the tail-hook, I might be able to help with some ideas," said Stephanie.

"Got 'em over there with my bags . . . gosh, I love it when ya'll talk that way. Let's go take a look see, okay" said Smith.

"Stephanie Reid, by the way, Smith. Please call me Steph. I have some background with aircraft engineering, if you're wondering," added Stephanie.

The group was breaking up in different directions and Jerome was already starting to log into his encrypted mini-pad attached to his sat-phone. Sloane walked over to Jerome with the angry look of a jilted lover, turning him around by the arm to look at her.

"Listen . . . Coach . . . I'm going to tell her, if you don't. Steph is going insane and about to burst . . . take care of it . . . Team Leader . . . and don't even think about trying to pull rank on me with this one," Sloane said, and stormed away.

Jerome was trying to assemble all of the pieces in his head, including the ones he did not know yet. He knew Sloane was right. He should have had a better game plan for getting Huiwei introduced to her estranged sister. He had his first cognizant introspection of the whole androcentrism debate, realizing there was no debate. Still, he first needed to call Commander Thomas. The contact information was now shining up from his pad screen. He could face his *maleness* later, he concluded.

"Commander Thomas . . . Commander Xi here . . . I hope the reception is okay

. . . I don't think we can stay safely connected for long. I have some questions if you don't mind," said Jerome.

"Call me Eric, please . . . good to hear from you. Is your package safe?" said Eric.

"It is . . . Jerome, please . . . we need to leave Disneyland as soon as possible. A mutual friend, it seems, mentioned you might have your hands in this mess. What's this about an aircraft carrier?" asked Jerome.

"So . . . you've met Smith . . . don't let him fool you . . . All-Conference linebacker at Baylor . . . didn't want to risk a head injury in the NFL . . . opted for a doctorate in aerospace engineering at Texas A&M. He should be a Captain by now, most see him that way anyways. He won't take off the overalls, however. Says he doesn't know what he'd do with clean fingernails, and all that saluting." Eric explained.

"He does seem like an interesting fellow," said Jerome.

"My brother, Carlos, is a Marine Major and F-35 fighter trainer down in Pensacola. As it happens, he's been working with Israeli fighter pilots on a new two-seater version. He jumped at the chance for a rendezvous with the Ford and his new Panther. He got me here and volunteered to wing-off with Smith. Carlos . . . Baylor track of all things. He said Smith was the best supersonic RIO he ever had . . . and hoped their conversations weren't being recorded, from the head-coms," said Eric.

"Smith has more details, so I'll try to keep it short and sweet, and hope we don't have ears, yet. The USS Ford, newest carrier, advance aircraft systems, still working out the kinks and not operationally deployed yet. We're sitting in the Pacific, east of Japan. Your friend has information badly needed, and her bosses are seriously frowning on that. Can't land her in the Philippines or a land base . . . too many employees of her boss just about everywhere. You can't fly back over the mainland, unless you had an unsanctioned fighter escort, and limits on your flight range. Gulfstream's not set up for refueling. Risky . . . but it's the best shot with short notice and a team of some pretty good gray-matter looking at the options," explained Eric.

"How's the World doing, by the way? If I recall your field is bio-weapons and micro-biology . . . we'll figure out things here," replied Jerome.

"Not good, and things are getting ready to get a lot worse I predict. If your friend is as good as I've been told, she can explain it to you. In the meantime, Smith has some virus test kits there, with a reactive agent and a portable analyzer. Prototype . . . blood-serum based, much like a diabetic finger-prick kit, with slower results. We don't know how accurate they are, yet, but everybody should test anyway. Smith knows the protocol.

That whole R.E.M. song . . . *'it's the end of the world as we know it,'* has some new meaning for us, now. We need the information," said Eric.

"We're on it. Thank you, Commander . . . except, now, I've got that song stuck in my head . . . thanks," concluded Jerome, and he ended the sat-phone call.

40

Smith explained to the team that the USS Gerald R. Ford was the newest aircraft carrier in the United States Naval fleets. "Bush – 43 got the ball rolling and it was commissioned in 2017 by Trump-45, it was going into its third-year of testing before operational deployment. I work on the kinks."

"Abandoning steam generators and diesel motors, the Ford has an electromagnetic aircraft launch system, EMALS, for take-offs and an advanced arresting gear, AAG, for catching planes on landing. The EMALS uses a rail-carriage, attached to the aircraft. The carriage is potentially adaptable to different types of planes, and in 92 meters, that's 300 feet, of runway, can accelerate a full-payload fighter to over 150 mph, or, 240 kph, if ya' like, with large capacitors feeding a linear induction motor – a rail gun. Spool-up the capacitors again, shoot another one off the deck – like popping tin cans with my sling-shot as a kid."

Smith continued on with his mental side notes. "Some 13-year-old kid in Kansas . . . second-place in a science fair a few years back, using an old photography flash capacitor, shooting metal projectiles 'cross the damn gymnasium without a sound. Listed a bunch of big-boy applications, including fighters off an aircraft carrier. Got noticed by a DOD Admiral who was in town and went to see his niece's entry on bacteria resistance to penicillin – some smart kids out there. Kid said he read a lot of Orson Scott Card and the new Harry Potter book. Said he couldn't call it a *rail gun*, or he'd get kicked out of school. Snowflake principal almost disqualified his entry."

"Likewise, the AAG uses an advanced, turbo-electric motor and sensing monitors ta' allow the catching-cables more accuracy in connecting with the tail-hooks hanging down from the landing aircraft, computing the slack allocations for the type of plane, flight conditions, and hopefully avoiding the damage and risks from the jolting deacceleration from the cables, also with a shorter landing distance."

Stephanie and Smith were already pouring over the schematics, like two ducks to a pond, and assessing the tools and welding equipment in the hanger, plus what Smith was able to bring with him. *"Evidently, the best blind-date for two aeronautical engineers was a set of blueprints and an impossible task,"* thought Jerome.

Jerome slowly strolled over to the engineers, waving to Huiwei and Sloane to join the party.

"Smith . . . you're still keeping track of the test kit results?" asked Jerome.

"All done. All negative. A prototype, but at least it's some relief, 'specially for Huiwei," responded Smith.

"We can't lose focus on the various tasks at hand. You two have your work cut-out, and do not hesitate to ask for an extra hand when needed. Sloane, you've been pouring through the Gulfstream manuals and planning how this proposed landing might even work," said Jerome.

"We got it under control Commander, and we'll probably need some extra hands ta' holt' some things in place once we get goin'," responded Smith.

"Excellent. Nonetheless, I would not be human keeping a certain matter on the back-burner any longer. I know we will need to take a break, and I only ask that you can get your heads back in the game as soon as possible," said Jerome, with confused eyes staring at him, except for Stephanie's.

"Huiwei . . . I would like you to meet your sister Stephanie Lee Reid," announced Jerome.

Stephanie leapt up like a frog on a hot skillet, embracing a stunned and confused Huiwei, as her tears were finally undammed.

"Sister?" was all Huiwei could say as she finally hugged back and joined in the tearful introduction.

Jerome could barely keep from crying himself, and he saw that Sloane was already joining in the group hug.

"Please . . . don't consider me the ass I may be . . . you two need to go over there and say what you need to say. Sloane . . . you need to coordinate with Smith, here, on how this whole thing is going to work. Our clock is still ticking," said Jerome.

Huiwei looked up with her tear-streaked face, "We'll talk about your ass later

. . . and whether it needs a good kicking, or something else . . . thank you Jerome," she said.

41

The Gulfstream was finally taxied out to the tarmac. Jerome sat in the co-pilot seat, still amazed that Hong got clearance without anyone having to enter the diplomatic terminal.

Jerome was glad Sir Harold had not put any restrictions on his foreign currency requisition request, and the courier was prompt in getting to the airfield in Northolt. Hopefully, not needing any more Yuan, Jerome was generous to Hong, even though he had not requested a payment. He should be able to support his parents, now, even if he calls in sick for the next year. Jerome thought he more than earned it.

"Tower cleared us for the runway Commander. Are you ready?" said Sloane.

"You have the ball Lieutenant Commander. I'll be glad to leave sovereign territory, but I think I should be more concerned about our landing," responded Jerome.

"Steph and Smith make a good team . . . if you couldn't tell. Huiwei built a handheld transmitter to release the tail-hook, if it works, we'll be fine," said Sloane.

"Some maintenance fellow at the hanger will be upset with Huiwei's scavenging . . . by the way . . . I never did ask . . . have you ever landed on an aircraft carrier?" he asked, with a tone of concern.

"Emergency landing of an F-35B, lucky or unlucky artillery frag, depending on your point of view. I don't think a STOVL vertical landing is in the cards with this bird. I am looking forward to adding this to my unofficial flight resume . . . already have a speed record this trip," responded Sloane.

The Gulfstream took off without incident and was gaining altitude reaching the northern end of the Taiwan Straight.

"What the hell is that?" asked Jerome, pointing to the water below.

"Looks like an exploding boat about half way from Fuzhou," observed Sloane.

"It does. But why is that PLA sea patrol boat moving away from it and not intercepting it?" said Jerome.

"Don't know, sir . . . never trained with the PLA Navy . . . I imagine they do things differently, like everything else," said Sloane.

Stephanie opened the cockpit door and stuck her head in, "We've got about forty-eight hundred kilometers to go. I wanted to let you know, we're going to try to get a little kip in. Let us know when you're getting close or if you need something. I brought you some bottled water, here. Sorry, Jerome, you'll have to wait for one of my killer martini's," said Stephanie.

"Thanks, Steph. We'll be fine. Get any rest you can," responded Jerome.

"Jerome . . . thanks . . . I mean helping me find my sister. I hope you're not one to keep a chit-list, because I obviously owe you a lot," added Stephanie.

42

"Yes . . . of course, I know Captain Lóng Qing, Admiral. I imagine most senior MSS officers do, including yourself," answered Major General Lú Ho-sun.

"She called you recently, correct?" asked the MSS, PLA Admiral.

"As a matter of fact, she did . . . but evidently you already know that. I've consulted with Captain Lóng on several matters over the years. Given her Party contacts, I tend not to put her on hold," said Ho-sun.

"And the nature of her call?" asked the Admiral.

"She wanted a contact to acquire a non-military boat in the Taiwan Straight. Something about a technology company . . . a client . . . since she has one foot in and one out these days. I tend not to ask more questions than necessary, given the nature of her operations," replied Ho-sun.

"Did you discuss Major Zhu?" asked the Admiral.

"Oddly enough, yes . . . briefly. Captain Lóng said we might have a mutual acquaintance, Major Zhu . . . she was his mentor years ago, and said she had been unsuccessful in trying to reach him. She wanted to recruit his help on something, the way I understood it. I told her, in confidence, that he had been detained in Wuhan and might be unavailable for some time. I presume she understood the innuendo . . . she was an MSS interrogator for a number of years, I believe. I don't know if she pursued it . . . I had no idea Zhu was up to something. That's already been fully reviewed," explained Ho-sun.

"I don't think Captain Lóng will be calling you in the near future," stated the Admiral.

The Admiral nodded his head at two military guards. They moved quickly, pulling Ho-sun out of his chair and securing his hands behind him.

"What's going on Admiral? This is outrageous," exclaimed Ho-sun.

"I think we may need to pursue this discussion in a different venue. I believe we also have questions regarding the operations team understanding from you regarding a vaccine for this virus, as shown in the original protocols," responded the Admiral.

Ho-sun tried to show a vain intent to struggle as the guards quickly escorted him out of the room.

43

About three-hundred kilometers away from the coordinates for the USS Gerald Ford, Jerome went back to the cabin to check on his team. He did not want to wake them with the shock of the intercom. They were all awake, some more than others. He smiled, seeing that Steph was now sitting next to Smith, as opposed to Huiwei, who was just waking up.

Smith stood up and let out a big stretch, cleaned up and no longer wearing his overalls. Jerome did not completely understand American football, but thought Smith would be a formidable flanker on any rugby field.

"You don't happen ta' have any of that martial arts training, do ya', Smith?," asked Jerome, with his Texas drawl.

"Nope. Tried it a few times in some combat training. Found out it was easier if I just tackled 'em and put 'em outta' their misery real quick like. Seemed to work . . . why, ya'll expecting a fight?" responded Smith.

"Nah . . . no fightin', just tryin' ta' figure the depth of my martial arts team," said Jerome.

"Hey . . . Jerome . . . no offense . . . don't talk like that in a Waco bar . . . or yer' gonna' git a Lone Star bottle over yer' head . . . besides, trust me, the gals will love ya' for the whole James Bond thing," said Smith, a bit sheepishly.

Stephanie and Huiwei were doing their best not to laugh out loud.

"Noted . . . evidently, some people like to talk behind my back. Well, heads up, we're about 300 kilometers out . . . so, time to get ready and buckle in," announced Jerome, still smiling himself.

"I think it's best if ya' made yourself comfy back here, Commander. It's self-serve, this leg. Right, Steph? I best ride shotgun with Sloane. Things could get tricky, and best if I'm on the com with the bridge and tower," said Smith.

"You're right. Go buckle-up. I'll stay back here and practice on my drawl with these two," said Jerome.

"Nooooooooo," said Stephanie and Huiwei in unison.

Smith went to the cockpit and strapped himself in to the starboard seat.

"So . . . you know how to fly this bird, Chief Warrant Officer Raymond Ludwikosky?" quirked Sloane.

"I've put a few planes on the flight deck safely . . . but this Gulfstream is your baby. Once we make contact with the tower, everybody on that end is gonna' feel a bit more comfortable hearing my voice. I think we can tag-team this rodeo just fine. Ya'll just focus stayin' on the bull, it's gonna' be tricky, but your probably way ahead of me on that part," said Smith.

"I can land just about anything, but you're going to know the fine tuning on speed, altitude and approach, especially coordinating with the tower on wind and weather conditions. Keep your eyes on the instrument panel and coach away. My ego can take a little break," said Sloane.

"Then let's land this bird Lieutenant Commander . . . Yahoo!" exclaimed Smith.

"Hey . . . did you tell him about the whole Texas drawl thing, like we asked you?" she asked.

"Yep . . . I think I kept a straight face, weren't easy . . . but ya' should'a seen the look on the cowboy's face . . . priceless . . . I think he took it well," responded Smith.

"About *twenty miles* out, I'm going to drop the tail hook . . . provided this garage door opener that Huiwei built will work. If it don't we go Plan B," said Smith.

"Got it. *Thirty-two kilometers* out you're dropping, fly-by to verify it's down. If not, touch-and-go to get a feel for the runway, then hope they can clear enough planes to use the long-deck length, hoping for a drag approach and throw the reverse thrusters full. I'm betting on Huiwei, your knowledge of the AAG and Steph's smarts," said Sloane.

"Hey . . . you guys came up with the Imperial system first . . . should'a kept it, besides just your local road signs. At least a pint is a pint in a London pub. Metric makes no since to a carpenter . . . it's hypocrisy . . . ya' know our boy Jesus was a carpenter . . . anyways, carrier's not deployed yet and has minimal aircraft, if we gotta' go Plan B . . . fuel time, will be our bigger concern," Smith said.

"A Baptist preacher and an engineer . . . my, my, Steph is walking into a hornets' nest," smiled Sloane.

"What? . . . Steph ? . . . hey . . . just fly the plane Gossip-girl," he said smiling back.

The hook dropped and Sloane circled back to make her approach. She could hear the constant chatter between Smith and the tower, but she was able to wash it out and focus on her visual and the signals Smith was giving her. Sloane was glad he was there and it quickly seemed like they had done this a hundred times before. It seemed he knew what she was thinking before she thought it.

The hook caught, she slammed the reverse thrusters, and with a sudden deacceleration, it felt like a long rubber band stretch, without the snapback.

They both just sat staring silently out the windshield. Sloane felt like she might need to pry her fingers open having expended all of her muscle strength gripping the yoke.

"Hot damn . . . now, that's what I'm talkin' 'bout . . . I owe ya' another one Big Man!" Smith hollered, breaking the silence.

"Wahoo . . . ro . . . de . . . damn . . . o!" returned Sloane, popping her harness off and reaching over to hug her co-pilot.

The team deplaned to a boisterous group of sailors in an assortment of colored vests and the many that came rushing out on deck. The joyous roar seemed to easily pierce the noise of the 35-knot wind from the open ocean and the headwind direction of the carrier.

They were set up in the VIP quarters on the carrier, reserved for members of Congress or dignitaries who decided to drop in. The team had some time to decompress, and were treated to meals of their choice by the galley crew run by the exuberant, Chief Warrant Officer Amanda Cook, a graduate of the Escoffier School of Culinary Art, who took her galley as seriously as the most demanding gunnery, Chief Petty Officer. The incredible array of fresh desserts defined, *chocolate to die for*.

Huiwei, Jerome, and Eric spent a significant amount of time in the ship's war room going through collaborated debriefing sessions with the British and United States intelligence officials, on secured lines. Huiwei downloaded her files on the carrier's computer server, and prepared overview, slide presentations, for the intelligence services, never certain of interception technology capabilities.

Huiwei was relieved that her immediate ordeal, for now, was over. She struggled with feelings that she was a traitor to her country and her years of service. Stephanie was her crutch, being patient with her emotions. It seemed like they had known each other as sisters for a lifetime. The more she learned about her parent's secrets, and their plights, the easier the transition became.

The officials and epidemic experts explained, in depth, how her actions will likely save millions of lives around the World, and allow governments to better prepare for the economic and political shockwaves. Her heart sank when she was told that it appeared there was no vaccine, or treatment drug developed in China.

She knew that only a few would know her story and the real facts underlying what was already being referred to as *the likely* pandemic. The public, the politicians and the diplomats *could never handle the truth*, as the movie line goes, she thought.

The temptation to take advantage of a crisis would be too strong for those seeking power and control. Even with the hard facts, they would still twist and dance around them, for their own gains. Huiwei also came to grips with the reality that the People's Republic would never be fully exposed. The competing economies simply would never be able to deal with it, and conventional warfare, along with China's belt-and-road strategies, were left for emerging nations, not World powers.

Huiwei knew from her own projections, that social, economic and political upheaval were still inevitable. Media sources would strategically choose sides, and an audience wanting to find comfort in the religion of politics, to reinforce their perceptions, would believe them. Bat soup and innocent animals would continue to be the proverbial scapegoats.

Some regions will likely experience civil unrest, and many would still die from the virus and the aftermath of violence, suicide and drug addiction. Toilet paper, bullets and expired antibiotics may replace modern currency for some.

Intellectually, she regretted that she discovered things too late to better model the potential outcomes with the actual facts she now had with her intervention. Yet, she was not sure it mattered. She could watch the unfolding of the human comedy in real time, without her crystal ball.

Huiwei and Jerome finally found time for a stroll on the enormous deck. Jerome affectionately looked at the ocean wind blowing her hair and breathing the salt air.

"Huiwei . . . you know you probably saved the World and maybe be the most heroic person in all of history . . . whose name will never be known," said Jerome.

She made a quick laugh, "Is that the epitaph for my tombstone?"

"Perhaps . . . better than anyone else could deserve . . . but I intend to make sure that day is very far in the future," he replied.

Huiwei stopped and turned to Jerome, putting her hands around his neck, pulling his lips to hers. She really did not care what any observer might think.

"Does that mean you're planning on sticking around for a while?" she said, looking into his eyes with her hands still clasped behind his head.

"Seems as if it's not much of a choice . . . more of an order . . . perhaps you'll meet Sir Harold someday . . . very fond of your father, too, it seems," he responded.

"So . . . I'm your mission now! You know I can still kick your butt," she retorted, withdrawing her hands.

"Oh . . . I don't know how to break this to you . . . but you most definitely are my mission . . . I suppose it's up to you how long I'm deployed," he said.

Jerome wrapped his arms around her waist, pulling her to her toes, with a long kiss, and all the passion he could muster.

"Nice counter move cowboy," she said catching her breath. "Where do we go from here," she asked.

"Hawaii would certainly be a nice place to celebrate my new assignment, or, even a wonderful cottage outside of Bath. However, you are a walking security risk and a target of one of the most powerful governments. Right now, they're assessing locations," he said.

"Europe? Antarctic? Small island off the Argentina coast?" she asked.

"The States most likely. Top of the list so far is Fairbanks, Alaska, or Manhattan, Kansas. A bit of remoteness from the coasts, proximity to military resources, and perhaps an academic position for you . . . once your new identity has been established," he said.

"Do I get a new pair of ruby-red slippers?" she responded.

"You know the story? . . . and Toto too, if you like . . . I haven't been able to own a dog since I was a young boy," he smiled.

"We had a copy of *The Wizard of Oz* hidden in our dormitory room as a girl . . . practiced English for the new girls at night . . . most girls wished to go home, too," she smiled.

Huiwei reached for another kiss, with Jerome holding her tight, as she clicked her heels together, twice.